DEATH AT TIDAL CREEK

Also by Caleb Wygal

Mytle Beach Mystery Novels
The Brass Key (Short Story Prequel)
Death on the Boardwalk
Death Washes Ashore
Death on the Golden Mile
Death on the Causeway

Lucas Caine Novels
Moment of Impact
A Murder in Concord
Blackbeard's Lost Treasure
The Search for the Fountain of Youth

DEATH
AT TIDAL CREEK

A MYRTLE BEACH MYSTERY

CALEB WYGAL

FRANKLIN/KERR
KANNAPOLIS, NORTH CAROLINA

Copyright © 2023 by Caleb Wygal.

Visit the author's website at www.CalebWygal.com

This is a work of fiction. Names, characters, places, and incidents are products of the author's imagination or are used fictionally and are not to be construed as real. Any resemblance to actual events, locations, organizations, or persons living or dead, is entirely coincidental.

All rights reserved.

Published by Franklin/Kerr Press
1040 Dale Earnhardt Blvd. #185
Kannapolis, North Carolina 28083
www.FranklinKerr.com

Edited by Lisa Borne Graves
Cover photo by Dave Gombka
Cover art and design by Mibl Art
Author photo by Pamela Hartle
Interior design by Jordon Greene

Printed in the United States of America

FIRST EDITION

Hardback ISBN 979-8-9887979-0-6
Paperback ISBN 979-8-9887979-1-3

Fiction: Cozy Mystery
Fiction: Amateur Sleuth
Fiction: Southern Fiction

For Mounia Belkasmi.
Thank you for everything and for introducing me to Moroccan coffee.

DEATH AT TIDAL CREEK

> Good work. Keep on it. If you hear my name, let me know.

> Will do.

> Has Clark been to the courthouse?

> No.

> Let me know if he does ASAP. Take all precautions.

> There's not much he can do.

> Don't sell him short. He's smarter than you presume.

> I understand. What if he learns what Autumn knew?

> Then he'll suffer the same fate she did.

END OF TEXT MESSAGES

CHAPTER
TWO

"Who's that guy?" Andrea asked before sipping from a tall beer glass.

"You don't know who he is?" her much older friend, Karen, said in a mixed accent of New York and Indiana. I mentally referred to her as not-from-work Karen because when Andrea had first talked about her, I thought of my employee.

Andrea stared at the musician like a star-struck teenager. He was perched on a stool with an acoustic guitar in hand. The handsome man sat in front of a gathered crowd in the brew house area of Tidal Creek. "His hair is magnificent."

I took a pull from a frosty Beam Reach IPA and then answered, "Greg Rowles. He's all over the place. Billboards, TV, commercials, various music venues."

Andrea leaned to the side and squinted as though that would give her a better view. "Oh, I thought he looked familiar. He's a talented singer."

"Headlined at the Alabama Theatre for years," Karen said. "Won Star Search back in the 90s."

This was the second time Andrea and I had seen each other outside of our neighboring stores on the Myrtle Beach Boardwalk. The first was when we went to lunch at La Vinotinto. Since then,

DEATH AT TIDAL CREEK

we'd had coffee at the bookstore a few times. This summ
shaping up to be one of the busiest in Myrtle Beach histor,. vve
were getting slammed by tourists and regulars at the bookstore,
and her business was taking off as well.

Upon sitting down and meeting Karen for the first time, she
held up her Breezy Blonde Ale and informed me she liked to be
punctual so she could start drinking early.

Andrea and I were busy business owners who led busy lives.
Over this past weekend, she suggested meeting here at Tidal
Creek Brewhouse in Market Common for dinner and a beer. Since
Tidal Creek's chef, Chad, had appeared on a Cooking Channel
show called Chef Swap, the brewery had become a food destination
with some of the finest, freshest beers in the Grand Strand.

Tidal Creek was a happening place with events occurring on
most days. This evening was no different, with local legend, Greg
Rowles, performing. I had met him on one other occasion when
Autumn and I had appeared on a local television show he co-hosted
with Audra Grant. They'd invited us there to talk about our new
book store. We'd credited Rowles and Grant for helping to create
buzz for our fledgling store. Autumn and I had filled in in a pinch
when the lead in the Gladiator Games Dinner Show, Connor
West, was supposed to appear, but had to cancel at the last minute
because of an injury he'd suffered during a performance.

Rowles started playing "Danny's Song" in the military cargo
hauler-sized opening at the mouth of the actual cavernous
brewhouse. Behind him, tall steel silos lined the wall to the right,
filled with grain, fermenting beer, and gallons of the finished
fresh product. The left side held equipment for roasting coffee
beans. Sometimes the two sides intertwined in making a coffee
stout beer. We listened for a few moments before Karen and

Andrea resumed their conversation about life at the Paradise Hideaway condominium in Market Common.

A typical June day in the Grand Strand had brought several pop-up thunderstorms. A deluge of rain and gusty winds left behind a few downed branches and large puddles in the parking lot. We sat on one side of a long picnic table, all on one side, near a row of tall silver fermenting grain tanks. We reserved the other side of the table for Karen's roommates. She owned the four-bedroom presidential penthouse suite at the top of the Paradise Hideaway, courtesy of a deceased rich husband.

Andrea joked to me that other tenants in the building referred to Karen and her roomies as the "Silver Girls," a modern-day reincarnation of *The Golden Girls*. They lived together like the beloved cast of the classic television sitcom, and as Andrea said, they even resembled that group, and all but Karen had silver hair.

I hadn't met the others yet. Andrea had gotten to know them since she moved into her new home. They even babysat her daughter, Libby, occasionally. She informed me the four women had become surrogate grandmothers to Libby. Two of them were due to arrive. The oldest of the roommates was at home taking care of Andrea's daughter.

On this Wednesday evening, people packed in at Tidal Creek. As Independence Day approached, tourists flocked to the resorts, beaches, and restaurants. I spotted a few locals in the crowd. It was easy to pick out the tourists. They wore shirts and hats with "Myrtle Beach" screen printed on them. Locals rarely wore clothing from local gift shops. We lived here already. Why advertise? The Visit Myrtle Beach people already did a fine job of getting the word out about our stretch of The Grand Strand.

As Rowles crooned a baleful tune, two more members of the

Silver Girls appeared from around the corner of Tidal Creek. They navigated the tables toward us where the taller one led the way and the shorter took up the tail.

It was a sticky June evening, typical of Myrtle Beach. Andrea and I were dressed in light clothes. The Silver Girls were dressed for late fall. What age does your internal thermometer beg you to turn the thermostat up to eighty, like my mom and dad?

I was a little more formally dressed than normal with a striped Brooks Brothers polo and navy chino shorts. Still wore flip-flops.

Andrea wore clothes like what she would wear to her job at Coastal Décor. A tasteful light green blouse, pearly skirt, and flat sandals. Two threads of curled blond hair fell over either side of her face and brushed against her black-rimmed eyeglasses. The rest of her hair was plaited in a complex braid. She drew more than a few looks from the men who passed by. Not going to lie, it gave me a confidence boost knowing she was here with me and not with them.

"Karen," the taller one, with shoulders back and chin held high who seemed like the natural leader of the Girls, said as she approached our table. "You're ready to go."

"Just getting started, Dot." Karen smiled and surveyed the men in the area. "Just a little liquid courage is all."

Dot scoffed. "Since when do you need help to talk to other men? You're like a real estate agent trying to sell a house. You're on the market and want any available man to know you're likewise available."

Karen's eyes hardened for a beat, but she recovered and said, "I'm just a woman who likes to have fun. C'mon. Dot, Violet, sit." She pointed at the bench seat across from us and tipped her head at Rowles. "I was here first, so I got the good view."

"I'll say you got a good view," Violet said as she sat across from me. "But I'll take this one."

Dot sat down next to Violet and set a frosty pint glass on the table. She gave me a once-over. "For once, I agree with Violet."

I blushed.

"Sorry we're late," Violet said. "My curling iron wasn't heating up."

Dot rolled her eyes and said in a low tone, "She forgot to plug it in."

Violet clicked her tongue. "I'm doing things like that more and more."

Andrea and I shared an expression of concern. The Silver Girls didn't seem as worried.

"You've always been that way," Dot said.

"Yep," Karen agreed.

Violet shook her head and sipped her red wine.

"Have you told this to your doctor?" Andrea asked, dropping poor Violet a lifeline.

"I have," she said. "Even been tested, but they couldn't find anything wrong with me."

Alzheimer's disease ran in my family. My grandfather and his three brothers were all struck with the same disease. I wondered if Violet may be in the formative stages of it. It wasn't my place to suggest such a thing. We just met.

To Andrea, Dot said, "You didn't tell me this date of yours was so handsome."

Andrea ran her hand through my arm. "Didn't feel it was necessary. You'd see for yourself."

I didn't need a mirror to know my cheeks were a vibrant shade of red.

"Aww, look," Karen said. "We're embarrassing him."

Andrea came to my rescue and changed the subject. "How was Libby when you left?"

Dot smiled. "She and Ma were playing with her dolls. Doing some sort of game show."

"Sounds about right," Andrea said.

I squeezed her arm in a silent "thank you." "She has an active imagination. You should see her play with my employee Karen at the bookstore."

"That's right," Violet said. "You own the one up on the Boardwalk. Next to Andrea's business."

"Yup," Andrea said. "It's where we met. I was a tea girl in his coffee world."

I had a drink of the Beam Reach. "Now, now. I like tea. It's just that I much prefer coffee."

She glimpsed across the table at her upstairs neighbors. "He's a bit of a coffee snob."

I showed my hands in mock surrender. "Guilty as charged."

Greg started playing "Wayfaring Stranger", and everyone stopped to listen.

Karen craned her neck and surveyed the patrons, some sitting at their tables, leaning against a half wall listening to music, or carrying their glasses in one hand and dog leashes in the other while strolling out to the beer garden.

The sun tucked itself behind the buildings that made up Market Common. Myrtle Beach's Uptown Downtown as they referred to it. The Market Common was a collection of businesses, boutiques, and restaurants with residences above set on an old military base next to the airport. It was a destination for shopping and dining for those who wanted to stay away from the hustle and bustle of downtown Myrtle Beach and Broadway at the Beach. Tidal Creek wasn't technically part of the Market Common proper. It sat on the other side of the street from the official boundary.

I enjoyed coming to the area. It had a relaxed vibe different from the Boardwalk. A pleasant refinement of pace for me. It didn't hurt that Andrea lived in a condo behind the Barnes & Noble a few streets over. We had seen little of each other outside of work, but it was comforting to know she lived in between my house in Surfside and the bookstore.

Karen swiveled her attention back to the table as Rowles ended the song, drawing the loudest applause yet. He thanked the room and excused himself to take a break and go refill his glass, although I'm sure many of the ladies surrounding the area wouldn't have minded doing that for him.

"There's several familiar faces here from the Hideaway," Karen commented.

"There usually is," Violet said, and lifted her chin to point over Karen's shoulder. "Dick and Janet are over there. Looks like their son and his wife are in town."

Dot elevated her head above the table like a giraffe, searching for a better view.

Karen turned, waved, and swiveled back. "I wonder where their daughter is?"

"From the way Janet talks," Dot said, "probably at some bar in North Myrtle hunting for her next boyfriend. I saw Paul and Marge huddled together near the bar when I came in."

"Louis, Reggie, and Carl were all sitting at the bar, too," Violet said.

Dot said, "It's like half the condo is here."

"Ha! You're saying it's a normal evening at Tidal Creek,"

Karen said.

Upon my first impression, Dot didn't seem like a woman who smiled much. She seemed more serious and straight-laced, but here she grinned and picked up her glass. "It is."

I sat back and enjoyed listening to the Silver Girls gossip about their neighbors. My mom and dad were the same way in their neighborhood. One eye was on the TV and the other on the street to see what their neighbors were up to so they could spread rumors and conspiracy theories about it later.

At once, Karen's gaze fell on something she didn't care for. Her face darkened.

Dot caught the shift in the mood. "Karen, what is it?"

"Him," she answered, and inclined a furrowed brow at the other end of the brewing area.

The door at the other end separating the dining room bar area and the brewhouse opened, and a hefty man entered. He had slicked back hair. It had streaks of gray in contrast with strands of black. His jaw was set in a perpetual scowl. A tall mug with a foamy head to it was in one hand. The other was shoved down in a pocket in his khaki shorts.

Karen took a long pull from the mug. "Here comes trouble."

CHAPTER THREE

THE OTHERS TWISTED to see who Karen was talking about and spun away.

"What? Don't want him to see you?" I said with a smirk.

"Nope," Violet said. "He's the head of our HOA. He's strict, but a pleasant person to be around."

"Know him well?" I asked.

"Well, no, I don't," Violet answered and winked at her roommate across the table, "but he'd like to get to know Karen a lot better."

Karen held her chin up high and nibbled on her bottom lip. "Yes, he would. I'm just playing hard to get."

The wrinkles on Dot's forehead creased like valleys. "Hard to get? Since when have you ever been hard to get? You put yourself out there the moment they placed your husband in the ground."

"Hey now," Karen retorted, "my private life is none of your business."

"It is when we have a shared wall," Violet added. "However, you haven't been cavorting around as much lately."

Karen bent to one side. "Nothing's tickled my fancy."

"Yes," Dot said and rolled her eyes, "tickling is a different way to put it."

Andrea squirmed on the bench seat. I felt her discomfort and shared it. Nothing like hearing women your mom's age discuss their inner love lives in front of you.

Thankfully, Dot changed the subject. "Be that as it may, the man runs the building with an iron fist. Stanley is the kind of guy that when he walks into a room, no one says hello, but when he leaves, everyone says goodbye. You'll get a letter from the association for even the slightest violation, like what happened with Ma."

She began to say more, but the man stopped at our table.

"Evenin' ladies." His paunch draped onto the tabletop as he leaned forward. "And I use the term loosely. Karen, you look lovely this evening."

The man was of average height and wore a navy Hawaiian shirt with white pineapples printed on the fabric. The shirt was tight around his bulging midsection but loose around the back. A sagging pair of Bermuda shorts no doubt gave the people sitting at the table behind him a delightful view of a half-moon. He wore identical flip-flops to the ones I wore. I couldn't nail down the accent, but if I had to, I would say it was somewhere between Queens and the Hamptons on Long Island. His gray hair was slicked back, making his bulbous nose stand out. It was misshapen, like his ears, which led me to believe he either used to be a boxer or had been in a lot of fights.

Karen patted her hair and flashed a demure smile. "Why thank you, Stanley. Just something I threw on."

"Hello, Stanley," Dot said. "I see you're being your usual gregarious self this evening."

He stood straight, chuckled, and sipped from his mug. "I'd

join ya, but I must make my rounds, ya know. If you don't mind, Karen, maybe I'll circle back around, and I'll buy you a drink later."

"Oh, Stanley. You know the way to this woman's heart," Karen said.

Dot cocked her head to one side. "With alcohol."

Mine and Andrea's heads rotated from one side to the next, like spectators at a tennis match.

Karen drew her light coat tighter around her shoulders. "I didn't say it was complicated."

"I'll just do that. See you soon, Deary." Stanley said and trudged off, stopping a few tables away and struck up a conversation with Dick, Janet, and son and daughter-in-law.

"He's been after Karen since he moved into the building," Violet said.

"How long ago?" I asked.

"A few years ago. Before Covid," Violet answered, measuring time as many did post the pandemic and lockdown of 2020.

"Interesting fella," I said. "If he's as strict as you say, why was he elected the head of your HOA?"

The corner of Dot's mouth curled upward. "It's simple. No one else wanted the job."

"Oh," I said.

"When our previous president died of a stroke," Violet explained, "the remaining members of the board called an emergency meeting to elect a new president. No one seemed to care because everyone in the building had few problems with the way it was being run."

"Eugenia was a good one," Dot said.

Violet and Karen raised a glass.

"Stanley was new to the building," Violet continued, "and was one of the few people outside of the board who attended. None of us went. When it came time to nominate a new president, none of the then current board members wanted the job, so he raised his hand and said he'd do it."

After finishing the last of the Beam Reach, I asked, "What qualified him to run it?"

"He said he ran a much bigger HOA at his apartment complex when he lived on Long Island," Karen answered.

Great. I nailed his accent. I'd high-five myself, but I didn't want to look weird in front of Andrea. "That'll do it."

"Yup," Violet said and had a sip of wine. "Fast forward to now, and he's still running it. He's just overly picky."

Dot leaned in. "I heard he used to work for the mob."

"Right," I said drawing out the word, then stood, and collected Andrea's empty mug. "Want another?"

"I do," she said and joined me. "Let's go see what else they have. Maybe get some food to soak up this alcohol. I hear the chef's pretty good."

"He makes a great burger," Violet said, and smacked her lips. "Almost like back home in Gilboa when our farmer neighbor Ollie used to slaughter a cow every other year. Talk about fresh burgers."

Andrea and I stared at Violet in horror.

Dot waved off her comment like swatting a fly. "Ignore her. She's always telling stories about her days of growing up in West Virginia. Her squirrel hunting stories are a hoot."

"They can be a bit much sometimes," Karen said, "but occasionally there are some gems."

Violet's eyes lit, and she said to her silver-haired companions,

"Oh, that reminds me. Did I ever tell you about the time Squirrelly and I got into an abandoned coal mine near Cowen?"

Andrea and I took that as our cue to leave. As we moseyed into the dining room, she patted her stomach. "Suddenly, I'm not in the mood for a burger."

"Me neither," I said. "Let's see what else is on the menu."

Our date ended a few hours later, after a few more beers and sharing a generous helping of shrimp and grits. Stanley had come back around and squired Karen away to the bar.

Andrea had to get back to put Libby to bed. I walked Andrea to the front of the Paradise Hideaway complex, where she gave me a peck on the cheek before saying goodnight.

I floated on the air back to the Jeep. On the way home, my hand would stray to the side of my face, remembering where her lips met my skin and relishing a delightful evening.

Our night was ending, but for others at Tidal Creek it was just getting started, but for two of them, it would be their last night on Earth.

CHAPTER
FOUR

"Mmm, Clark. What's this?" Winona asked after smacking her lips while cradling her personal Harry Potter mug between both tiny hands. The red splotch on her forehead lifted. She stood on the other side of the coffee counter in my bookstore, Myrtle Beach Reads. There were some weeks when I spent more time here than at home, prompting me to call it my "home away from home."

"Moroccan coffee," I answered.

She cocked an eyebrow. "Moroccan?"

"Yes. The headmaster of Libby's preschool is from there. I went with Andrea one afternoon to pick up Libby and struck up a conversation."

Winona raised an eyebrow. "And knowing you, the conversation drifted to coffee."

I grinned. "Naturally. She had a distinctive accent. I asked her where she was from. She said Morocco. I asked her what she missed most about her homeland. She said the pastries and coffee."

"It's delicious, whatever it is." She took her mug and crossed the store to the other counter where the staff rang up books for customers and kept track of special orders and inventory.

Myrtle Beach Reads sold mostly new books, but we sometimes accepted trade-ins if we thought they would sell. While my deceased wife, Autumn, could spend hours in a used bookstore, she didn't desire to have stacks and stacks of used books no one would read. She wanted to optimize our square footage and pack in as many sellable books as possible. It didn't mean we wouldn't accept a rare old Nora Roberts mass market paperback on occasion, though. There was still an audience for her books, my Mom included.

I trusted the keen eyes of my staff, except for Humphrey because he didn't know the difference between Grady Hendrix and Jimi Hendrix, to turn down books likely to collect dust on our shelves. We sent them to the Back Again Bookshop with the cast-offs. I'd met the owners. A lovely couple from the state of Washington. The wife Kelsey had a discerning eye on what books they accepted. However, if her husband, Aaron, was there, I've been told he'll accept anything if you were nice to their shop cats, Caramel and Midnight.

If there was ever a lull in a summer week, it came on Thursday mornings. This was a time after the vacationers taking long weekends left and before the next wave of tourists came into town. I enjoyed working Thursday mornings to get the payroll done and to take care of other business-related items. If those tasks were finished in short order, I'd work on writing books.

On one of those late-week mornings last week, I took my brother Bo's advice and logged into Autumn's social media accounts. The passwords were all saved on her laptop I had dusted off from a closet. I scanned all her messages and activities but found nothing suggesting why someone would kill her. I'm not ashamed to admit I shed a few tears, reminiscing about the pictures she had posted of us on her account.

I realized I'd spent much of the last year speculating not only about if Autumn had been murdered, but also who might have done it and why. What I hadn't considered was how it could have been done. There were no marks on her body. I had her cremated and her parents and I spread her ashes three miles out in the Atlantic in International waters. There wasn't a body to examine for signs of foul play.

That left one possibility in my mind. One Agatha Christie was famous for. Poison. The line of thought opened more questions if that was the case. How was the poison administered? When was it administered? Who possessed such knowledge?

Those questions still rattle around my brain daily. I had to find who did this.

Before my escapade with food bloggers Shelly Garland and Brian McConnell over Memorial Day Weekend, I'd had writer's block. My first book went well, and readers (and my publisher) expected the next in the series. The problem was that I didn't know what to write. I had a late-fall deadline looming. Then, during one slow evening in the store, when Andrea was here sipping on some Earl Grey, she suggested basing a story on the Connor West case. It was a lightbulb moment.

I set to work on it the next day and have made steady progress. My early working title for it was *Death of the Gladiator*, but I wasn't sold on it.

The bell above the front door jingled and in came Andrea. Since moving to the area from Missouri, she'd gained a bit of a tan. Now, she appeared pale, and I didn't think it was from the wrong shade of makeup.

She moved at a quicker pace than normal across the store to me. "Morning," I said. "The usual?"

Instead of returning the salutation, answering my question,

or telling me how handsome I looked, or how wonderful yesterday evening was, she asked, "Did you hear what happened?"

"That's a broad question. Can you narrow it down?"

"With Stanley."

"Who?" The name rang a bell, but I wasn't making the mental connection this early in the morning. I still needed my second cup of coffee.

"The guy in my condo everyone hates."

"Oh, the HOA guy? The guy who came by and flirted with Karen?"

"Yeah. Him."

"What about him?"

"He's dead."

I rested my hands on the counter and expelled a long breath. Her hands wrung together.

"Dead? How?"

She studied the ceiling and had a long blink before answering. "They found him and one employee dead at Tidal Creek."

I had a sharp intake of air and felt the color drain from my face. No wonder she looked pale.

"How did they die?"

"Someone shot them."

"That's horrible. Do they know who did it?"

"Don't know. They haven't released any details beyond what I told you."

A few minutes later, we sat at a table in front of the coffee counter. She idly stirred honey into a cup of Earl Grey, while I held a cup of coffee before me. Steam curled up toward the ceiling from both cups. Winona assisted a cluster of tourists who came in together searching for area guides. Tony Bennett sang about leaving his heart in San Francisco over the speakers. Traffic flowed by on Ocean Boulevard outside. Another busy day was in the works.

"Who found them?" I asked.

"I'm not sure who it was. They haven't said. I've met most of the people who work there."

"Becoming quite the regular, aren't you?" I tried to smile.

She tried as well, but it wasn't genuine. How could it be? Even though she and the other people who lived in her building didn't care for Stanley, he was still a human being.

"I end up there a couple days a week," Andrea said.

"Who was the other victim?"

"I think her name was Emilie."

I remembered her. She ran Tidal Creek's social media accounts and worked behind the bar at other times. It seemed like she was fresh out of college because she and I had conversations about her going to Coastal.

"They have an area inside where Libby can play."

I ran a finger around the rim of my coffee cup. "Maybe I can join you again one of those evenings."

She flashed a genuine smile. "Libby would enjoy that." She tapped a fingernail on the counter. "Look, I gotta get back over there. Just thought I'd come in and tell you. Thought you might find it interesting."

"I do. Thank you." I said the word "you" in a higher pitch, like I didn't quite mean it.

"Anytime. See you later."

"You bet."

Her hand lingered on the counter for a moment longer before withdrawing it and leaving.

We'd reached a point where I didn't charge her for tea anymore. Her having an excuse to come in here was a small sacrifice for the lost profit. Normally, her appearances lit up my day, but news of Stanley's death threw a wet blanket over everything.

It seemed like every time I heard about a murder taking place in Myrtle Beach over the past year, I got sucked into it somehow. Why did this feel like it would be no different?

CHAPTER FIVE

I FOUND MYSELF glued to the TV and internet for the next few hours, hoping to find updates on Stanley's murder. There were few. Even though I only met the man last evening, his death cast a shadow over me. Knowing you saw a person within hours and feet of their murder will do that to you. It's like thinking, *had I been there a little later, it could have been me.*

The other victim was a young woman named Emilie. A recent graduate from my alma-mater and Tidal Creek's social media guru. According to the staff, she tended the bar whenever she felt like it and didn't appear on their weekly schedule. The owners knew she worked hard and would earn her pay, one way or the other. She was beloved by Tidal Creek employees and anyone who had gotten a beer from her. Me included. I'd had a few conversations with her since she started. She was smart, funny, and had an infectious smile.

Any time someone meets an untimely death in the way Stanley and Emilie did, it's a tragedy for someone. In Stanley's case, it might be a relief to the people who lived at the Paradise Hideaway. In Emilie's, those who knew her well said she would have had a bright future ahead of her. Based on our conversations, I agreed. She would be missed.

According to an article, Stanley spent most of his life on Long Island in a little hamlet named Hicksville and was a retired sanitation worker who had worked in Queens. He was sixty-three years old upon his death and lived alone. From Andrea, I learned he took an early retirement after he and his wife divorced, and it was a clean break.

The police had released few details of the shooting. As much as I wanted to talk to her, I would not call Detectives Gomez and Moody hoping for gossip. According to reports, the shooting occurred minutes after the brewery closed, after the last of the staff had left for the night.

I drove slowly by Tidal Creek that afternoon on Johnson Avenue. An Eagles tune about takin' it easy played through the car speakers. Yellow caution tape encircled the entire complex. Rows of police vehicles and anonymous black sedans took up all the parking spaces on both sides of the street. A teal Jeep Wrangler almost identical to my black one but with a wheel cover displaying a Tidal Creek crab logo was the only vehicle out of place.

Just because the location was blocked off, it didn't mean I couldn't see what was going on. Most details of the actual crime hadn't been made public, which was odd at this point. There should be at least a statement by now. Was it something gruesome? Or did it go deeper? Was Stanley's murder part of something larger? They hadn't said where at Tidal Creek the murder took place or who discovered the body.

My mystery-writing brain made up several scenarios, of which none were likely true. As I cruised past the grassy area of the beer garden and performance stage, I noticed a mob of crime scene technicians huddled around a squared area with high horizontal weathered wood slats. Climbing vines wound their way up the enclosure through the cracks between wood. The area separated the parking lot from the beer garden on the back side against the dog park. Beyond was a row of trees bordering the business next door.

The targeted area was where the workers at Tidal Creek took the trash. The concentration of personnel led me to believe the area had something vital to do with the crime. Two doors at the front of the enclosure were open. I spotted the edge of a dirty green dumpster inside.

After passing by Tidal Creek, making my way to the end of the street and the back of Market Common, I noticed Gomez's blue Camry parked near what looked like a dingy, white-bricked distribution center for several businesses. My breath caught, knowing she was in the area.

My mind flashed back to the scene a few weeks ago when we were on our way back from Charleston in the pouring rain after solving the death on the causeway case and pulled into a gas station parking lot. There, we confessed our feelings for each other, kissed intensely for too short a period before she revealed she was engaged to be married to someone else. She'd fought back her attraction to me because she was involved with another man but slipped (which was what led to our brief make-out session), before doing the right thing.

She dropped me off at home later, which led to one of the longest, most restless nights of my life. I had spoken to her one time since then when she gave me the contact information for Detective Banner's wife.

Back to the present. I reached the end of the street. Across from me was the 1229 Shine restaurant. A large mural of someone in an old-time diving bell mask made the reconfigured military building stand out on the street. Behind that was the FOX WFXB studio, where Autumn and I went for the *Carolina AM* program filming with Greg Rowles and Audra Grant.

I tapped the steering wheel, pondering my next move. If I turned left, I would drive past Paradise Hideaway, Barnes & Noble, and out to Farrow Parkway. Going right would dead end at a tall chain-link fence bordering the perimeter of the airport.

The parking lot for 1229 Shine was fuller than usual for this time of day. No doubt, it was the result of an overflow of people who went to Tidal Creek for their day drinking who couldn't get into their usual hangout. Shine had an enormous bar, taking up much of the interior space of the restaurant. I didn't feel like drinking beer. Had more than enough last night, but I was craving some sweet tea and their mouth-watering bang bang grouper bites. It was a healthy enough lunch. Autumn would disagree if she were here. Even three years after her death, her voice still sounded in my conscience. She would call me a fool for the thought, but order a basket for herself.

My work at the bookstore was done for the day. I had no other obligations or plans. Why not?

I drove straight across and parked in the tightly packed gravel lot. I passed an older couple coming out in a good mood. The husband had his arm around the small of his wife's back as he guided her to a tricked-out golf cart.

The man had a white goatee and said to me, "Enjoy. They're on top of their game today."

"Usually are," I returned. "Thank you. You as well."

They motored off as I opened the front entrance. The packed bar stretched out before me. A dining area with glossy wood tables lay to the right of the host stand. I made my way to an empty seat at the end of one corner of the bar and sat on a soft stool before nodding at the bartender who had made eye contact with me.

As she approached, a man to my left said, "It's Clark, right?"

The man sitting next to me on the stool where the sides of the bar met on the corner was none other than Greg Rowles, with a hamburger between his hands and a half-drunk beer beside him.

CHAPTER SIX

"*Didn't I see* you last night at Tidal Creek?" Greg asked and took a large chomp of the burger.

"Yeah, you did. I was there on some type of weird group date."

The bartender waited for me to speak to her, tapping her foot with a menu in her hand. I said, "Oh, excuse me. I'm sorry. Can I get a sweet tea and an order of the bang bang grouper?"

"No problem," she said and sauntered to the other end of the bar, where she entered my order into a POS screen.

"The girl you were with was a looker," Greg said after the bartender was gone. "Don't tell my wife I said that."

I held up my hand. "It's between you and me. I'm amazed you remembered my name."

He pointed at the side of his head with the perfect hair. "It's all up here. I never forget someone who's been on my show."

"Wish I had your memory," I said, although I heard people say the same thing to me. "Enjoyed listening to you play last night."

"Good, good." His head bobbed as he reached for the beer. "I like to play a gig here and there now and then."

"Miss performing at the Alabama Theatre?"

"Sometimes, but I have another project I'm working on up in North Myrtle."

"The Greg Rowles Legacy Theatre?"

"That's the one."

"Cool. I believe you were playing at the Alabama Theatre when I entered Coastal Carolina."

"When was that?"

I told him the year.

He guffawed. "Get out of here. Talk about making a man feel old."

"Sorry."

"Don't mention it. With age and a long-standing job comes the knowledge that someday the kids in the seats might have kids of their own watching you. Can't tell you how many times I had people in the audience tell me they remembered watching me as a kid when they used to vacation in Myrtle Beach with their parents. Now, they're the parents."

"The world works in funny ways sometimes."

"Tell me about it."

We chatted for a few minutes about this and that. The server delivered my meal during the conversation. When I was halfway finished and we seemed to be getting along, I took it as the perfect time to segue into the events that happened last night after Andrea and I left Tidal Creek.

"Did you hear about what happened over there?" I pointed out the window in the general direction of Tidal Creek.

He pursed his lips. "Yep. It's a shame. A darn shame. I'd met Emilie. She was the one who poured my beers last night. I didn't know the man who died, but I remembered seeing him when they described him to me."

"How late were you there?"

He peered at the ceiling for a moment. "Around nine. Right before they closed."

"Did you play for that long?"

"Nah. After I was done, I had some dessert and met with my hair stylist, Tony, to strategize about my upcoming haircut," Rowles said.

I was sure his beautiful mane of salt and pepper hair took some work. He probably had his barber on call. If I had hair like his, I would. I have a full head of hair, but Greg's hair would make most men envious.

"What do you remember about the guy who got killed?"

Greg pondered the question as he sipped his beer. "He was getting around, talking to anyone who would lend an ear. Seemed like a helpful guy."

"What makes you say that?"

"They made a last call and started collecting garbage from the can outside. Emilie came in with a heavy trash bag she could barely lug, and he volunteered to take it out to the dumpster for her. I overheard him tell her he'd help with the rest of her duty. I assume it was because it was still wet outside from those afternoon storms we had yesterday, and he didn't want her getting soaked and muddy. Then they went outside."

"Those were some bad storms we had," I said. "That was nice of him."

"I had the impression it was something he did. Seemed like he was familiar with where to go."

"I wonder if he got free beer out of it."

"Wouldn't surprise me," Greg said. He had an easy laugh, but it grew strained when talking about last night.

"Was that the last you saw of them?"

Greg finished his beer with one gulp and set the glass on the bar top. "Might have been the last anyone saw of them."

It wasn't the last time. Whoever killed Stanley was the last person to see him alive. The question was: did Greg see the killer? He seemed like a guy who would have connections at the PD. It wouldn't surprise me if his number was in the chief of police's phone.

I didn't get to ask him. Greg excused himself, saying he had to go record a commercial for Beach Ford, and left the restaurant. The bartender came and asked if I wanted a refill on my iced tea. The front entrance opened and two people walked in. An attractive, but short, redhead and her much taller husband. I knew they were married because I had met them before. The wife rarely spoke, but her husband was annoying. He seemed to pop up like a bad penny.

He scanned the room, tugged on his wife's elbow, and pointed at me. After saying something to the host, they headed in my direction.

The bartender stood in front of me, waiting for directions.

I said, "Can I get a to-go cup for the tea and my tab?"

"Sure thing, handsome. Be right back."

I reached for my wallet and pulled out a twenty and a ten. Should be more than enough to cover the bill and leave a generous tip.

"Clark!" the man who just entered the restaurant said as he pulled out a barstool for his wife to sit next to me in the spot Rowles vacated.

"Caleb," I said. "How are you?"

"Fantastic," he said. "Grammy is watching the munchkin, so we can enjoy an afternoon out. Going to be awesome to finally sit down and talk to you."

The bartender returned with a tall white cup with a lid, straw, and the check. I took the cup, glanced down to make sure I estimated my check right, dropped the two bills on the table, and told her to keep the change.

Caleb had sat down next to his wife. "You're not leaving, are ya?"

I held my hands out, palms up, and scurried away. "Sorry, gotta run. Enjoy your afternoon."

As they receded behind me and I wound through the tables to the door, I overheard Caleb say to his wife, "Man, that was my chance to pick his brain about his murder cases."

I couldn't leave 1229 Shine fast enough.

CHAPTER
SEVEN

THE FULL REPORT of the murders broke that evening, or at least what the police wanted to reveal. I watched Erica Sullivan of *WMHF News* report the details on the TV in my living room. My feet dangled off the end of my recliner. I made myself a steak quesadilla for dinner and settled into what promised to be a quiet evening at home by myself. As every evening had been since Autumn's death.

"We initially told you about this next story this morning, and now we have more details," she reported, as I stuck a cheesy bite in my mouth. The screen cut to photos of Stanley and Emilie that looked like social media profile pictures before the images ran to long-range shots of police investigators working the crime scene at Tidal Creek. "A member of the kitchen staff found Emilie Smith, twenty-two, and Stanley Griffin, sixty-three, both of Myrtle Beach dead at Tidal Creek Brewhouse in Market Common. A staff member taking out the trash found the bodies around eleven this morning. Police say both victims were shot at close range. The coroner estimates the time of death was between nine and eleven on Wednesday evening. Tidal Creek closes at nine and the owners tell us the last of the staff leaves half an hour later. The police say they have no suspects at this time."

It wouldn't put it past the police to announce they had no suspects when they did. They didn't want the suspect to know they were under suspicion.

The feed shifted back to Erica. "Griffin, a retired sanitation worker from Long Island, moved to Myrtle Beach four years ago. He lived alone at a complex in Market Common, and according to the staff at Tidal Creek, was a nice person who often helped them collect the trash. A daughter and son who both live in New York City survive him. Smith was born in the Upstate in Greenville and was a recent graduate of Coastal Carolina University. She worked as the social media manager at Tidal Creek. We'll pass along more details as they emerge."

Erica threw to the weatherman, who had one of the easiest jobs in America this time of year. The weather in Myrtle Beach was mostly the same from late-May to early-September. Hot, muggy, a chance of afternoon storms, and always keeping an eye out on the lower Caribbean for signs of tropical formations. The first official day of summer was last week, but unofficially the hot season in the South began mid-April.

A chill coursed through me. Stanley died within hours of me meeting him. Violently. Greg told me he saw Stanley taking out the trash at Tidal Creek before they closed. The area where it seemed like the police were investigating where Stanley would have gone to throw the bag in the dumpster before the staff left.

Was someone waiting there to ambush him? How would they have known he would be the one coming? He didn't work there. The killer must have known Stanley's pattern of volunteering to take out the trash. But why had he done that? He retired from driving a trash truck. Maybe he did it for old times' sake. Force of habit? If the killer knew that Stanley helped take out the trash, wouldn't they have known another employee at Tidal Creek would also enter the garbage corral at some point? That meant that whoever did this would have known that there would be collateral damage.

If the killer wasn't there for Stanley, then whoever the intended victim was worked at Tidal Creek. I've been there enough to have casual conversations with several members of the staff, but not enough to be on a first name basis with anyone. None of them seemed like they would have enemies, especially Emilie. They served beer and food for a living. Who wouldn't fancy being in their good graces?

I wouldn't have done it before hearing Erica Sullivan's report, but now I thought about reaching out to Detective Gomez and prying. The problem was this wasn't my business. Yes, I found identifying murderers gave me a certain pleasing sensation. After Autumn's death, I hated to see anyone's family cope with the sudden loss of a loved one with no closure like I had. Seeing Paige Whitaker's husband after her death had driven me to act, knowing she'd left him and young kids behind. It broke my heart.

I know it's the police's job to find the bad guys, but if I came into a situation where I could help, then I would. And did.

Stanley was divorced and had two, I assumed, grown children. Unless he and his ex had a very late start on having kids.

On a whim, not expecting to get a reply, I sent a text message to Phil Moody, not Gomez. The crotchety old detective, with a penchant for inhaling enormous meals and grunting answers to questions, would sometimes feed me information.

I finished the quesadilla and washed it down with a Pepsi. Not the healthiest of dinners, but I'd make up for it with a long bike ride on the beach in the morning.

After piping some classical music by John Allen Howard through the stereo speakers on the wall, I cracked open a new Nelson DeMille book. After reading a few pages, my cell phone buzzed. It was Moody.

He replied to my original question about what happened at Tidal Creek. He texted:

> Guy took two shots to the back of the head. Girl got one to the chest. Messy.

My jaw fell open. Thinking about the way Stanley was shot, I replied:

> Execution style? Like a mafia hit?

He sent:

> That's what it looks like to us.

When I met Stanley, he seemed like a nice guy out for a good time. Perhaps too good of a time. I recalled a story from the late 2010s in Myrtle Beach involving a mid-level drug runner who got arrested as part of an organized crime case. There's been rumors of a Myrtle Beach Mafia for years, but it mostly centered on a good-old boys' network. Nothing like drug running.

The man who killed the notorious crime boss, Carlo Gambino, back in the 1970s hailed from Myrtle Beach. Those were the only ties I was aware of between Myrtle Beach and the mob, besides two mafia-themed restaurants named Wiseguys and Luciano's. They had good pierogies.

Dot mentioned that Stanley had suspected mafia ties from his previous life up North. It's possible his former lifestyle followed him here.

I texted:

> Any suspects?

His response:

> No comment. Don't tell anyone about the method.

By "method," I assumed Moody meant how Stanley was killed—er, executed. I thanked him for the info, set the phone down, and went back to the book. After re-reading the same paragraph three times, I closed the book and set it down.

So, not only did a man I met last evening get shot a few hours later, someone apparently executed him like he was in a Godfather movie.

Stanley retired early from running a trash truck in Queens. What kind of "trash" was he disposing of? Did the mafia pay him to look the other way when Stanley found a body in a dumpster? He seemed like a talker who liked to drink. He could have gotten liquored up, spilled the beans, and told someone some old garbage pickup stories he was supposed to have kept secret.

I watched the Godfather movies years ago and read a few of the books by Mario Puzo. That was the extent of my mafia knowledge. It was possible someone caught wind of Stanley saying something he shouldn't have said and got passed up the chain of command.

A chill coursed through my veins.

The mafia in Myrtle Beach? The Grand Strand has thousands of stories and colorful characters. Why not add some well-dressed gun-toting gangsters?

This was one case I didn't want to get involved with. It turned out I wouldn't have a choice. The case came to me. Just not in the way I expected.

CHAPTER
EIGHT

A FEW DAYS passed with no reported updates on what happened to Stanley and Emilie. What Moody told me about the circumstances of the murder hadn't made it to the public. I was sure the police didn't want to set off a firestorm with details and potential mob ties.

On Saturday morning, I went through the inventory of overstock books in the backroom, seeing if there were any I could remove and donate. Humphrey poked his head into the stockroom door and told me I had a visitor. His face held amusement.

He led the way out to the sales floor. Sunlight streamed through the front windows as it did this time of morning. It was especially harsh when there were no clouds in the sky.

A shapely silhouette stood in the glare. Streams of light passed by her before disappearing into the air. She canted her hips to one side. One foot tapped a steady rhythm. By now, I would recognize this person anywhere.

"Andrea," I said. "Good morning."

Eschewing a greeting, she said, "Clark, I need your help."

***

A FEW MINUTES later, she held a cup of tea in front of her on one table between the coffee counter and checkout counter. A closed file folder lay on the table between us. I held a cup of fresh-brewed Birchin Lane coffee in one hand. The other arm dangled over the back of the seat next to me. Humphrey tended to an older couple wearing MIT shirts, looking for books on engineering for their grandson. My gangly employee was in over his head. The only thing he could engineer was a peanut butter and jelly sandwich.

"What's up?" I asked Andrea.

She sighed, took a sip of tea, then said, "You remember Stanley was the head of our homeowners' association?"

"I do."

"Last night, we had an emergency HOA meeting in the rec room to figure out who would take over."

"Ah." I groaned. "Can't beat quality time like that with your neighbors. I'm sure it went smoothly."

Andrea wasn't in the mood for my brand of humor. "It didn't. They hadn't had a meeting since Covid started a few years ago. With that going on and no one craving to be congregated together because of it, they let it all be."

"Sounds like my community." I took a sip of coffee and listened.

She wrapped both hands around her mug and leaned forward. "Every member on the board except for one trustee, who forgot she was a trustee, had either died or moved away since they elected Stanley."

I held up my hand. "He basically ran the building by himself?"

"That's the gist of it. He took care of everything. Had no issues with the landscaping and maintenance not getting done. Stanley was handy with a hammer and did many of the tasks himself."

"Did he charge the HOA for his services?"

She pursed her lips. "I don't think so. I've only had time to scan the most recent bank records."

I tipped my head forward. "I'm sure you'll find out."

"That's part of the reason I'm here." She puffed some air, causing one of the curled blonde locks of hair hanging over her face to shift back and forth.

I took my arm off the seat and set it on the table before me. "Did you say, 'bank records?' You took a role on the board?"

She rolled her eyes. "I did. I already regret it."

"What happened?"

"Only five people came to the meeting out of the hundred or so who live in the building. Two of them came hoping for free food."

"Did you have pizza? I bet people would have come out for some pie from Ultimate California Pizza."

She gave me a flat look. "They closed, remember? Libby was not happy."

"Oh, right," I said. "I wouldn't be either."

She did a half eyeroll. Maybe now wasn't the time for my corny jokes.

She said, "Yes, we had food. Not pizza, you dope, but that's not the point. The other three, me included, ended up assuming temporary spots on the HOA board."

"I surmise that if you have the bank records, you're the treasurer."

"Temporarily. We're going to hold another, better organized meeting next month after we have time to sort through the mess Stanley left behind."

I cocked my head to the side and raised the coffee mug. "Mess?

I thought you said Stanley had everything under control?"

"By all outward appearances, yes. He did. Then we started going through the mail collected since his death and found overdue utilities and taxes. It's already a mess, and we've just started sorting through it."

"Who owns the building? Shouldn't they be responsible?"

Andrea gave me an exasperated look. "You would assume so, but they're in the Czech Republic and unreachable."

I drank from the mug. "So, you're not here for idle chit chat?"

She grabbed my hand. "Clark, I need your help with this. I'm in over my head. You're better with numbers than I am. I told the temporary board president and vice president about this, and they told me to handle it."

Andrea's palm was clammy. Her fingers folded over mine. She had me and knew it. There was no way I could turn her down.

I drained the last of the coffee. Inventorying the stockroom could wait.

I got to my feet with the empty mug. "Let me get another cup. This might be a long morning."

The relief in her eyes was all I needed. She mouthed, "thank you."

Little did I know I was about to in get way over my head. It's a nasty habit I needed to break before it broke me.

CHAPTER
NINE

IT DIDN'T TAKE long to understand why Andrea was so perplexed. She said the bank records only went back three months, and there was a balance of less than a thousand dollars on the most recent one. What Stanley left behind made little sense. Something wasn't right.

She sat across from me with a hand on her forehead, flipping through the few sheets of records. We had ordered pizzas for ourselves and my staff and Andrea's from the nearby Pizza A La Roma to be delivered. She had a new employee, a retired Spanish teacher named LaDonna, to help her mind the shop and spruce up the photography in her Instagram feed. Andrea's daughter, Libby, was in daycare at Small Wonders in Market Common. Life in the store went on around us. Humphrey and the other members of my staff left us alone. I had to snag the occasional break to serve coffee to customers.

"When was the Paradise Hideaway built?" I asked.

"Twenty-eleven, if I recall," Andrea answered.

After drinking a second cup of coffee while sitting at the table with Andrea, I switched to water. My doctor warned me I couldn't live on coffee alone, and I needed to drink more water. I argued that water was one of the two ingredients in coffee, and I would be fine. She didn't think it was funny, but I did as the doctor says. *Mostly.*

"When did the homeowners' association take over?"

"Twenty-fifteen when the building was sixty percent occupied."

I shifted in the seat. "So, there should be records going back at least eight years."

"I would believe so." She took a sip of lukewarm tea. "The police gave us copies of everything they took in regard to Stanley's role with the HOA so we could sort out the mess. We also couldn't find any recent tax bills or returns."

"Sounds like Stanley was bad with his record-keeping."

"Yeah, but he supposedly came qualified for the role. What was he doing these past few years?"

It was a rhetorical question. There was no way I could answer it, but it was a valid argument. Why assume the role if you would not honor it? Like, if Stanley started fulfilling his duties and found he was in over his head like Andrea, wouldn't he have told someone?

I held up a finger. "If Stanley knew these members of the board were dying off or moving from the building, why wouldn't he at least send out an email saying so? I know Covid limited the amount of one-on-one contact and communication, but he should have at least told someone."

"That's the thing," she said. "No one in the building would have cared. It wasn't their responsibility. The attendance at the meeting last night echoed the sentiment. The people who live at Paradise Hideaway don't covet extra responsibilities. They want less. Have a good time and enjoy their retirement."

"What percentage of the residents do you think are retired?"

She cocked her head to the side and thought about it for a

moment. "I'd say seventy. Seventy-five."

"Wow. That means the other quarter of them are working age and have jobs."

"There are families. We always have a few kids running around the pool. Libby has a few little friends she plays with. Not many."

The bell on the front door jingled and a delivery man came through the door carrying an insulated pizza delivery bag in one hand. I got up and met him at the door. I already paid the bill when I ordered the food but had to sign and add a tip.

He left. I took the pizzas to an empty table in between the counters and set them there. La Roma had included a stack of napkins and plasticware which I laid beside the stack. I told Humphrey and Karen to help themselves. Andrea grabbed herself the narrowest slice of their house special pizza, while I opted for the largest.

After we had taken a few bites, I said, "Let's recap what we have."

"Let's do it," Andrea said with a half-full mouth.

I counted off by raising a greasy finger. "Bank statements going back three months. There's less than a thousand bucks in the checking account. The most recent tax record is three years old."

"Which would have been before Covid started."

"Right. And you have a partial sheet of people who have paid their dues."

She washed down the pizza with another drink of tea. "That's another confusing part. The people he has listed as paying are ones who paid their dues by check, which are less than half of the occupants. Which means most people didn't pay."

"Do you have an online payment portal?"

"Yeah, it's how I paid. It went through PayPal."

"How come he didn't record payments coming from there?"

She lifted her shoulders to her earlobes. "Beats me."

I stared at her for a moment. You could say what you want about her stunning looks and glowing personality, but sometimes the elevator didn't always go to the top floor. I wouldn't tell her that. "Did you check the PayPal account?"

"I didn't."

If I could have rubbed a hand over my face without insulting her, I would have. Perhaps she hadn't had time to check. "Do you have those records?"

"Not in the folder. He left behind the username and password though."

I wiped my hands and mouth with a napkin. "Hold on, I'll be right back."

I went to my office and retrieved my laptop. After getting it up and running, I asked Andrea for the login info. She dug through the file folder and pulled out a sheet containing usernames and passwords for the various online accounts associated with the HOA and scanned the sheet before passing it across the table.

She tapped a finger on a grouping on the center of the paper. The username email address was:

ParadiseHideawayHOA@gmail.com

"There it is."

"Thanks." I lifted the paper and went to the PayPal website where I logged in.

Her brows knitted together. "Something seems weird about that address."

"How do you mean?"

She crossed her arms, studied the screen, and nibbled on a

fingernail. "I'm not sure how, but it feels wrong somehow."

"If you figure it out, let me know." When the account information loaded, the balance showed in big numbers on the left side of the screen. "Uh oh."

Andrea leaned forward. "What is it?"

I swiveled the screen around where she could see it. Her eyes went big, and she gasped, before sitting back in her chair.

She raised her voice. I couldn't blame her. "Account closed?"

* * *

IT GOT WORSE. I logged into their bank next.

She came around the table and sat next to me so she could see the screen better. After seeing the balance of the bank accounts, she held her head in both hands.

"How in the world?" she muttered. "Some people pay their dues monthly, quarterly, and yearly. It varies depending on each tenant's situation. I've met most of the people in the building. Like I said, most are retired."

"How do you pay yours?"

"Semi-annually. Once in January. Once in July."

"So, you were getting ready to send in the one for July?"

"I paid it early, a few days before his death."

I, too, stared at the screen in wonder. The HOA checking account had less than three hundred dollars in it when there should have been thousands. If nothing else, the record of Andrea's payment should be listed somewhere. How many others in the building paid twice a year like her? Transactions for payments from people like Andrea, and the ones who paid monthly and quarterly, should show, since we were at the end of the second quarter. A stirring in my gut told me we had only scratched the surface of whatever misdeeds Stanley left behind.

My finger traced the screen and scrolled through the list of transactions.

"I see multiple check deposits like there should be," I said, "but don't see any funds transfers coming over from PayPal. Do you think he was paying some bills directly from there?"

She snorted. "He may have. I wish I knew how many people paid with a check versus online."

"Did Stanley send out statements?"

"He would." She cocked her head to the side. "I'd get mine once a year. We have a community bulletin board in the lobby where he had a sign posted reminding people to pay their dues."

"Let me guess, the sign stressed paying dues online for ease?"

She stared at the ceiling for a moment, recalling how Stanley worded the message. "You're right. It says something like 'Pay your dues online!' and gives the PayPal email address for where to send the funds."

"Except the PayPal account is closed."

I still had their PayPal account open in a separate tab. I clicked back on it. At least I could see past statements, despite the account being inactive. The most recent statement was three months old. The last few statements showed the money in the account dwindling down. The last transaction showed thirty-three cents being transferred to his checking account.

Andrea leaned in for a better view. I took a nibble of pizza while she tried to make sense of what was on the computer screen. She wore a light, intoxicating, flowery perfume. I would have allowed her to lean closer if she wanted to, but now was not the time. Unless she desired to make it the time.

"These all seem normal to me. Looks like he was paying the utility bills from here." She stopped speaking for a moment as she scrolled up and down again and again through the list of transactions. "Huh."

"Huh, what?" I asked.

"Odd. He paid the Santee Cooper bill three times that month, all in differing amounts."

Santee Cooper was our local electric company. I paid them for my home, Myrtle Beach Reads, and the still in the works, Garden City Reads location.

"You're right, that is weird," I said. "I pay mine once a month. Why would Stanley pay three times? Did he get behind and make three separate payments in the same month?"

Andrea gobbled down the last of her first slice. She concealed her mouth while she chewed. After she swallowed and washed it down with a gulp of tea, she said, "Click through the other statements on there."

We spent the next hour sorting through all the transactions we could find. Humphrey ate half a pizza. A few customers received slices when they jokingly asked if the pizza was free. I didn't mind.

I started a spreadsheet, collecting the various transactions from both accounts in one place. It painted a messy and incomplete picture. If Stanley closed the PayPal account, then the money had to be going somewhere. But where?

They say to follow the money in a criminal investigation. It looked like the trail had run dry, but like an expert hunter, I had a few tricks up my sleeve.

CHAPTER
TEN

THE FIRST NATIONAL Bank of Myrtle Beach sat on Oak Street in a building that used to be a Pizza Hut, near the courthouse where Autumn used to work. It was easy to tell because of the signature roof style. I always found it amusing when banks referred to themselves as "First National" anything. Going nationwide was a lofty goal, for sure, but it made these banks sound more important to customers. The FNB of MB had two branches.

Andrea and I took the quick trip there after bashing our heads on the table in frustration. *Kidding.* We wanted to, but we weren't getting any answers staring at the computer screen. Andrea had tried calling the bank, but after going through an endless number of submenus with the automated phone system that the bank employed and not being able to speak to a living human being, we gave up and hopped in the Jeep.

Through many of the networking events I had attended over the years, I had made an acquaintance with the FNB of MB president. He was a reader of political history who came to the bookstore often.

We entered the front door of the bank. Any visible signs that this used to be a pizza restaurant vanished. The bank replaced the dining room, salad bar, and kitchen with comfortable carpeting, modern lighting, a long counter separating the bank tellers from customers, and a wall of offices to our right. Advertisements for various bank offerings, including mortgages and business loans, were scattered around as were photos of friendly looking families enjoying their time together—no doubt because they kept their money at this bank. The characteristic aroma of baked pizza clung to the walls and ceilings. No amount of odor-dampening primer could get the distinctive smell out of here. I wasn't complaining as it harkened me back to our enjoyable lunch.

I greeted the bank guard with a nod. He stood hand over wrist next to the door. His eyes narrowed. Or tried to, that is. The left one seemed to have a mind of its own. He studied me with a stern expression for any hint of trouble and nodded back. Then he appraised Andrea, tipped his head, and smiled. "Ma'am."

She returned the smile, which I'm sure made his day. "Hello, sir," she said.

Andrea led the way forward. I glanced back at the guard. He gave me an approving nod.

I couldn't recall the last time I had set foot in a bank. My bank had eliminated many of the teller positions over the years and preferred for their customers to do all their transactions through ATMs. It didn't bother me. Sometimes, I preferred less contact with people. I dealt with enough of it at my bookstore.

A host station stood between us and the cash counter. Behind it stood a tall, razor thin man with bleach blond hair who appeared fresh out of college.

He greeted us: "Hello. Welcome to the First National Bank of Myrtle Beach." His voice was loud, but his tone was soft. His nametag identified him as **Tim**. "How can I help you today?"

I stepped up. "Hi, Tim. We're looking for Henry Slade. He in today?"

Tim's chin tilted up. He put a corded phone to his ear. "Uh, let's see."

To our right was a wall of five office doors with accompanying windows, except for the middle one. Each had a nameplate or division name on them. The second and fifth doors were ajar. Muted voices carried forth from within. The first and fourth doors were closed. Lights were off in those rooms.

The middle door, the one without a window, was closed. On it, a nameplate listed "H. Slade, President." A thin sliver of light streamed across the carpet from a crack under the door.

"He's here," I said while Tim listened to the phone.

"Uh, yes, he is," he said. "Who is asking for him?"

I told him our names, which Tim relayed into the phone. He took the speaker from his ear. "What is this concerning?"

"Access to a checking account," I said.

Tim waved his hand at the empty counter behind him where two bored tellers waited. "Sure, just step forward, and one of my colleagues can assist you."

"No, I need to speak to Slade." I leaned closer to Tim and said at a volume low enough so the others couldn't hear. "We discovered what we believe to be fraudulent activity connected to a business account. I know Slade. This needs to be kept hush hush until we know what we're dealing with."

I leaned back. Tim glanced at the guard behind us and back to me. I was careful not to peek back as well. I didn't want Mr. Stern Expression with the bulging biceps to perceive me as a threat.

Tim said a few quiet words into the phone, set it down, and

said to us, "Please have a seat over there. Mr. Slade will be out in a few minutes to get you."

He pointed to two soft navy seats next to the wall outside of Slade's office.

"Thank you," I said.

I followed Andrea to the appointed chairs and sat down beside her. The guard watched me sit. I think. The lazy eye threw me. He could also be staring at Andrea's legs, as I would have done had I been in his position.

Before we could get comfortable, the office door opened, and Henry Slade poked his head out.

"Clark, come in."

Andrea led the way into his cramped office. Two chairs sat before a desk. Three filing cabinets crowded next to the left side of the room. A bookshelf with various awards stood behind Slade's seat.

Slade himself was a shade above average height, possessed a muscular build, steely gray eyes, and short salt and pepper hair. I pegged him to be in his mid-thirties. With the premature graying hair, he would eventually possess the silver hair typifying a high-powered banker.

He sat down and gestured at the seats across from the desk. "Have a seat."

We sat. His gaze lingered on Andrea for a few seconds before saying to me, "Clark, how's it going? Haven't seen you around in a while."

I crossed my left foot over my right knee and got comfortable. "Staying busy."

"I'll say." His eyebrows lifted. "Been seeing you on the news. Haven't seen you at any Downtown Development meetings lately though."

I cracked a smile. "Oh, did you not hear? They blackballed me."

He leaned back in his chair with a playful smile and clicked on a ballpoint bank pen. "No, I haven't. What happened?"

I gave him the condensed version of being caught in an off-limits area at the OceanScapes Resort during the Paige Whitaker investigation and the owner of the hotel getting me thrown out of that specific group. At least he didn't have me arrested.

This was also the first time Andrea had heard the story. I tended not to bring up my one bad run-in with the law while trying to develop a relationship. Then, it occurred to me; perhaps Andrea might like a man with a bit of a rogue streak.

Andrea leaned away, wagged her head, and grinned. "Clark, you never told me that, you scoundrel you."

I rolled my shoulders backward. "Never came up."

She hummed something I didn't catch when Slade asked, "Who is this?"

I did a brief introduction between the two and laid out what brought us to his bank. I concluded, "Basically, we're trying to get the other bank records associated with their HOA account since all we have are three months' worth of bank statements. Your website didn't go back any further."

"Yes, I heard about his murder. Such a heartbreak." He flashed a smile at Andrea, while swiveling in his chair to face the computer on his desk. "Let's see what we can find."

"Thank you." Andrea gave him the account number.

He pecked at the keyboard. The glow of the screen illuminated his face. There were no windows in his office, and the one overhead fixture of fluorescent lights didn't brighten the dim room much.

"Let's see," he said. "Ah. Here it is."

"Here what is?" Andrea asked.

He took his fingers off the keyboard and laced them together on his desk. "This account *was* only started three months ago."

Andrea's face came together like she was sucking on a lemon. "Hold on. Wait. Our HOA has existed for several years." She pointed at the computer. "There should be all kinds of records on there."

Slade spread his hands. "I don't know what to tell you. That's all we have."

I said to Slade, "Could there be another account associated with Paradise Hideaway?"

"Hmm. Let me see." He returned to the computer and resumed pecking. He made a few sounds as his right hand would travel to his mouse and make a few clicks before going back to the keyboard. The pattern repeated itself over a much longer period than his initial search. "That's odd."

I hated hearing someone being questioned use the word "odd" in any investigation. It usually meant the mystery was about to deepen.

Andrea leaned forward. "What is it?"

Slade kept his focus on the computer screen. He confirmed that another checking account associated with the condo had been closed at the same time this other one was opened.

"What? Why?"

"I don't have an answer," he said. "But I can tell you he closed one account on March ninth around ten AM and opened this new one later the same afternoon. We require people who wish to close an account to come to the bank and sign release documents to get their funds. It also affords us an opportunity to keep their business or route it to another one of our services."

"Did he come back to open this new account?" I asked.

Slade shook his head. "No, he opened it online."

Beside me, Andrea muttered, "Oh no. Oh no. Oh no," over and over.

I rested a hand on her arm in consolation. To Slade, I asked, "How much was in the account he closed?"

"Let's see." After a few strikes on the keyboard, he said, "Fifty-three thousand, four-hundred and eighty-two dollars."

Andrea gasped.

My mouth fell open before I could form words. "Seems like a lot of money to be in a homeowners association account."

"Oh, you'd be amazed at what some of the upscale developments have in their accounts," Slade said. He lifted a finger toward the screen. "This is chump change compared to some of them."

If the acid churned in my stomach, I was sure it was causing Andrea's to do backflips.

She turned to me and said, "There's a significant amount of money missing. There was nowhere near that much in any of the bank statements I have from the new account."

I held out a hand to her. "Let me see those bank statements again."

She handed me the stack of papers.

I leafed through them, finding the oldest one, then studied the first transaction. "Here it is."

"Here's what?" Andrea said.

"The initial deposit into the account," I said. "I'm appalled that neither of us caught this."

She leaned over to get a closer view of the page. "What is it?"

"He only deposited a thousand dollars to start the account."

Her face grew red. "What happened to the other fifty-odd thousand dollars?"

It got worse.

CHAPTER ELEVEN

SLADE PRINTED OUT all the bank statements from the HOA checking account and put them into an expanding file folder with the bank's logo on it. We thanked him for his time and information and returned to the bookstore.

Andrea's body shook with anger. I tried calming her, but it had little effect.

We started at the top of the stack to the oldest records and started sifting through every transaction. The going was slow. Andrea had to leave to go pick up Libby at daycare. She said she'd come back and left me with the statements.

I poured another coffee and resumed my spot at the table. Traffic in the store was slow this time of the afternoon. Karen watched a Turkish soap opera on her phone behind the book counter. A cup of coffee sat before her. I eventually relented, after warning her several times not to watch videos while on the clock. If no one was in the store, and all the work was caught up on, I had no problem with her taking a break on the sales floor. I'm a good boss in that way. She was too valuable of an employee to have quit because I denied her the joy she received from watching partial episodes of *Aşk-ı Memnu*.

Month after month of statements ran together. Various regular transactions for power, water, landscaping, taxes, etc. became predictable on certain days of the month. Throw in the odd repair paid to contractors too. It took me ten minutes of this to realize I was searching in the wrong part of the timeline. I tabbed through several pages, skimming the dates, skipping ahead to when Stanley Griffin took over.

I sorted through the first two years of statements under his watch as the HOA president without incident. Then, in October of last year, I noticed an entry for DirecTV. I underlined it with a blue pen. To my knowledge, Paradise Hideaway didn't have community television provided to its tenants. The bill was for a hundred and twenty-five dollars, more like a personal bill.

In November, the DirecTV charge came again. As did entries for gas stations, a restaurant in Market Common named Gordon Biersch. December's statement was a menagerie of dealings. DirecTV again, Travinia Italian Kitchen & Wine Bar, Barnes & Noble, Orvis, and the Uncommon Chocolatier. All businesses in Market Common. I'm sure the residents of Paradise Hideaway wouldn't have appreciated Stanley living high on the hog on their dime. In January, he flew to New York. March led him to Cancun. Hotels were included in the charges. I didn't see any payments for tax preparation during the last two years.

Like air escaping a tire with a nail in it, the daily account balance slowly drained until it got inflated again by the tenants' payments coming in.

I wasn't certain of what point the last of the HOA board members died or moved. At some point, Stanley figured there was no one watching over his shoulder, and he could get away with using the HOA debit card here and there. I underlined all these transactions for Andrea to see.

December threw in another wrinkle. Stanley's same excessive spending still occurred, but for some reason, the power company, Santee Cooper, started charging the entire building multiple times per month. I counted five transactions in December, six in January, seven in February, and eleven in March before he closed the account. It made sense that Stanley would pay his personal power bills and the building power bills through the HOA. What made little sense was the extra transactions. Two per month had normal-looking payments in precise amounts, like $2,450.67 or $85.34. The others were in even amounts for several hundred dollars at a time.

I'd let Andrea call Santee Cooper. She would not be elated when she returned.

The front door jingled, and Libby came running in, giggling, with a unicorn backpack bouncing up and down on her shoulders. She made a beeline for Karen, who stowed her phone away. The two had become fast friends, although Karen was more of a grandmother to Andrea's daughter.

Two potential customers came in behind Andrea and Libby. With the little girl occupying Karen, it was up to me to service the guests.

As I stood and walked to the front, I passed Andrea as she reached our table and placed her pocketbook in an empty chair. She brushed my arm. Her hand was cool to the touch. "Find anything?"

I shifted my jaw and did an intake of air.

She read my expression. "Uh oh. Not good, is it?"

"You're not going to like what I discovered, nor will your neighbors."

She adjusted her cute librarian eyeglasses. "Fantastic."

Her levels of sarcasm approached mine. I found it endearing. "I'll be back."

She let go of my arm and retook her seat.

The customers were a retired couple from Toronto. The husband was searching for an action-adventure novel with regional ties. I pointed him to *Blackbeard's Lost Treasure* by Caleb Wygal. The wife wanted something with a touch of romance and family relationships. She left with titles by T.I. Lowe and Kelly Capriotti Burton.

After they had gone, I went back to our table. Karen and Libby were recreating an episode of *Peppa Pig* on the *Thomas the Train* table in the kids' section. The British narrator in my head went, "The talking pigs that took over the island of Sodor confused poor Thomas."

When I returned, Andrea's face was a dark shade of red.

I sat down across from her. "I take it you saw the transactions I marked?"

Her head rocked back and forth between both hands pressed against the side of her face. "Oh, my goodness. He was robbing us blind."

"So, you did see."

She gave me an expression informing me that now was not the time to attempt humor.

"Sorry."

"What am I going to do, Clark?"

I rubbed my hand across my jaw. There were two items on her task list as I saw them. One would be left for me to do, and I wasn't looking forward to it. "Do you have the power bills from Santee Cooper?"

"I do." She dug through the file folders until she found what

I asked for. "Here you go."

She slid a stack of ten or so statements across the table. I took them and found the account number and cross-referenced them to the bank statements. "It appears he was paying these bills on time. The entries on this sheet give the last four digits of the account number."

"What about the other Santee Cooper transactions?"

I picked up the January statement and ran a finger down the page, stopping on the first Santee Cooper entry. It occurred on the third, as did the one below it. The entries on the third of the month were labeled **Santee Cooper: Utility**. The other ones at random dates but in even amounts had the label of **Santee Cooper: Myrtle Beach**.

"These look like he was paying your bills and his at the start of the month."

"What about the other ones?"

"Beats me," I said. "They're in even amounts. Like he was making payments on something else."

"Like what? It's a power company. What would he have financed through them?"

I tilted my head to the side. "Dunno. Solar panels maybe?"

She shook her head. "We don't have those."

"Then your guess is as good as mine." I set the page down. "You need to call them and sort this out. Then call the police."

She rolled her eyes. "I wish I hadn't volunteered for this. I was afraid you were going to say that."

She bit her lip, causing her right cheek to dimple. A pregnant pause fell over our conversation as she awaited my next words. How could I resist?

"I could make a call for you," I said.

She flashed a toothy smile, came around the table, and wrapped her arms around my shoulders. A smidgen of spicy perfume accompanied her.

"Oh, thank you, Clark!"

"You're welcome."

She released the hug and retook her seat. "I don't enjoy talking to the police after what happened with my former husband."

I raised my hand while keeping my wrist on the table. Her husband got drunk at some honky-tonk when Andrea still lived in Missouri and wrapped his truck around a tree driving home. Andrea was at home with their newborn baby at the time, Libby. The last time she spoke to the police, it was about him. "I understand."

"Thank you. Thank you. Thank you," she repeated. "I owe you big for this."

"Don't worry about it. I'm glad to help."

"Still." She leaned forward and took my hand in both of hers. "If there's ever anything I can do for you, don't hesitate."

"I won't." Dreading the phone call I was about to make, I said, "Let me go back to the office and make a call while you contact Santee Cooper."

"Yay me."

I left her at the table with my laptop. I found it easy to get along with Andrea. Conversation flowed with ease. We were still learning things we had in common, of which there seemed to be plenty. She was a caring mother to boot. Her looks could stop traffic, but she didn't seem to flaunt it, normally wearing sensible attire. Many other women of her attractiveness level and shape would dress like they were hoping for a good time on a Saturday night. That wasn't Andrea. She was a refreshing change from some women who made passes at me since Autumn's death.

That was another thing. Andrea never made a pass at me. We meshed naturally. A rare occurrence in my lifetime. Our relationship had grown over the past few weeks. We hadn't defined it. *Yet*. But something was brewing. I believed we both felt it but hadn't voiced it. For now, there was no hurry. We enjoyed being business neighbors and seeing each other outside of our little strip mall on the southern tip of the Myrtle Beach Boardwalk.

Twisting the knob on my office door, I took out my phone as I entered and closed the door behind me. Dust motes floated through the sunlight entering through thin windows set high on the wall. Shelves containing various writing manuals and marketing books took up one wall of the narrow office. The office was small, but it never felt cramped. I spent little time here, only enough to do the paperwork needed to keep the bookstore running and do a little writing.

I pulled out the chair from behind the desk and sat. The chair creaked. The air-conditioning hummed from a grate in the ceiling.

I tapped on the phone screen several times, going into my call screen, then using the letters on the telephone keypad, I typed the numbers 4-4-6-2 to spell out Gina. The action brought up the phone number for Detective Gina Gomez.

A woman whom I solved a case with three weeks ago and had a steamy make out session alongside the road on the way home from Charleston, in a gas station parking lot, in the pouring rain.

She also had revealed to me she was engaged. Broke my heart. We hadn't spoken since that day.

My finger hovered over the dial button. It wavered before

hitting the back button four times and clearing out her name. This time, I hit 6-6-6 and Detective Moody's name appeared. Quite an ominous number attached to his name. I tapped the call button and released a deep breath.

The phone rang. My mouth went dry. I reached for a tepid glass, half filled with water and slaked my thirst.

When he answered, his tone was not what I expected.

CHAPTER
TWELVE

HE SOUNDED MORE jovial than anything, which for surly Detective Phil Moody, was disturbing. "Clark, what's up?"

I pulled the phone away from my ear and looked at it as though it might be broken.

Moody wasn't one to mince words, and I would not beat around the bush. Nor did I want to. The shorter this call was, the better.

"It's about Stanley Griffin."

An audible groan came through the receiver. "We can't let you in on this one."

"Trust me. I didn't mean to become involved, but we've uncovered a possible embezzlement from the homeowners' association he ran."

He grunted, which I took as a command to continue. I told him about helping sort through the bank statements of the Paradise Hideaway HOA and uncovering what I believed to be a misappropriation of funds, i.e. — theft, but left out Andrea's name. It was an unconscious decision.

He was silent for a moment. "You're telling me he stole fifty-K?"

"More."

"Good grief. That might explain a few things."

I sat back in the chair and crossed my legs. "Like what?"

"Hold on." I heard some swishing sounds come through the phone, followed by a door opening and shutting. "Sorry. Had to step outside."

If he was on the job, it meant he was about to divulge information the police wanted to keep quiet. Electricity shot through my veins.

It sounded like he was on a sidewalk on a busy street. The muted Doppler shift sounds of cars passing by made it difficult to hear.

When he spoke, his voice was clear, if hushed. He must have gotten a new phone with noise filtering. It seemed like he'd used an old-fashioned flip phone in the past. "There's a reason we haven't disclosed details of his murder."

Fearing a grisly explanation, I asked, "What happened?"

A siren zoomed by wherever Moody stood. I assumed at the police headquarters on North Oak Street in Downtown Myrtle Beach.

"We're operating under the suspicion this was a mob hit."

"Mob hit? You *were* serious in your text. Like the Godfather?"

He grunted. "Dead serious. He was kneeling when the shots came to the back of his head."

I gulped. "Execution style?"

"Yes. Griffin was wearing shorts and had abrasions and little bits of dirt and rocks on his knees. He was un-recog-niz-able if you know what I mean." He drew out the word to give it more gravitas. Point taken.

"I understand." A mental image flashed through my brain that would stick with me for a while. "What about the girl? Same way?"

"No. Shot in the chest from a distance of about six feet."

"This happened where they take out the trash? In the tall corral?"

"How did you know?"

"I happened to be driving by there during your investigation on my way to 1229 Shine."

We both knew my scoping out a crime scene was no coincidence, but he left it alone. "Mmm hmm. There were two bags of trash by her side. We presume she was taking out the trash and opened the corral as the execution was taking place."

"I can picture it," I said. "She comes in. Sees the hit going down and receives one to the chest for being there. Collateral damage."

"She took two shots as well, but that's what we believe happened."

"Why are you telling me this?"

He took a deep breath. "Because, until now, we were operating off the suspicion Stanley was a victim of a mob slaying."

"Isn't there a Myrtle Beach Mafia?"

The phone went silent. I almost thought the phone company had dropped the call when he said, "That's the rumor, but this doesn't appear to have ties to any of that."

His statement wasn't a denial that the Myrtle Beach Mafia didn't exist. "So, does my information alter your thinking?"

"Don't know. It could be he was a slimeball stealing money from his neighbors and the mob hit was separate."

"Are there any suspects?"

"There are. Can't tell you about them."

A large vehicle inched past wherever Moody stood.

I had to wait a few seconds until the sound died away before pointing out, "You've already told me a lot."

"It only scratches the surface. The mob may have followed Stanley from Long Island to Myrtle Beach."

"What? Did he accept bribes from the mafia to look the other way when loading up certain trash cans in Queens?"

"I can neither confirm nor deny."

My grip tightened on the phone. I was half-joking when I'd asked. "Not good."

"Not good is right. Gomez has spent hours on the phone with the Organized Crime Task Force in New York since the murders." A pause. "That's all I'm going to say."

We had reached a dead-end in that part of the conversation.

I asked, "What do you want to do with the information about Stanley?"

"I need you to bring it here to the station. You and whoever you're helping need to give us a statement."

I closed my eyes. "I was hoping you wouldn't say that."

"Tough luck, kid. When a person like you gets involved in criminal matters, you're going to come through here at some point."

I didn't like being referred to as a "kid," but Moody was old enough to be my dad. "Gotcha."

"When can you come? We need to get this on the books ASAP."

Libby might be okay staying with Karen for a bit while Andrea and I went to the police station. I glanced at the clock on the wall. Winona should arrive at any minute. The police station was a few blocks away, but in mid-afternoon traffic during the travel season, it could take forever to get there.

It occurred to me the police could gain access to the same records Andrea possessed. We could point them in the right direction and let them figure it out. With all that had transpired between Gomez and I in the past month, she and Moody might not be surprised if I dumped the records in their lap and walked away. The do-gooder part of me would not let the bitter part win. Stanley stole from Andrea, her friends, and neighbors. They deserved justice too.

"We could come within the next half hour."

"Good. I'll tell Gomez you're coming." He made a sound that almost sounded like a snicker. "She'll be glad to see you."

He hung up the phone. I didn't know what to make of his last statement. Was it sarcasm or genuine? Whatever the case, I had to suck it up and do the right thing.

My breathing quickened. I was about to introduce one woman who I was developing feelings for to another who I recently had similar deep emotions toward. That was troublesome enough.

What I couldn't figure out was why it worried me about what Gomez would think of Andrea and not the other way around.

No doubt about it. I was in trouble.

Sounds about right.

CHAPTER
THIRTEEN

BEGRUDGINGLY, ANDREA AND I had collected all the papers on Stanley's supposed crimes and hopped in the Jeep. We pulled into a parking spot facing the cumbersome police station.

Since getting to know Andrea, I hadn't mentioned the flirtation that went on between Gina Gomez and me. Especially not what happened coming back from Charleston. I wasn't one to kiss and tell. Gomez's name had come up when Andrea asked me about the murders I had solved, but I was careful to leave any flirtatious hints out of it. Nothing says "I like you" worse than talking about your romantic feelings for another woman.

The Ted C. Collins Law Enforcement Center on the corner of Mr. Joe White Avenue and North Oak Street was a muted government building made of brick. Bushes and oaks obscured the entrance.

Peeking through the windshield, Andrea said, "I suppose you've been here before."

"Once or twice."

She hadn't attempted to open the door, staring at the entrance with her jaw working back and forth. Delicate hands clutched folders between them. They shook.

I reached over and placed a calming hand on hers. The

tremors ceased. She turned to me. Her chin quivered. Fear filled her eyes.

I tried to give a reassuring smile. "I'm going to be with you the entire time. I've done this before. We'll go to one of their offices, not an interrogation room, and tell them what we know and try to answer questions they may have. We'll sign our names to a statement and leave them to it."

She swallowed. "I hope that's all it is."

"Honestly, this is going to be the simple part."

Andrea faced me. "What's the hard part?"

"When you have to tell the people in your building that Stanley stole their money."

She fidgeted and adjusted her glasses. "This is more than I bargained for."

I realized right away it had been the wrong thing to say.

"That's what everyone has to say at some point in their lives." I strengthened my grasp on her hands. "I'll be by your side the entire time if you want me to be there."

She leaned forward and kissed me. It was brief but electric.

Licking her lips, she reached for the door handle. "Thank you, Clark. Let's do this."

She exited the vehicle. I was almost too stunned to move. Talk about throwing someone a curveball at the last minute. Now, facing Gomez was going to be even more difficult.

I touched a hand to my mouth, savoring where her lips met mine, leaving behind a hint of bergamot from the cup of Earl Gray tea she'd had before we left.

* * *

A+ter what seemed like an eternity of watching her wait on the sidewalk, I eventually joined Andrea on the concrete.

"Here we go," she said when I stopped beside her.

"That's the spirit."

She clutched the file folder in both hands as we walked side-by-side to the entrance. Traffic in and around the precinct flowed like a swiftly moving stream. Petty crimes and misdemeanors this time of year kept the three-hundred member police department busy. It fell to Gomez to investigate murders, thefts, and other assorted unsavory felonies.

I held the heavy steel door open for Andrea to enter. She thanked me, and we entered a cramped lobby. Various types of people waited in uncomfortable chairs atop black and white checkerboard tile flooring. The place smelled of BO and cheap cologne. One woman dressed in gray business attire and blue glasses sat straight in her chair with a manila folder in her lap. An older man wearing a rumpled suit beside a young man slouched down in a chair tried to talk sense into his client. An older couple, looking like they just rolled out of bed, conversed in hushed voices. I wondered if they were here to see an inmate or called in for questioning. Either way, I kept my distance.

Officers escorted criminals locked in handcuffs down hallways stretching from either side of the lobby. I saw a few familiar faces in uniform. No one gave me a second glance. A lone woman sat behind a desk on the other side of a bulletproof plexiglass barrier. The glow of a computer screen reflected on thick glasses. Dark hair streaked with gray was pulled back in a tight bun.

Her arms rested on the desk. A cup of steaming-hot coffee sat beside her. She did not seem enthusiastic about her job. Can't say I blamed her.

"Help you?" she said as Andrea and I approached the desk.

"Yes," I said, "we have an appointment with Detective Phil Moody."

The woman tilted her head forward and regarded us over the top of her reading glasses. After a moment, she picked up a telephone and hit three numbers on the keypad. Andrea squirmed beside me. She couldn't stand still.

I rested a hand on her arm. She stopped. I leaned in close. "You've done nothing wrong. There's nothing to be nervous about. Relax."

She gave a tight smile. "Thank you."

The people greeter behind the desk said a few words into the phone and laid the receiver back in its cradle. She pointed to the chairs along the wall. "Wait over there. He'll come get you in a minute."

"Thank you," I said, and we retreated. The woman took a sip of coffee and then folded her arms in front of her on the desk and resumed her vigil like a gargoyle on a Gothic cathedral tower.

Various people occupied all the chairs. Which was fine, as I preferred to stand. Andrea seemed to have the same notion.

We waited for about ten minutes before someone came to get us, but it wasn't Detective Moody who appeared.

The long legs of Gina Gomez wearing a dark pantsuit brought her down the hall to our right of the lobby. My heart fluttered a beat. I wondered what hers did upon first seeing me. The smile on her shapely lips compressed into a thin line at first sight of Andrea. The two had not met.

"Clark," Gomez said upon reaching us. "Who is this?"

No "Hello," "Long time, no speak," or "I've missed you." Straight to the point. That was the Detective Gomez I knew. Off the clock and out of her signature navy pantsuits, Gina Gomez was easy to get along with. She possessed an edge ingrained in her after years of training. Her dad was also a detective in New Jersey. Must be in the blood.

I shifted my feet. "This is Andrea Crispin. She bought the furniture store next to the bookstore. I've been helping her sort through HOA records left behind by Stanley Griffin."

Gomez gave Andrea a quick appraising once-over and stuck out a hand. "Hi, I'm Detective Gina Gomez."

"Pleased to meet you," Andrea said, taking her hand for a brief handshake. "Clark has told me about you."

Gomez glanced at me. "Nice. Clark is always keen to help others. Gets him in trouble sometimes."

Was that a veiled warning?

Before I could say anything, Gomez cocked her head backward. "Come with me, please."

She pivoted on her heel and turned her back to us. Andrea looked at me. I rolled my shoulders. Even for the business-like Gomez, she was in an icy mood. It could be the monkey wrench we were about to throw in her case, but it could also be from Andrea's appearance. Both physically and her being here with me.

The long afternoon was about to get longer.

* * *

AFTER PASSING THROUGH a veritable maze, Gomez led us to her office. Moody was already there, staring off into space. He grunted when we entered the room. His gaze lingered on Andrea for longer than I felt comfortable. She didn't seem to notice.

"Have a seat," Gomez said, gesturing at two chairs on one

side of her neat desk. A window with cheap blinds let in slivers of sunlight. A desk, four chairs, three filing cabinets, and a brag wall containing her various qualifications and certificates comprised the cramped room. She said to me, "Close the door."

I would have preferred leaving it open with the thought of four bodies squeezed in close quarters, and Moody's tuna breath would have made for an unpleasant ambience.

I was wrong on both counts. The A/C was cranked too high, bringing me back to days of the frigid house Autumn liked to keep. Moody sucked on a minty Lifesaver. They didn't offer us anything to drink.

We sat on one side of the desk. Gomez and Moody sat shoulder to shoulder on the other side. His chair didn't match the other three, leading me to believe they brought it in from another office so no one would have to stand during our statement.

Gomez placed a recording device on the surface of her desk. "I need to record this." She pressed a button on the recorder, clicked the computer mouse a few times, sat back in her office chair, and poised her fingers over the keyboard.

After establishing the time and date of the interview and stating all our names, Gomez guided us through a barrage of questions about how Andrea and I uncovered Stanley Griffin's embezzlement from the Paradise Hideaway HOA. The interview moved fast, as did Gomez's fingers. If Moody did the typing, we might be here for days. After some initial nervousness, Andrea slowed down and told her side of the story. Moody kept quiet the entire time.

Whatever hint of jealousy Gomez showed upon meeting Andrea ebbed. The attractive newcomer sitting to my left transformed from possible competition to a witness in Gomez's eyes. At least, that's what I liked to believe.

When Andrea and I finished and Gomez punched a few more entries, she took her fingers off the keyboard. "Is Clark your boyfriend?"

No, really, she didn't ask that. It's just what I imagined her next question to Andrea would be. I wouldn't have been shocked. Instead, Gomez asked, "Did you see Stanley around the building much?"

"Not a lot," Andrea said. "Sometimes he'd be around the game room, shooting pool or lounging out by the pool outside."

Gomez made a note. "Was he ever with anyone?"

Andrea twisted her lips. "I can't recall anyone from outside the building. He played pool with various other guys in the complex and tried to chat up all the single women anywhere near his age when he sat out by the pool. Seemed like he mingled with everyone. I can't recall anyone he cavorted around with more than the other."

"No suspicious figures around?" Gomez asked.

Andrea shook her head. I was content to listen, as was Moody.

Gomez readied her fingers on the keyboard. "Did you have any clue he was stealing money from the HOA?"

"No. None," Andrea answered. "I barely knew the man."

"Did you ever speak to him?"

Without helping it, Andrea had to smile. "Yeah. I did. When he would see me with my daughter, he always greeted her and told her a joke."

Gomez lowered her fingers on the keyboard and changed her formal tone. "Aww. How old is she?"

"Four."

"That's a great age," Moody said, surprising everyone in the room.

DEATH AT TIDAL CREEK

We all stared at him like he'd grown antlers.

"They've all been great, so far," Andrea said.

Moody grated a laugh. "Just wait until they hit double digits."

The thought of Moody being a parent was something I had never considered. I knew little about him, but him having kids? It was a scary thought.

Andrea giggled. "Trust me. I'm in no hurry to get there."

With the formal part of our verbal statement concluded, Gomez switched off the recorder.

The small talk was great and all, but I didn't want to be here any longer than necessary. However, I couldn't help myself. If we were here, our conversation wasn't being recorded, and the mood had loosened. Maybe their lips had as well.

I uncrossed my legs and sat forward. "On the phone, Moody had mentioned that maybe the mob had followed Stanley here. What makes you think that?"

Gomez glared at her partner. "He frequented a restaurant named Luciano's. Heard of it?"

"Yeah," I answered. "The Italian place up near The Dunes."

"Yup." She glanced at the recording device, perhaps to make sure it was, in fact, turned off. "We've learned the owner, Lorenzo 'The Meatball' Bruno, retired from the Frontino crime family over a decade ago."

My brows came together. "I thought once you were in the mafia, you only left on a slab. How did he get out?"

"That's if you took part in a murder," Moody answered.

Gomez picked up the line of thought. "Right. From what they can tell, he was a capo."

"What's a capo?" Andrea asked.

Gomez laid the pad and pen on the desk and crossed her

arms. "Bruno was thought to have headed a crew. He operated a sort of family within the family. By day, he held a legitimate job as a construction manager. At night, Bruno would report to an underboss or even the don himself on occasion."

"What type of illegal work did he do as a construction manager?" I asked.

Gomez twisted a hand from under a crossed arm. "The crimes he was alleged to have committed weren't done on the job. He held a legitimate, tax-paying job, but they suspected him of having padded contracts and equipment orders to skim money off the top. They only gave contracts to certain hand-picked businesses who had gained favor with the family. He saw to it the contracts got carried out and any competing contractors or bids got snuffed out."

A tremor ran through Andrea's voice. "Did they kill people to get what they wanted?"

"Unconfirmed," Gomez said. "People disappeared, though. It's difficult to convict someone of a murder if you don't have a body."

Andrea and I made eye contact. The nervousness that had subsided after she got to tell her story had returned with a fury. She trembled with the understanding we may be entering dangerous territory.

"How did he get out?" I asked again.

This time, Gomez answered. "Someone in the crime family falsely accused him of being an informant. He told someone at the Organized Crime Task Force that after the accusation, the family did their homework and cleared him. After clearing his name, he couldn't trust anyone and walked away without repercussions. No one knows what happened to the accuser."

"Why do you believe he still has connections?" I asked.

"The Task Force has tracked members of the Frontino gang to Myrtle Beach," Gomez said. "The family checks in from time to time to make sure Bruno isn't spilling the beans, so to speak."

"Ah." I wouldn't consider that "staying connected" to the Frontino family, but Gomez might not be telling us everything. Gomez didn't have to tell me any of this, but she had. Even though a rift had come between us, she still trusted me with confidential information, but would only tell me so much. It meant something. Didn't it?

"What does this have to do with Stanley?"

Gomez leveled her gaze at me. "Stanley was also a member of the Frontino crime family."

CHAPTER
FOURTEEN

A CHILL WENT down my back. "That's, uh, suspicious."

"That's our thought," Gomez said.

The initial shock wore off and my mind cleared. "Is there more to it than they may have known each other in the past?"

Gomez held up two fingers. "We believe Griffin reported to Bruno."

"What's the other thing?" Andrea asked.

"Bruno threw Griffin out of his restaurant the night before his death."

I sat up straight in the chair. "And you believe Bruno, or someone associated with Bruno, tracked Stanley down and did the deed?"

"That doesn't leave this room," Gomez said.

The implications that a mafia hit occurred in Myrtle Beach could hurt the area in several ways. With the way *The Godfather*, *Goodfellas*, and *Scarface* brought organized crime into pop culture, it wasn't a leap to believe hysteria around the mafia could swell. Businesses would get apprehensive about expanding. Prospective businesses would look for opportunities elsewhere. Residents would think twice before going out. Tourists would be hesitant to come to Myrtle Beach if they thought they would get caught in the crossfire.

Gomez slid a business card across the desk to Andrea. "Keep an eye out for strangers in and around your condo for me. If you see anything, call me. Don't hesitate."

With trembling fingers, Andrea picked up the card, adjusted her glasses, and studied it. "I will."

"Good. We're going to step up the police presence around your condo until this boils over."

Andrea's shoulders sagged in relief. "Good. Thank you."

"That's what we're here for," Gomez said.

"What now?" I crossed my arms.

"Give me a few minutes to finish typing up your statement so you can sign it," Gomez said.

"Thanks," I said.

Andrea squirmed in her chair. "Is there a bathroom near here?"

"Yes." Gomez turned to her partner. "Can you escort her?"

Moody grunted and stood, as did Andrea. Minus the grunting. "Right this way."

I stood to let Andrea follow Moody from the room, leaving Gomez and I alone.

After Andrea shut the door, Gomez said, "You two seem chummy."

"We get along." A lump formed in my throat as I rubbed the back of my neck. The desire to escape tempted me to excuse myself to the restroom to avoid this awkward conversation, but it had to be done.

She pulled her navy jacket tight. The engagement ring on her left hand sparkled. "I'm sure."

Gomez wasted no time in dredging up fond/bad memories. If that's where she desired to go, I could play the game as well.

"How's things with your fiancé?"

Her eyes narrowed. "We're good." She laid both hands on the desk. "Look, Clark. I'm sorry about what happened. I shouldn't have led you on."

"Thank you." To show her I didn't place full blame on her, I said, "I should have kept my hands to myself. I knew you were in a relationship." *But I couldn't help it*, I wanted to add.

"Can we try to get back to the way we were before?" She fiddled with her shirtsleeves. "I hate to have left things the way they were, but I was embarrassed. My behavior wasn't acceptable."

I held a hand to my chest. "Neither was mine, but yes, it would be nice to speak to you again with no awkwardness."

"No more awkward than this conversation?"

I chuckled. "Yes, something like that."

Andrea and Moody returned, bringing an end to our private chat.

"Almost done," Gomez said as Andrea resumed her seat.

I didn't know how that could be true since the detective hadn't typed a word the entire time we were alone in the room. However, Gomez remained true to her word, and seven minutes later, Andrea and I signed our names to official statements and exited the police station.

After we climbed back into the Jeep, there wasn't any mention of giving our statement and what the police might do with it. Andrea had been quiet since coming back from the potty break and her cheeks remained red. She broke her silence. Before we exited the parking lot, Andrea said, "You didn't tell me you had a little thing with Detective Gomez."

A tingling sensation swept up the back of my neck and spread to my face. My hands tightened on the steering wheel as I looked for a gap in the traffic on Joe White Avenue. I swallowed and avoided the question. "How did you know?"

"Moody told me on the way back from the bathroom." Andrea crossed her arms. "How come you didn't tell me this before now?"

I flipped my blinker and bolted, making a left-hand turn in the Boardwalk's direction. I didn't believe in getting revenge, but Moody's action made me surmise a few ideas of where to hide his body. "It didn't come up."

Her voice rose. "Didn't come up? You couldn't have told me there was a gorgeous detective at the police station you just *had* to talk to about this? And you may have had feelings for her?"

Still avoiding her question, I said, "What did Moody tell you?"

She huffed. "You two were comfortable around each other, and you had been on a date, and she talked about you in glowing terms when you weren't around."

At that moment, I'd forgotten about Gomez and mine's date-cut-too-short to a gala at the Chapin Art Museum. It got cut short because the managing director of the gallery gave us key information about a suspect in an ongoing case, which we had to rush out and track down, ending our date early. It had gone well before that. Quite well. At least Moody didn't know about Gomez and me stopping alongside the road for a brief but steamy make-out session. At least, I hoped not.

"Let me explain," I said.

In a stern tone like she was counseling her daughter, Andrea said, "Please do."

"First, I can't comment on what Gomez says about me when I'm not there. You'd have to ask her about it."

Andrea's arms loosened from their grasp of each other.

I continued. "Second, she called me at the last minute to accompany her to a fashion gala at a museum. It was the last minute because she and her boyfriend weren't talking to each other, and powers-that-be pressured her to have a date. Third, they got back together and are now engaged."

She considered my words. "Okay then. Thank you for telling me."

"I'm sorry I didn't tell you before now."

"You should be."

As we pulled to a stop at the light to cross over Kings Highway, I wondered what Andrea's jealousy meant and how I felt about it. Here we were. Two people who had known each other for only a few weeks, had been on two dates, and were now somehow involved in a murder investigation together. Albeit, on the outside looking in. We got along well, and I hated to admit it, maybe better than Autumn and I did in our first few weeks after meeting so long ago. That was a different life. We were different people. In the here and now, this new woman sitting next to me was becoming an important person in my life. Would it lead to something romantic? I think we would both agree it was moving in that direction, but after our individual pasts, neither of us was in a hurry. Yet another thing we had in common.

What to do about *us*?

Azure skies were above. Traffic flowed in a never-ending stream. A scattering of tourists drifted up and down the sidewalk. Myrtle Beach was primed to set records this year as far as the number of visitors was concerned.

I reached over and laced my fingers between hers. She looked down and placed her other hand over ours. She gave a wan smile.

"We good?" I asked.

She nodded in confirmation. "Yeah. We're good."

"Good."

The light turned green. The Jeep rolled forward.

As did our relationship.

CHAPTER
FIFTEEN

A WEEK WENT by. The police arrested two associates of Lorenzo Bruno in a conspiracy to commit the murder of Stanley Griffin with Emilie Smith being in the wrong place at the wrong time. Bruno and two men who worked at his restaurant were at Tidal Creek the night of the murders. Bruno's "associates," who worked at his restaurant, each held lengthy criminal records. They had released few details of the crime to the public. It was unknown to me what connected them to the killings.

If more than one person tracked Stanley down to the garbage corral behind Tidal Creek, one man may have been behind Stanley when Emilie walked in on them. Two possibilities occurred to me: Stanley's murderer may have shot Emilie when she appeared, or one of his associates did, or the same person killed both. I didn't know the forensics of this case, but police investigators would be able to tell if they used the same gun for both shootings.

Stanley's only son came down from New York and sorted through Stanley's belongings after the police had done their job. No word on if he planned to sell the place.

Andrea and I dug through more bank and tax records and uncovered over twenty thousand in embezzled funds from Stanley Griffin. We still hadn't figured out why he paid Santee Cooper several times a month in what amounted to another thirty K. We called the power company and visited account representatives to figure out where all the money was going. They checked our records against theirs. Half the transactions were valid. The ones in even amounts baffled them. They didn't receive those funds, which meant thousands of dollars were unaccounted for. We still didn't have an answer.

I informed Gomez of this, and she said Stanley was probably using those funds to pay the mafia off.

We brought in the other two temporary members of the Paradise Hideaway HOA board, Paul and Janet, and told them about the crime. Both were present at Tidal Creek on the evening of Stanley's murder. Janet was the temporary president, while Paul maintained the role of secretary. Together they organized another HOA meeting, but this time they went door-to-door, passing out invitations advising residents to attend with the vague explanation that dues were going to be discussed. With many of the people who lived at the Hideaway retired and living on a budget, one way to bring them out was to hint that their money might be affected.

On a Monday evening, we met in the Paradise Hideaway commons area. The large open room had floor to elevated ceiling windows, coastal décor, a pool table, ping-pong, and multiple tables for eating, playing mahjong, cards, chess, board games, and puzzles. Twin ceiling fans with palm frond blades hung on the ceiling. They remained off, lending a stuffiness to the room. At least Andrea and I felt that way. Many of the older women wore light jackets or cardigans. The high today in Myrtle Beach was ninety-five degrees, which meant the A/C was pumping but the summer sun blared through those windows, creating a greenhouse-like situation, trapping the heat in.

I stayed at the back of the room sipping on iced tea and studying the community info board, paying close attention to the sheet with instructions on how tenants paid their dues. As I studied those instructions, part of it seemed off to me. I took my phone and snapped a picture. I'd ask Andrea about it later.

She invited me for moral support, but I had no dog in this fight. I've attended HOA meetings in my neighborhood for pure entertainment value. They often have epic shouting matches between neighbors. At those, the results directly affected me. Tonight, I could be a fly on the wall and enjoy myself.

Several attendees were present at Tidal Creek on the night of Stanley's death, like Paul and Marge, Dick and Janet, and the Silver Girls as Andrea referred to them. Karen, Violet, Dot, and Dot's mom, Beatrice. For the rest of the thirty-odd present, it was my first time seeing them. One younger couple came with their young son. He and Andrea's daughter, Libby, played games on the floor. They might need earmuffs when the adults started shouting. Several older couples were also scattered around. Some sat by themselves, others congregated in cliques. A long-haired young man with Coke-bottle glasses wearing a mechanic uniform stood against a wall alone. His mouth remained open. Either he didn't have the wherewithal to keep his mouth closed or he was trying to catch flies. A woman I took to be his mother sat at a table next to the wall and instructed him to stop slouching. Moms will mom until the day they die.

Andrea, Janet, and Paul stood at the front of the room, speaking amongst themselves. Paul was a paunchy fella with a comb-over dressed like he had just stepped off a golf course. Janet had curly blonde hair and wore a navy pantsuit like what Gomez would wear, except Janet's legs weren't anywhere near as long, nor did she fill it out in the same way. Her lips were pressed tight when not talking, showing premature wrinkles above and below.

When the clock on the wall reached 6:28, Janet cleared her throat and announced in an authoritative voice, "We will start the meeting in two minutes. Please help yourselves to refreshments if you haven't already done so. Thank you."

I stood next to the refreshments table. Three people hurried back and poured drinks. One guy took five cookies and a can of Coke.

When the clock hit 6:30, and not a second later, Janet said, "This meeting will now come to order."

Janet and Paul took turns going over the details of what led to this important meeting in case anyone present had been under a rock. During their narrative, Andrea added nothing. Her part was coming. She held a stack of papers between her hands. They shook. She bit her lip and watched the two temporary leaders as they laid out the sequence in which this meeting would take place, leading to a vote of a formal board. They glossed over the coming revelation having to do with the bank accounts.

Then the fun part of the meeting began. The airing of the grievances. This derailed whatever schedule the temporary HOA board had planned. I came at Andrea's behest, but this was the fun part. In appraising the attendees, I had the feeling Maury Povich or Jerry Springer could find a multitude of content in this room. I just hoped that the attendees would take it easy on Andrea.

A woman, with braided gray hair and an overbite, raised her hand. Janet, to her detriment, called on her. "Yes, Marge. Do you have a question?"

The pudgy woman stood and held a wrist over a hand in

front of her. "Yes. I have a question about holiday decorations."

Janet, Paul, and Andrea shared a look. Paul said, "I'm not sure we're the ones with those answers. You'll have to wait until we elect a formal board."

The woman stamped her foot. "I will not wait!"

The three temporary board members recoiled. Janet stumbled for words. "Uh, yes, go ahead then."

"That lowlife Stanley fined me for having a pumpkin outside my door on November 2nd, two days after Halloween. Are you all going to be that strict?"

Several among the gathered crowd echoed the woman's sentiments. Janet said, "He fined me as well, but it is written in the bylaws not to have holiday decorations up more than one day after the holiday takes place."

Others piped up and said Stanley had fined them twenty-five dollars for similar violations after Christmas. I knew HOAs could be strict, but that seemed absurd.

Janet held out a calming hand to the original complainant. "After the board goes to a formal vote, I'm sure there might be some leeway in handing out fines."

The woman's face reddened. "He didn't even warn me. Just slipped an envelope under my door with the fine and instructions on how to pay it."

"I'm sorry. We had no control over how he ran the association during the Covid years." Janet waved a hand, encompassing everyone in the room. "All of us seem to get along in peace. Paradise Hideaway is a wonderful, laid-back place to live. The next committee will try its best to let everyone live in peace if the look of the building doesn't get out of control."

That seemed to quell the woman's complaint. She thanked

Janet and sat back down.

A tall, dark-skinned man, wearing a trucker's hat, stood next. I recalled seeing him at Tidal Creek the night of Stanley's murder. Without waiting for Janet to recognize him, he said, "My name is Carl Rhodes. I live in 203. And I also have a complaint about Stanley."

They'd let the gate open. If they let one woman grumble, they couldn't deny anyone else. A parade of stingy fine complaints followed.

Carl complained he was fined for installing parquet floors, an apparent violation of building standards.

All the Silver Girls, except for Karen, had a complaint about Stanley's management.

Violet rose, "He fined me for walking my dog, Daisy, before seven A.M. If the possibility of my wittle Daisy barking was the reason for the rule, then why can the landscapers start mowing and using their leaf blowers before seven?"

That rankled feathers. Several were upset by the conflict in codes. I didn't enjoy being awakened by the landscaping crew that serviced our neighborhood ungodly early in the morning. Apparently, Stanley didn't like early risers.

Dot's diminutive mother stood. She had short, curled white hair, and thick glasses, which magnified her eyes, and wore a creamy knitted shawl around her shoulders. Her voice was raspy, but there was some spunk behind it. "That slime bag fined me for planting purple tulips in our window box, and he didn't open the pool until ten. One reason we moved here was so I could get in early morning swims."

A litany of stories about stiff fines followed. Some I agreed with, others seemed way too strict for what was basically a retirement complex, with a few exceptions.

I locked eyes with Andrea and wondered if she was thinking what I was thinking. None of these fines ever showed up in the accounts. Stanley must have pocketed all the money.

If those assembled were already up in arms about Stanley's strict style, wait until they heard what Andrea was about to say. Talk about adding gasoline to the proverbial fire.

CHAPTER SIXTEEN

AN HOUR PASSED as Janet and Paul allowed everyone to complain. Stanley had more enemies than friends.

When everyone had said their piece, Janet introduced Andrea to go over the accounts. She searched the back of the room for me. I held a fist up to my chest. My way of telling her she has this, and I was here for her. The gesture seemed to have its desired effect.

She took a step forward. "Hi, I'm Andrea, and I'm still new to the building. I haven't met all of you yet, but my daughter and I have felt very much at home."

The Silver Girls sat together at a table near the front. Violet said, "And you've been wonderful to have. We love you and especially your daughter."

Her words brought a smile to my face. There's something to be said about having good neighbors. I've lived in my house for over a decade and there are still people who live close by I've never spoken with. In my defense, the residents at Paradise Hideaway lived in closer quarters and had areas like this rec room and the pool outside to mingle. My neighborhood had no such amenities. I had a lake behind my house and a kayak to use on it. It was all I needed. At least, that's what I told myself.

As I looked around the room at the camaraderie shown to each other, it caused me to wonder if living in isolation since Autumn's passing had been the best way to get over her death. The people who worked for me at the bookstore had been amazing in the aftermath, particularly Karen and Margaret, but I could have been better off being around people and having support when not at the bookstore rather than holing up in my quiet house.

I snapped back to the present when Andrea said my name. She went over how much money was in the accounts during my rumination, when she gestured to me standing at the back of the room. "I asked my friend and fellow business owner, Clark, to help me sort through the bank and tax statements."

Many of those gathered turned to peer in my direction. Murmurs of assent rippled through the crowd.

One man said, "Hey, I've seen him on TV. He's the guy who solved the Connor West murder."

"Oh yeah," his wife said. "Thought he looked familiar. Wasn't he also involved with the composer's death on the Golden Mile?"

By now, my name and face had registered. I sought no accolades or recognition from what I had done in those cases. The media came to me in the aftermath.

One woman who remained hidden called out, "Hubba, hubba!" causing my face to flush.

"Leave him alone, ladies," Andrea said, drawing their attention back to the front. "He's mine."

A smattering of "awws" emanated from the gathering.

Now having gained a bit of confidence, Andrea stood straighter. "I brought Clark in because something baffled me in the accounts. There should have been more money."

"Say what?" a man, who I recalled from the night of Stanley's death named Reggie, called out.

Andrea's shoulders slumped. "Yeah, when we began investigating the homeowners' association accounts, we noticed records for the checking account only went back three months."

A woman with a wrinkly face crinkled her face further. "There should have been years of records."

"You're right." Andrea held up a stack of papers. "These were all we had. I retrieved the list of passwords from Stanley's records and went to access the account online, only to find the account was closed."

The room erupted. Fifty people raised their voices at one time, causing Andrea to shrink back. Janet and Paul did their best to bring things back under control.

Paul stepped up beside Andrea and addressed the gathering. "This is just the start. Prepare yourselves for some bad news. You must let her get through this because it's very complex. Then we'll answer any questions you may have." He turned to Andrea and held out a hand to the room. "Please, keep going."

Andrea tried to put on a confident smile. "Not only that, but the most recent property tax receipt was three years old, and we only had what we speculate is a partial list of you who had paid their dues."

The residents of Paradise Hideaway looked at each other in confusion. Many were asking each other the same question: "I paid my dues. How about you?"

It seemed almost everyone in the rec room should have been current on their dues.

Violet held up her hand. "Why do you think it is a partial list?"

Andrea laid the papers on the table in front of her. "Clark

did the math. If our dues are a hundred fifty dollars a month and there are sixty of the seventy-five units occupied, then we should have received nine thousand dollars a month or one hundred and eight thousand dollars a year in payments. What we have only accounted for an average of three thousand over the last five months."

Dot did the quick math in her head. "So, you're saying thirty-thousand dollars is missing? Outrageous!"

The room descended into chaos. People shouted at Andrea, Paul, and Janet as if it were their fault. Andrea appeared on the verge of tears as the vitriol spewed.

I set my tea down and jogged around the edge of the room to the front and joined the temporary three board members. The volume of caterwauling residents was so loud it caused the floors to vibrate.

I waved my hands up and down and shouted, "Calm down! Everyone, calm down!"

The buzz in the room subsided after catching their attention.

When the sound level subsided enough to be heard, I said in as authoritative a voice as I could muster. "You have every right to be upset. I would be too if I lived here."

"What did Stanley do with the money?" Beatrice demanded, fingering a string of pearls around her neck.

Several others joined in with the same demand.

Andrea, Janet, and Paul did not respond. Andrea's eyes were rimmed with tears. Janet and Paul looked like deer caught in headlights. They got more than they bargained for when signing up. They didn't ask for this treatment. I was a neutral party in all this. Maybe the throng wouldn't demand my head on a stake if I said a few words.

"The short answer," I said, "was he used your checking account as his personal one and paid bills and bought things with it."

"What?" Dick yelled. "I agree with Dot. That's outrageous."

I shoved my hands in my pockets. "It is. He broke the law and Andrea and I have filed a report with the police. They are investigating and are going to bring in the FBI and IRS." Heads bobbed. That seemed to quell some anger. I continued, "The bank statements only give us part of the picture. He was paying sizable sums of money to the power company. Before you ask, we don't know why and neither do they. Andrea has spent hours on the phone and in their offices trying to figure out where the money was going."

A man wearing a quarter-zip golf pullover and Whispering Pines golf hat raised his hand. I pointed at him, and he stood.

"Name is Joe Brunson. I live in 204 with my wife, and I'm a retired banker." He crossed his arms. "On these banking transactions to the power company, there should have been account numbers listed alongside them where the payments went. Why is it so difficult to determine where the money went?"

I looked at Andrea. She stepped forward. "Yes, Mr. Brunson. We know he paid the correct utility bill on the third of every month. Like clockwork. Then he would make other payments throughout the month on a different account. The people I spoke with at Santee Cooper could not trace this other account."

Joe crossed his legs. "We paid how much to this other account?"

"Thousands," I said, throwing the room into another ruckus. I waited for the buzz to die down. Once it did, I continued, "We went to your bank and spoke with the branch manager and asked why there were only three months of bank records. It turned out Stanley closed your account one morning and opened another one that afternoon. We believe this was because he'd planned on hiding what he was about to do with your money. What that is, we don't know everything yet. The authorities are investigating."

Janet came and stood by my side. "There is an insurance policy we have covering embezzlement like this. We hope to recover most, if not all, of the money Stanley stole. The bank and IRS are going through it all with a fine-tooth comb to determine the totality of the crime. And yes, it was a crime. We've all been robbed."

Someone at the back of the room piped up. "Maybe he deserved to die!"

It was a disgusting thing to say. What was equally disgusting was that many agreed with the rabble rouser. As I stood there watching those gathered bicker and gossip about Stanley and his crimes, I wondered if anyone here had learned about his actions and took matters into their own hands.

CHAPTER
SEVENTEEN

THE MEETING CONTINUED for over an hour. After everyone cooled down, they came to a vote and elected a formal board. Andrea was more than happy to step aside from her role as temporary treasurer and let another sap sort out the mess. The "sap," in this case, was the retired banker present at the meeting, Joe Brunson. However, he was due to go on a two-week Viking cruise in Europe with his wife and would get with Andrea when they returned. If anyone was qualified to maintain account records, it was him. Janet and Paul took the "temporary" tag off their titles and became elected officials. The residents of Paradise Hideaway must have known enough about them to entrust the management of the building to them.

Few threw their hats into the arena when the formal voting had begun. The Silver Girls had shown no interest in becoming board members.

Beatrice invited Andrea, Libby, and me up to the Silver Girls third-floor unit afterward. Although Karen owned their four-bedroom apartment, she didn't seem to mind when her roommates invited people over.

We rode the elevator together up to the top floor. The Silver Girls gossiped among themselves the entire way of what they thought of Stanley and what he had done with their money. When we got out, I followed everyone down a short open hallway to their room. A soft breeze whispered through the area. Each apartment had a window by the door, almost like a motel. All had a window box with uniform-colored flowers. Libby and Andrea held hands as they walked in front of me. The little girl had been well-behaved during the HOA meeting. Even during the shouting matches. I would look over at her when the venom was spewing to see Libby laying on the floor, scribbling with a crayon in a coloring book with a contented smile. Andrea had done a good job of raising her.

Their door lay at the end of the hall. A window with a flower box containing the "criminal" purple tulips stood on the wall to the left of their door. Dot entered a code on a keypad and unlocked the door, allowing everyone to enter.

A tile foyer greeted us upon entering. The Girls took off their jackets and hung them on a rack by the door. As this was the top floor, the vaulted ceilings overhead made the unit feel larger than it was. Tasteful coastal decorations gave the home a cozy feeling. The foyer let out into a grand living room. A modern kitchen was set off to the right. A door behind the kitchen was ajar, giving a glimpse of a bedroom within. On the opposite side of the apartment was a hallway leading to four more doors.

At the back of the apartment were expansive picture windows, providing a stunning vista of Market Common. A sliding-glass door led out to a large, enclosed balcony overlooking the pool. It had lounge chairs and an outdoor table and chairs on it.

Violet darted to a door on the left side of the house, while Karen headed straight for the kitchen, calling out, "Who else needs a drink? We all deserve one."

Libby raised her hand. "Me! Me! I'll have some Kool-Aid."

Karen twisted and gave the little girl a warm smile. "Not the type of drink I was talking about, but anything for you, Junebug, as long as your Mama doesn't think it's too late."

She tilted her chin to Andrea for approval. She and I both looked past Karen and out the picture windows. The sun had set over Myrtle Beach. Splashes of orange and blue clouds hung over the sky.

Andrea's nose twitched. "It's fine. If she gets all riled up, she can sleep here tonight."

Karen put her arm around Libby and gave her a squeeze. "This little one is welcome here any night. She's our collective grandbaby."

Dot and Beatrice echoed the sentiment.

"That's right," Beatrice said. With the way her glasses magnified her eyes, it gave them an almost comical appearance. It was hard to take her seriously. The rhinestone covered fanny pack she wore everywhere didn't help her almost comical appearance. "She's slept in all of our rooms at some point."

"I assume Libby loves doing sleepovers," I said.

Libby hopped up and down. "They're the best!"

The girl followed Karen into the kitchen. Dot waved an arm at their well-appointed living room. "Go ahead, Clark, Andrea. Make yourselves comfortable. I'll get you something to drink."

Violet had reappeared, cradling a jittery, small, white Maltese. An engraved collar identified her as Daisy. Violet leaned in. "Then you can tell us all the things you weren't allowed to say at the meeting."

Andrea and I shared tight smiles. There was much that we couldn't and wouldn't say.

A few minutes later, with drinks in hand, we sat in the living room. I sat in a white recliner swirling a glass of merlot while Beatrice, Dot, Karen, and Violet squeezed in together on the sofa. Libby sat on the floor with her legs tucked underneath her, scribbling at a coloring book. Andrea sat cross-legged next to her in front of me. If I needed to get up, she'd have to move. I was satisfied with where I was for the time being.

"I should have known Stanley was up to no good," Dot proclaimed. "Didn't like him from the start."

"Oh, come on." Karen batted a hand. "Stanley had his good qualities. You just didn't see them."

Beatrice interjected, "Kind of like how Stanley craved to see everything of you."

"Ma! Please." Dot gestured at Libby. "There's a child present. Watch what you say."

"Listen here," Beatrice said, "when you get to my age, you can say what you want when you want."

Violet sipped from a tall glass. "Isn't that why they kicked you out of St. Olaf's church?"

"No," Beatrice snapped. "Father DeMille didn't like that I was watching a New York Giants game on my phone during his sermon."

Dot rolled her eyes. "It didn't help when you stood up and let out a loud cheer in the middle of it."

Beatrice blinked. "Hey, I shouted 'Hallelujah' at least."

Violet placed a hand over her eyes and shook her head. Karen sipped her wine. Dot glared at her mom in disbelief. I stifled a laugh.

"Ma, you just can't do that," Dot said.

"What?" Beatrice's scratchy voice raised an octave. "It was

years ago. Eli Manning threw a game-winning touchdown. I can't help it if the NFL schedules games in London that interfere with morning mass."

Dot looked at Andrea and I and tilted her head forward. "Ma is a hard-core Giants' fan."

"Back in Gilboa, the preacher would sometimes have to talk over the sick goats and pigs," Violet said.

Everyone whipped their heads to the native West Virginian sitting at the end of the couch and waited for an explanation.

"The community vet didn't work on Sundays," Violet said. "Some farmers would bring their sick livestock to church claiming they had to keep a close eye on them but hoping Dr. Jeter would take pity and check out their animals after church."

Dot's mouth fell open. "Nothing like a Violet story to break up a conversation."

Violet looked forward, not seeming to grasp the dig at her. The woman seemed like she spent plenty of time in her own little world.

To get things on track, I said, "So Stanley had his good qualities and terrible qualities, and some of you mentioned them during the meeting. Was he really that picky?"

"He fined me for having tulips in the flower box on the window by the front door in the hallway," Beatrice said.

"Tulips?" Andrea said. "What's wrong with tulips?"

Beatrice folded an arm over her wrist. "He said they were an unapproved color, but he was cross after I yelled at him for throwing me out of the pool."

Dot turned to her mother. "Ma, you climbed the fence before the pool was open."

"Hey, I can't help it if I like to get my swims in to start the day. It's what keeps me young."

"You're ninety. You'll catch pneumonia," Dot said.

Beatrice batted a hand. "Whatever. I grew up swimming every morning at Gaiola Park in Naples. Besides, Stanley was nothing more than a fly in my ointment."

In studying the small woman, a person would presume she was weak and frail. Maybe she was compared to fifty years ago, but Beatrice seemed like a tough woman.

"Besides," Beatrice said to Dot, "you were the one who called the cops on him."

"Say what?" Andrea said.

"I was hoping to forget that. Thanks, Ma." Dot put a hand to the side of her face and said to Andrea and me, "The four of us weren't here one day, and he let in a guy who used to work for my former employer to search for documents they thought I kept after retiring."

"Seems rather drastic," Andrea said. "What was so important about what they thought you stole?"

"I was a secretary at a security firm." Dot stopped to sip her wine.

"They were really fancy-schmancy," Beatrice said.

"I don't know about that," Dot said.

"What do you mean, you don't know about that?" Karen said to her friend. Then to us, "Her company catered to the elite. Like celebrities and politicians."

"She loves telling the story of how she met both George Bushes. Junior and Senior," Violet added. "All because of her employer. Well, *former* employer."

"Ah," I said. "And they thought you kept something incriminating after you left?"

Dot tilted her head. "Look, we offered protection to high-profile people. Sometimes they would come to Myrtle Beach and cut loose. We were invisible to them but kept files on their movements. Let's just say some of them were here to have too good of a time, if you know what I mean."

Myrtle Beach was not immune to shady elements taking root in the city. All of us in the room, except for Libby, understood.

"Got it," I said. "I assume, as the head of the HOA, Stanley had access to all the units in case of an emergency or to investigate violations, but how did he explain letting this guy in?"

"He played stupid is what it was," Beatrice said.

"How so?" I asked.

Dot explained. "We had all gone out to lunch. Went to Travinia's. When we came back, our door was open, and Stanley was standing over there in the foyer. He told us the guy below us was complaining of a water leak, and he came and knocked on our door, but no one was home and called the maintenance man."

I leaned forward. "Was there a water leak?"

"Nope," Dot answered. "Not only that, but his maintenance man was in my bedroom when we came home."

"Do you have an ensuite?"

"No. I do not. No plumbing in my room," Dot said. "When the guy came out from my room, I thought I recognized him, but he faked an accent and told Stanley there was no leak in broken English. Then he rushed out of here as fast as he could."

"How do you know he was fake?"

Dot raised her eyebrows. "He didn't have any tools with him when he left."

"Oh," Andrea and I said at the same time.

"What did you do after that?" Andrea asked.

Dot's head vibrated in a herky-jerky rhythm. The movement of someone so aggravated that they were about to pop a blood vessel. "I called the police."

I sipped my drink. "What did they say?"

Dot sighed. "Stanley's, quote, unquote, plumber was long gone. They asked the guy below us if there'd been a leak. He said there was, although I don't know if they found any evidence of one."

I considered the situation for a moment. "Do you think your former employer paid Stanley to let the guy in and gave some money to the guy downstairs to go along with it?"

"I had that thought." Dot pointed at the floor. "The guy and Stanley were friends. Wouldn't have shocked me."

"How long ago was this?"

"Been over a year," Dot answered. "It wasn't too long after I retired when it happened."

"I knew of people back in Naples who got whacked for less," Beatrice said.

"Ma!" Dot shouted and then gestured at Libby. "Children are present."

Andrea's mouth hung open. Mine might have too.

"Let me apologize for my friend here," Karen said, the Southern hospitality seeping into her voice. "Beatrice doesn't have a filter."

Beatrice wasn't apologizing. "If you grew up where I did, you wouldn't have a filter either."

"Mom and Dad migrated to the States from Italy in the 1940s," Dot explained.

"Got it," I said.

"Stanley was nit-picky with everyone in the building," Violet said, "except for Karen."

Karen smiled and puffed up the back of her hair. "What can

I say? We can't all be perfect like me."

Beatrice's lips vibrated. "Whatever toots."

From there, the conversation descended into a good-natured back-and-forth of verbal sparring between the Silver Girls. Andrea and I finished our drinks, thanked them for the hospitality, and quietly exited their apartment.

I carried a sleeping Libby back to Andrea's residence two floors down. It was the first time in my life that I'd carried a sleeping child. Libby wasn't much bigger than a toddler and weighed next to nothing. She curled an arm around my neck and breathed warm snores into my skin.

Andrea opened the door to Libby's room, and I laid her as gently as I could on her bed. I had no nieces or nephews. The meager number of the friends I had kids. With the ones who did, they never tasked me with getting this close to their kids. I had enjoyed being around Libby since she and Andrea came into my life. For the first time in my forty-plus years of life, I felt what I could only label as fatherly affection for someone else.

Andrea held my hand back to her front door and thanked me for carrying Libby down. She gave me a kiss on the cheek and thanked me for everything. As the elevator descended, my mind was somewhere else.

I didn't know how to place this thought and these feelings. They were something I had hoped to share with Autumn.

Those thoughts were obliterated a moment later when I reached the lobby.

CHAPTER EIGHTEEN

THE ELEVATOR PINGED before the silver doors swished open. I exited and strode through the lobby. The rec room lay off to the left on my way out. Its doors were open, and I spotted a few gray-haired men playing pool and some others bunched around a table playing cards. My parents would have been in bed hours ago. The scent of Libby's hair still lingered against my skin.

As I reached to open the door to the front entrance, a voice shouted from the direction of the rec room, "Clark! Clark!"

I stopped. The overbearing mom who had counseled her long-haired son to stop slouching during the HOA meeting scampered toward me from the rec room as fast as her chubby legs would carry her. She tottered with a hitch in her giddy-up. I met her halfway.

When we met, she was out of breath. I took it bursts of speed like she'd just done weren't an everyday thing. Her appearance suggested a sedentary life. She wore designer glasses and a shirt with "CCU MOM" on the front. She smelled of cigarettes.

"Clark, I'm glad I caught you," she said with a native Carolina accent. "I just had to meet you. My name's Marie. I love your book."

This woman was the second person to approach me in public since my book was released. The first time it happened, I thought someone had figured out I was a ghostwriter. Before I wrote my solo book, I wrote books for a well-known adventure writer. He was getting up in years with more ideas than he could churn out and wanted to get as many books published as possible before he died, so he farmed out his plots. I was one of his crops. No one knows what books I wrote. I was under contractual obligation not to reveal who I wrote for. The royalty checks were nice, but after Autumn died, I ran out of steam and felt the urge to leave a mark for myself. One day, Margaret suggested I write mysteries based on cases I'd solved. Write what you know. Unfortunately, I knew murder.

"Oh," I stammered. "Thank you. I'm glad you enjoyed it."

"Are you writing another?"

"I have some ideas for more. I'm under contract for three, so I must do at least two more."

"Great," Marie said. Her eyes lost focus on me and darted around the lobby, looking for something or someone. We were the only two people present. Her hands wrung together in nervous tension like she had something else to say. She stood between me and the front door.

"Have a nice night." I tried to skirt around her.

She side-stepped and continued to block my path. "I'm sorry. There's something I need to tell you."

It was pay week, and I had to be at the bookstore early the next morning to run the payroll. The clock on the wall showed it was near midnight.

"Okay," I said. "Like what?"

Her fingers continued to interlock. She leaned forward. "My son, Colton, used to date the girl who got murdered when they were in college together."

"You mean, Emilie?"

"Yeah. Her."

If I would have had a piece of candy in my mouth, I would have choked on it. The mental picture of a cute girl like Emilie attached to a withdrawn, gawky young man like Marie's son didn't compute. To each their own.

I'd spoken to Emilie during several of my visits to Tidal Creek. She ran their social media accounts and tended the bar when it suited her. Her gig at the brewery was her first job after graduating from Coastal Carolina. She was thin with long hair and had big brown eyes. Cute. Perhaps a little out of the bespectacled, gawky Colton's league.

"It's such a tragedy," Marie said while looking away.

"Absolutely. To have a life taken so young," I said. "Is that what you wanted to tell me?"

"Oh, no, no. Well, yeah, but there's something else."

"Like what?"

"I saw you leave with that adorable mom and daughter."

"Andrea and Libby."

"Yeah, them. You seemed like you were following the Silver Girls."

I nodded.

She held her hands in front of her. Her fingers interlocked so tightly the tips of them were red. Whatever she had to say was making her a nervous ball of energy.

"Sorry. I have anxiety," she said. "Real bad. It paralyzes me. Everything scares me. It took all of my courage to attend the meeting tonight, but I just had to. My stomach was tied up in knots the whole time."

"Why did you have to go? Couldn't your son have reported

back to you?"

"Well, see. That's the thing. Colton ain't a real good communicator. Know what I'm saying? Besides, I knew they were going to talk about Stanley, and I'd heard through the grapevine many people here didn't like him. Especially the women. He made it a point to try to fine every single one of us."

"Us. Who do you mean by 'us'?"

"Mostly us single women. We don't have a man to go nose-to-nose with him. He probably thought he could get away with picking on us."

I scratched the side of my jaw and thought about that for a moment. "Did he try to fine you?"

Her head bobbed. "Fined me fifty bucks because the letters spelling our last name on our mailbox were the wrong font."

Outside of the complex, near each of the main entrances, were small, covered pavilions containing all of the mailboxes. I'd been with Andrea when she checked her mail. Each had a standard room number above the keyhole, but many residents had added their last names as well. A way of bringing a sense of community.

I stifled a laugh. Marie was being serious. "The wrong font?"

"Yeah." She blinked several times. "I picked out some letters from Dollar Tree and slapped them on there. He sent me a letter with a copy of the page out of the restrictions and covenants guide showing the allowed letter fonts."

"And yours didn't match?"

She crossed her arms. "Nope. They do now for whatever it's worth."

The clock on the wall struck midnight. I needed to hurry this along.

"What does this have to do with the Silver Girls?"

Getting to the point wasn't high on the list of Marie's priorities. If she got as anxious as she said she did, then it took a lot of courage for her to wait down here for me to come back down. Whatever it was she had to tell me, she must feel it was important.

"I have trouble sleeping at night. I stay up late." She pointed to the ceiling above our heads. "Colton and I live right up above the lobby. Some nights, I'll sit by the window in my bedroom and watch people come and go. It calms me. You saw the residents here and how old most of them are. Most are in bed by seven."

"Which means there are few people coming and going late at night."

"Correct. It passes the time watching. Some nights, I don't sleep at all and see people emerge from the building in the wee hours of the morning."

"Do the Silver Girls stay out late?"

"The only one I ever see come in after nine, ten o'clock is Karen."

I bobbed my head. "I don't know much about any of them, but that seems fitting."

"I don't know them well either. She and Stanley came home late together often over the course of several months."

"They were dating?"

Beatrice had wisecracked upstairs that Stanley wanted to "see more" of Karen. Perhaps he had succeeded, and Karen kept it quiet.

The elevator chimed. Marie whimpered and looked over my shoulder. I turned to see a haggard man get off and saunter in the direction of the courtyard at the rear of the lobby.

After he was gone, Marie took a deep breath and answered my question. "Seemed like it to me. I saw them kiss and hold hands while walking through the parking lot. Never saw them do that during the day."

"Like they were hiding their relationship." From the way Karen told it, she and Stanley weren't friendly with each other. At least, not on that level.

"That's how it seemed to me. Anyway, the night before the shootings, I saw them arguing in Stanley's car."

"What time was this?"

She glanced at the smartwatch on her wrist like it would tell her. They're not that smart. "Wasn't real late. It had just gotten dark. Around nine, nine thirty maybe. Couldn't hear what they were arguing about. They were sitting under a streetlight, so I could see everything. At one point, Karen slapped him hard in the face. Then she got out of the car before he could say anything else, slammed the door, and rushed inside."

"What did Stanley do then?

"He rubbed the side of his face where she'd slapped him and watched her run inside. After she came in, he sat there for a few minutes before throwing his car in reverse and left."

"How long was he gone?"

"After all the excitement, I couldn't sleep. He came back around midnight."

"How did he appear when he got back?"

"Drunk."

This time, I did laugh. "Couldn't walk in a straight line, could he?"

"No. We get two assigned parking spots per unit. It's a good thing the people who have the parking spots next to his were out of town from how he parked his car so crooked. He uses one spot for his car and the other for his golf cart. Almost hit it that night. It's a wonder he made it home from wherever he went."

"Did you see him and Karen together after that?"

"Nope."

"How long ago was that?"

"You say this happened the night before Stanley's death?"

"Uh-huh."

A tingly sensation worked its way down my spine. No wonder she hadn't seen them together after the altercation. "Got it."

Before I could reconcile this new information with what I already knew, she said, "Here's the thing. The reason I had to talk to you. It has nothing to do with Karen."

"What is it then?"

"I watched Violet shoot Stanley."

CHAPTER
NINETEEN

I HAD TO shut my mouth to keep from catching a fly. It took me a moment to realize she had stopped talking and was waiting for me to say something.

"How come you haven't told this to the police?"

"They never asked."

"Don't you gather this is something they need to know?"

"I do but was hoping you could tell them for me. Do you really believe I would voluntarily approach the police?" She curled an arm around her stomach. "Just thinking about doing that makes me want to throw up. I rarely ever leave this place. It's just too overwhelming. Besides, I know you solve murders. Thought you might use this and see if Violet did it."

"What do you mean? You said you saw her shoot him."

Her lips twisted together. "Well, not literally."

I did everything in my power to keep my eyes from rolling. "Okay. Tell me what you saw."

She rubbed her hands like she was applying lotion. "So, it was early one morning, I think, a few days before his murder. Like around sunrise. It was a night where I didn't sleep."

"You were watching the parking lot?"

She shook her head. "No. I was watching the sunrise. The

reason we picked our unit was because it faces the east, and I can watch it every morning. Anyway, Violet was out walking her dog. Stanley comes out and confronts her. I couldn't hear what they were saying, but he kept pointing at the dog and the watch on his wrist. Led me to believe he was getting onto her for walking the dog so early. They go at it for a while. At one point, he threw his arms up in consternation and marched away. Violet watched him go and raised her hand and shot him with a finger gun."

"And you believe she shot him in real life because of this?"

"Dunno. I don't know about you, but why pretend to shoot someone in the back if you weren't pondering at that moment you would like to see them dead?"

The woman had a point. Was it motive? I couldn't see Violet murdering Stanley over a confrontation about her dog, but there could have been other times they clashed. I wasn't a pet owner, but I knew some who valued their dogs or cats over other family members.

Marie continued wringing her hands. "Anyway, just thought you should know."

"Thank you." *I think.* "Do you know the Silver Girls yourself?"

"Not really. I mean, we've said hello to each other in passing, but I keep to myself."

If I were a person fraught with anxiety like Marie, I could see where she would be the ultimate introvert. Talking and meeting anyone had to be out of her comfort zone, but if her anxiety controlled her as much as she claimed, then it wouldn't be debilitating if she could come to the HOA meeting earlier. She would have known going in that she'd have to be around her neighbors. Something here wasn't jiving.

I studied her and tried to gauge how to use this information.

"I have a few friends inside the police force. Would you be comfortable telling them what you told me?"

Her neck muscles tensed, and eyes widened at the suggestion. "I don't know. I'd be mortified."

"I know a very nice detective named Gina Gomez who could come to your home and speak to you." I wouldn't suggest Moody coming along. He'd spook about anyone. "I would be there too."

Her eyes bore into me for a long second. "Well, maybe. I suppose it would be alright."

I got her phone number, thanked her for the information, and promised I would be in touch with her the next day.

After climbing in the Jeep, I searched out the windshield for Andrea's apartment. The light in the bedroom flicked off.

At twenty minutes after midnight, I sent Gomez a text message before driving away from Paradise Hideaway. This had been one of the longest evenings I could remember having for a while. I was usually home and in bed by ten every night.

This night was clear. There wasn't a cloud in the sky. A crescent moon shone overhead. A bright star hovered near it. Jupiter, I believed. I'd always had a fascination with astronomy and liked to know what was going on with the stars and planets. If I had my pair of binoculars with me, I might have seen the four Jovian moons accompanying the large, bright planet above.

Streetlights lit the way out of Market Common. A few windows in the apartments above the businesses glowed from within. Neon signs on the businesses cast multiple colors onto the streets below.

As I pulled up to the stoplight at Phillis Boulevard and Farrow Parkway, I looked right at an empty lot. I flashed my left blinker and waited. No one was around. To my left was a building containing a Berkshire/Hathaway Real Estate and a Santee Cooper

Credit Union. I peered forward at the lights reflecting off the lake on the other side of Farrow when a thought screamed in my head.

I jerked my head back to the left at the Santee Cooper Credit Union. Beside the door was an ATM machine. I shook my head out of respect. What a sneaky man. A piece of the Stanley puzzle just locked in place.

* * *

My phone buzzed on the way home as I drove on Kings Highway back to Surfside Beach. I pulled up to a red light at the Lakewood Campground/Neighborhood Wal-Mart intersection. The same one where I saw Brian McConnell before chasing him through Surfside and Garden City before ending in crash and explosion. I involuntarily grabbed my chest where I had suffered broken ribs during the incident.

To get my mind off that catastrophe, I picked up the phone off the passenger seat. Gomez had replied to my text:

> Call me tomorrow afternoon.

The light turned green. I was less than five minutes from home. She could wait. As I let off the brake and the Jeep started moving, I thought about what Andrea's reaction would be if she knew I was texting Detective Gomez this late at night, even if it was only about a case.

After I got home and locked the door, I flicked on a lamp in the living room and sat down on the couch. I stared at the phone in my hands. On the screen was my text message chat with Gomez. At the top of the screen was Brenda Banner's contact information

Gomez had given me, which had led to a meeting with Brenda where she told me about the evening her deceased husband investigated Autumn's death. That came after Gomez had told me her version of that evening's events.

I pieced together that the then lead Detective Banner didn't always operate within the lines, and on the evening of Autumn's death, his behavior suggested he was being influenced by someone else outside of the department. Gomez said he kept her at arms' length from the scene and he spoke on the phone to someone in hushed tones. Banner kept meticulous records, and his wife showed me the phone records from that month.

On the night of Autumn's death, he made three calls. All those calls went to the same phone number that had sent Autumn threatening text messages the day before her death. Messages she didn't tell me about. Messages which could have been traced had we gone to the authorities about them. Once I discovered them, it was too late.

After discovering Banner had been in contact with Autumn's intimidator, I had gone down a rabbit hole trying to figure out why they were sent to her. The phone number had been disconnected. How long it had been disconnected, I could not discern. Nor did I learn who owned the number. My belief was the messages and calls came from a burner phone.

Autumn never told me much about the cases coming through the courtroom where she worked. She clerked for Judge Whitley, the Chief Municipal Judge of the City of Myrtle Beach. Most of their cases concerned motor vehicle infringements, such as moving violations, breaking fishing laws, etc. I had gone back and looked at the docket of cases going through Judge Whitley's courtroom around that time but saw nothing unusual. Nothing that would lead someone to threaten and then kill Autumn. I had even spoken to one of her coworkers. She couldn't recall anything strange happening at the time.

One person I hadn't spoken to was Judge Whitley herself. I had tried, but she was a tough woman to reach. If I had a job where I fined and sent people to jail, I'd make it tough for people to reach me too.

After glancing at the ceiling to strengthen my resolve, I replied to Gomez's text:

> I will.

As I tried to fall asleep, I couldn't stop reflecting on the events of the evening and wondered if Stanley rubbed one of the Paradise Hideaway residents in such a way that someone sought revenge.

Way in the back of my brain, a little voice asked, "What if it *was* one of the Silver Girls?"

CHAPTER
TWENTY

THERE'S NO REST for the weary or a small-business owner. Duty called as much as I would have loved to have slept in. I awoke with thoughts of last night jumbling around in my head. No one seemed to have liked Stanley. Of course, those at the HOA meeting airing their grievances about the dead man could have been a vocal minority. It gave me pause.

All four of the Silver Girls, Violet, Dot, Karen, and Beatrice, all had clashes with Stanley. The peeping Tom, Marie, witnessed Violet pretending to shoot Stanley in the back. He had violated Dot's privacy by allegedly allowing her former employer into her room to snoop around. Karen and Stanley had what seemed like a secret fling, ending with her slapping him and storming off the night before his death. The surprisingly spry Beatrice got into it with Stanley after climbing the pool fence before it was open, and he slapped her with a fine over tulips.

If someone were to dig deeper, what other motives could they find for killing the former HOA president?

I had to admit, though, if Stanley was mobbed up from his job on Long Island, and said something to someone he shouldn't have said, then a whack job could have been the result, meaning Gomez and Co. were on the right track.

On the flipside, let's say I wanted to kill Stanley. He'd fined me for something silly and threatened to have me evicted over it. Maybe we'd almost come to blows. If he was gone, then perhaps I had a better chance of persuading the next HOA president to be more lenient. At the age of many who lived at Paradise Hideaway, they might have hoped this was their last residence before finding a new address in the Great Beyond. Let's say I knew enough about Stanley to be aware of his possible mafia ties from up North. Pop culture educated plenty of people well enough to know that, unless you were going to give a man cement shoes and throw him off the Springmaid Pier, a gangland execution of Stanley would be just what the doctor ordered to obfuscate any investigation.

After opening the store and getting the coffee going, I went next door to Coastal Décor. The store was full of tasteful furniture, decorations, and knick-knacks with a beachy theme. She gained most of her business from people buying condos in the resort towers along Ocean Boulevard. The store smelled of caramel and cinnamon.

No one was in sight when I entered. A muffled electric bell sounded in the back office as the door closed.

"Just a moment," Andrea called from the back. "Be with you in a minute."

I didn't respond but headed to the rear of the store and knocked on the open door frame to her office. Her back was to me at an organized desk. The computer screen showed an open email. With one hand, she pecked a response to it at the keyboard. The other held a half-eaten apple fritter. Her guilty pleasure. I wasn't close enough to be able to read the screen's contents. Not that it was any of my business.

"Brought you something to go with the pastry," I said.

She jerked in her chair and minimized the program on the computer, leaving a background picture of her and Libby. She pivoted in her chair and touched her chest. In a breathless tone reminding me of playful Marilyn Monroe's, she said, "Oh, Clark. Sorry. Didn't know it was you."

A quick study of the office showed no live camera feeds of the store's interior. Apparently, it was easy to catch her off-guard if she was focused.

"How could you? Here," I held out a cup with a lid on it. Curls of steam came through the drinking slot. "Earl Grey from the Charleston Tea Plantation."

She smiled, reached for the cup, and accepted it, but remained seated. "My favorite. Thank you."

"Of course, a hard-working mom and business owner such as yourself might need a morning pick-me-up."

She flashed a knowing smile. "Aren't you sweet? You're starting to get me."

"A little." I held my thumb and index finger close together. "Did you get much sleep?"

"Yeah. After you put Libby to bed, I wasn't far behind her. Neither of us changed into our jammies."

"Libby was out cold."

"She had been up way past her bedtime."

"I know you're busy, but I have to tell you about what happened after I left."

"After you left?"

I leaned against the side of the door frame and relayed the conversation with Marie.

She considered my story while blowing on her tea to cool it.

"I know who it is you're talking about. She has a son. Young guy, long hair. Seems like he'd be a regular at We Have Issues."

We Have Issues is a comic book store farther up the Boardwalk near the Gay Dolphin owned by my good friend Marilyn.

"I think so," I said. "Saw her telling him to stop slouching before your meeting began last night. Anyway, it seems like not only did Stanley steal from you all, but he also had friction with other tenants in the building. Did he ever fine you?"

"Nah, but then again, Libby and I haven't been there for very long."

"True."

Andrea leaned back in her chair and rested her elbow on the desk. Her eyelids were heavy, and her hair lacked the finish it normally did. I felt her pain. She still looked cute as she examined me. "Wait a minute. Are you saying someone else could have killed Stanley?"

"Maybe," I said. "There were a lot of people from your building present at Tidal Creek that night, and the two people charged with the murders are out on bail."

The news reported that the police released the two goombahs on bond after arresting them in connection with the murders.

"Meaning what?"

"Innocent until proven guilty. Unless they got caught red-handed and confessed to the crimes, they could stay out of jail and await trial."

"Ah." She sipped her tea. "Then they're out there somewhere."

"Yup."

She held the cup of tea up to her mouth and stared at the floor. Her left foot tapped a quick rhythm.

I crouched down to her line of sight. My knees protested

along the way. I put a hand on her knee. "They have no reason to bother you. You didn't know Stanley well enough to be aware of any specific mafia ties."

"I know, but what if he hid something in those HOA files linking our building to them?"

My mouth opened, but no words came out. I had considered that but hadn't voiced it to keep her from stressing. Too late. "We've been through them. Every page and then some. I saw nothing. Did you?"

She shook her head.

"Okay then," I said, trying to be reassuring, but inside, my stomach tingled. "Nothing to fret about."

She reached down and wrapped her fingers around the hand I had on her knee. Her hand was warm from holding the tea. "Thank you."

"Along those lines, I think I figured two things out. Another layer to Stanley's scheme."

She rolled her eyes. "Like what?"

I pulled out my phone and showed her the picture I took last night of the HOA payment instructions on the community board. "Is this the same PayPal email address that you had access to?"

She took the phone from my hand and enlarged the image. "Uh. No, that is not. I haven't seen this one."

"It was on the board."

"Yeah, but that doesn't mean I paid attention to it." She returned the phone and put a palm to her forehead. "I bet he created that one and switched where the money was going."

"Probably around the same time he switched bank accounts."

She pressed a hand to her forehead. "Ay-yi-yi. I have no idea what to do about that."

"The police would," I said. She gave me a flabbergasted look. I asked, "Might have to see them anyway. Do you still have the bank statements?"

"I do."

"Can I see them?"

"Sure." She spun in her chair and scooted over to a small filing cabinet and pulled open the bottom drawer. Her fingers riffled through the files before drawing one out and placing it on the desk. Leaving the drawer open and grabbing the file, she darted back to me. "Here you go."

"Thanks," I said, accepting the proffered manila file folder. Since I was already down on my knees, I remained there and placed the file on her desk and flipped it open.

"What are you looking for?" she asked.

"Those Santee Cooper transactions."

"What about them?"

"I might have figured them out."

After comparing the various entries, I confirmed my suspicions. Stanley was indeed a sneaky snake.

CHAPTER
TWENTY-ONE

I BID A fond farewell to Andrea and left her store, after making a call to Gomez. Andrea didn't protest before, during, or after the call, much to my relief. It was a call that had to be made.

The traffic on Ocean Boulevard was heavy, as expected, during the peak of the travel season. Cars of various makes and models puttered along in both directions, interspersed with the occasional golf cart loaded with tourists. Brave bikers and blissful pedestrians traveled about, taking in the sights and sounds. The clock approached noon. The sun was high in the sky, reflecting off a calm Atlantic across the street. Sea air drifted in a soft breeze, ruffling palmetto fronds.

From the covered deck at the front of The Shops on the Boardwalk, as our collective strip was labeled, we had a view of the Atlantic. I was grateful that there was a paid parking lot across the street instead of a towering hotel. A bright glint caught my eye from a car parked there. A black Lincoln with tinted windows sat almost straight across from the bookstore's front entrance on the other side of Ocean Boulevard. The sunlight high in the sky must have reflected off the driver's sunglasses.

I shrugged it off and went back inside the store.

A short time later, I sat at a table in the bookstore, awaiting a visit from Detectives Gomez and Moody. Steam wafted from a mug of coffee beside the file folder. Margaret and Winona were running both the book sales part of the store and the coffee counter. I told them to ignore me.

That was no problem for Margaret. She ignored me anyway and did her own thing. A small but intimidating woman, she was a lifelong librarian forced to take an early retirement. She had her own unique way of organizing the books, and I wasn't about to get in her way. Her way of merchandising the books worked. If it ain't broke, don't fix it.

Winona, on the other hand, peppered me with questions whenever she could. I had tasked her with running our second bookstore location, Garden City Reads. After months of inaction and waiting for permits to be approved, construction was underway on the interior of the spot my business advisor, Chris MacInally, and I had picked out near the pier. Garden City Reads was going to sell only books since there was already a coffee shop next door to it. It was a tough decision to make, forgoing coffee. I craved the beverage that fuels my days to be part of the bookstore brand, but I didn't want to compete with a fellow small business owner. Instead, the coffee shop owner and I had already agreed to help promote each other.

The bell above the door jingled announcing Gomez who removed a pair of sunglasses. She wore her usual navy pantsuit with her hair tied back in a ponytail. It only took her a moment to find me. I sat in the same spot at the same table where we first talked the day we met: the day of Paige Whitaker's murder.

I stood up as she arrived at the table. "Good morning."

"Same to you, Clark." She had a Jersey accent softened by years of living in the south. She got straight to business. No niceties today. "You said you had some things to tell us."

"Yes, I do." I gestured at the counter. "Coffee?"

She held up a palm. "No thanks. I've already had three this morning."

"Never stopped me."

She smiled for the first time since entering. "Sounds about right."

"How about water instead?"

"Sure."

"Where's your partner?"

"Moody? Oh, he had an appointment with his cardiologist in Charleston today at the VA Clinic."

"That's right. I remember him telling me before we wrapped the Connor West case, he had a heart that ticked like an '81 Yugo."

We stood less than two feet apart. I had gotten up because I assumed she would want coffee. She was close enough to where the scent of her perfume surrounded me. That smoldering fragrance and the sight of her caused me to get a little weak in the knees.

To keep from collapsing, I gestured to a chair. "Have a seat."

I went behind the counter, brought her back an ice water in one hand and my coffee in the other.

She thanked me for the water when I sat and asked, "What's up?"

Her voice carried a weary tone like someone at the end of their rope. Knowing she was engaged and there was another woman in my picture, I couldn't help myself. Gomez, Gina, sounded like a woman who needed someone to talk to. In a gentle voice, I asked, "What's the matter?"

Her voice sputtered. "Clark, I can't talk about it. Shouldn't talk about it."

This wasn't the first time she had said something similar to me and then gone against what she said. Then I said something I immediately regretted. "If you ever need someone to talk to, just let me know."

"Thank you." She paused. "Wouldn't your girlfriend have something to say about that?"

It was my turn to pause. Andrea and I hadn't defined our relationship. Contemplating our time together over these past few days, maybe it was time for a discussion.

Then I said the second thing I regretted. "She's not my girlfriend. We're friendly is all."

"Yeah, but I could see it," Gomez said. "The way you two were around each other. There's something there."

"I'm not going to deny that."

Her shoulders made the slightest of dips, but her face remained stoic. Before I could get to last night's events, this conversation had already gotten uncomfortable. She seemed to sense that and got us moving into familiar territory. Murder.

"You said you might have another suspect in Stanley Griffin's death and reckon you have an idea about where all the money was going."

"Yes." I related the evening's events, starting with the HOA meeting and the hostilities there, the payment email address switch, and finishing with Marie mentioning seeing Violet shoot a finger gun at Stanley's back mere weeks before his death.

When I was done, she said, "That's a lot to unpack. I'll get those email addresses from you and get our people on it. We questioned Violet when we interviewed all the current and former Tidal Creek employees, searching for motive. This didn't come up."

"I believe I know where those extra electricity transactions were coming from."

DEATH AT TIDAL CREEK

"Oh?"

"Yes. We were barking up the wrong tree. Remember, some payments to Santee Cooper occurred on the same date every month and were in varied amounts. Then the other ones came randomly and were even numbers."

"Right, and they had no clue where those payments were going."

"What if they weren't payments at all?"

"What do you mean?"

"What if he was hitting up the Santee Cooper Credit Union ATM at the end of his street and withdrawing thousands of dollars in cash?"

Gomez snickered at my suggestion.

"What?" I asked, a little perturbed by her reaction.

She took my drift. "No, Clark. Don't misunderstand. I'm not laughing at what you said. When you look at it that way, it's so obvious. I'll give it to him. Stanley was a clever man."

"Maybe too clever."

"That would explain where he was getting the money to repay the vig he owed."

I scratched my head. "The vig?"

"Yeah. The vig is short for vigorish. The Organized Crime Drug Enforcement Task Force in New York found Stanley had gotten out of the Frontino crime family on the condition he never talks about anything he saw and if he pays a vig every month to the family until the day he dies."

"Not optimal."

"Nope, but it was the path he chose."

"How did they find out about the vig?"

She explained that the OCDETF closely monitors the mail

going in and out of the Frontino family's various businesses. "The OCDETF told us they found envelopes coming from Stanley and going to a construction company containing cash."

"What did they do with the cash?"

"Oh, they let it go on. They didn't want to interrupt their business. They're looking for bigger fish to fry than a couple thousand dollars in cash from a retired sanitation worker."

Drug money, in other words. "Got it."

"Thanks for the information, Clark. I appreciate it."

"What are you going to do with it? Anything?"

"I'll ask Moody his thoughts and call the Organized Crime people. See if the amounts of cash correlate to some envelopes filled with cash they intercepted. We might talk to Violet again as well."

"What about Marie? She's the one who saw the comings and goings in the parking lot."

"Let me think about it."

"Is the reason you have to think about it is that you already arrested someone?"

"Partly. The other thing is we're stretched so thin. Budget cuts came down from the mayor's office, which have me and Moody burning the candle from both ends."

"I'm sorry."

"Yeah, like with Stanley. Just part of the job I chose. It's out of my control." She sighed.

That was one aspect of owning my business I enjoyed. I controlled everything to a degree. There was no need for me to be concerned about more work from my boss. I was the boss.

"You look tired," I said.

Her cheeks blushed on either side of a warm smile. In a

sarcastic tone and a break from her professionalism, she said, "Thanks for noticing."

"I've never seen you appear this out of sorts before."

She placed her right hand on the table between us. The other she kept at her side, hiding the engagement ring. Again. Out of sight, out of mind. I interpreted the gesture as an unconscious invitation on her part for me to grasp her hand and bring her some comfort. Earlier, we both acknowledged what was happening between Andrea and me, and I was all too aware of Gina's relationship status.

I glanced at the wall separating my bookstore from Andrea's business. She was on the other side of it at this moment. Gina's fiancé was also not present. Not that I had ever met him, anyway. It was just the two of us. Right now, a woman who I had shared a brief passionate moment with was sitting here with me, a mere twenty-four inches apart. Not separated by a wall, but by a table. It took everything I had to not take her hand in mine.

"I hate that for you," I said, keeping my hands to myself.

She didn't remove her hand from the table. "Thank you."

"Like I said, if you need to talk about it, you know where to find me."

"Thank you," she repeated. "I'll keep it in mind."

Something she said a moment before caused a *ping* in the back of my brain, but I couldn't find the source of the sound just then. "Did you say you might talk to Violet *again*?

She stared at me before answering, perhaps weighing how much she should divulge about their investigation. When she answered, it threw me for a loop.

"It's not the first time Violet's name came up in connection to this case."

CHAPTER
TWENTY-TWO

IT WAS MY turn to be silent. There might have been more to the batty woman from West Virginia than I'd thought.

I stared at Gomez for a beat before asking, "In what way was she connected?"

"Clark." She expelled a breath, crossed her arms, then pressed her lips together.

I knew what that meant. I crossed my arms as well. Two could play the game.

I leaned forward. "Look, you know me, and you wouldn't be here if you thought I couldn't add light to the case. I think the reason you're here and not at the station is because you don't want them to know you're talking to me. When Andrea and I came to the police station, you hadn't arrested anyone yet. Now that you have and had to let them out on bail, you need to see what I have to say before throwing a monkey wrench into everything."

She sat back in her chair and crossed her legs, arms still folded. "Can't put much past you, can I?"

"That's not a denial."

"No, it's not. You're dead on." She uncurled her arms and let one dangle while she placed the other on her cheek. "Violet used to work at Tidal Creek."

"I didn't know that. What does it have to do with the murder?"

"We don't know if it did, but it came up in our investigation when we spoke with the people there that night."

"Gotcha. How long has it been since she was an employee?"

"She worked in the kitchen for about six months after she moved here."

"How long ago?"

Her head tilted. "Three years. She and the rest of the women who live in her apartment have been there for about that long."

"The Silver Girls, you mean?"

Her lips curled. "Yes. That's what others called them during interviews. Fitting."

"Yes, it is."

After learning that animosity between several residents of Paradise Hideaway and Stanley existed, I'd grown more curious about the events leading up to and including the murders. I tried to probe. Like asking the prettiest girl at the prom for a dance, the worst she could say is, "No."

She'd opened up about the investigation. With her being more forthcoming, I went for it. "What time were they killed?"

"We still don't know the exact time of death, but they disappeared from the cameras about ten minutes before closing." She glanced to either side of her before coming back to me. "This doesn't go past you."

I sat up straight in my chair and uncrossed my arms. "Of course."

"Tidal Creek has some gaps in their security camera coverage. For one, they don't have a camera on or in their garbage corral. We know what time Stanley and Emilie left the building and started going around the property collecting trash, but not what time they opened the door to throw it away."

"Do they have cameras showing areas outside of the brewery?"

"They are all directed at the building, storage units behind it, and the beer garden. The area where they discard the trash is in the middle of it all. The perimeter tree line between there and the property beside it is also not visible. Emilie walked to the brewery. She lived in an apartment above Gordon Biersch."

Gordon Biersch was another brewery/restaurant in Market Common. You could almost throw a rock from one place and hit the other. The other part of what she said, about the camera coverage, suggested that someone could have snuck between the trees to gain access to the trash corral from the neighboring business. Interesting.

"Easy commute," I said.

"Definitely," Gomez replied. "She lived with some friends from college. Anyway, there wouldn't have been a vehicle for her to leave in the parking lot. Same with Stanley. He walked or drove to Tidal Creek. His cart and car were still at Paradise Hideaway when we went to inspect his apartment, so he had to have walked that evening."

"Did any angle show him arriving?"

"Nope. Only that he walked in the front entrance. We're not sure exactly where he parked if he came by vehicle."

"If he drove, is it possible someone took the cart back to his place and left it there as part of a coverup?"

"Likely not in this case. We found one set of golf cart keys hanging on a hook by his door and another in a kitchen drawer, along with his spare apartment key."

I recalled entering the Silver Girls' apartment last night. "He didn't need one. All the doors have a keypad. No key necessary."

"That's right. Less to keep track of for someone going out drinking nearby."

I raised a finger from where one hand was on the other elbow. "Except he'd have to remember his code. I'm sure that could be problematic if he indulged enough."

"Tidal Creek cuts people off when they've had too much to drink. Their staff is well trained. They'll even call an Uber for you if they don't think you should drive home."

"Good to know," I said. "How did you link Lorenzo Bruno's men to the scene?"

"Easy. They were there."

"Did they sneak in?"

She shook her head. "Nope. Bruno and two guys who work in his kitchen came and ordered a few beers. No sneaking involved."

"Did you see if they talked to Stanley?"

"There were cameras on them the entire time. As far as we could tell, the only time Stanley came close to them was to go to the restroom. They watched him enter, but he didn't acknowledge them. They left after he walked in. Stanley hung out in the beer garden most of the night around a fire pit."

I wondered if Gomez had seen me on my date with Andrea. If she watched every moment Stanley was on the premises, then she would have seen him stop by our table. If she wasn't going to mention it, neither was I. "Do you think Stanley saw them at all?"

"No telling."

"How did you link them to the crime?"

She sipped her drink. "Can't tell you."

That was disappointing. Apparently, there was a fine line between what she would tell me and what she wouldn't.

"Did you notice anything odd about the scene?"

"I'd never seen someone murdered in that manner in my time with the department," Gomez said. "My dad is a retired detective from New York City. He's seen it all, gangland executions included. When I told him about this, one thing stuck out to him."

"What's that?"

"The killer shot Stanley with a small caliber weapon. Dad said the mob likes bigger guns to make it difficult to ID the victims."

"Why?"

"Because when the mob does a double tap with a bigger gun, the victim's face becomes unrecognizable. That was the case here, but not to that extent."

I recoiled. "Oh. Moody mentioned that."

"Yeah. Many times, the mafia will leave their gun at a crime scene if they've taken steps to make it untraceable."

"Right. Like in The Godfather. Leave the gun. Take the cannoli."

Gomez's nose crinkled. "Something like that. The reasoning being if they leave the gun at the scene, it can't be found on the suspect later."

"Makes sense. Did they take the cannoli and leave the gun?"

"No. We haven't found a murder weapon."

Parts of what she was telling me weren't connecting, and perhaps she was holding out crucial information. My next question would be one of public knowledge. If not now, but sometime. "How did you get enough to make an arrest?"

She held up a finger with each word: "Means. Motive. Opportunity."

We sipped our drinks as I processed what she said. The three keystones to any investigation. Bruno and his men were at Tidal Creek that night. The opportunity. If they did shady things as many suspected they were doing, then the means was an easy one to connect, except for the part about not finding the murder weapon. Motive could have been for a couple of reasons. Either a command from the boss, a command from Papa Frontino, or the result of a fallout at Bruno's restaurant.

"That's great and all, but what about the others who fall into those categories?"

"Like whom?"

Time to throw this unspoken thought into the universe. There was no one around us. I leaned forward and said in a low voice. "The Silver Girls."

Gomez's head bobbed like she had a pop song going through her head. Up and down in a rhythm. "Believe me, we investigated them. *All* of them."

"And you found nothing?"

"I didn't say that."

"What did you find?"

"Like you had mentioned. A good amount of motive, but sometimes, we couldn't find opportunity, nor did we find evidence any of them owned a gun. Not that they couldn't have acquired one by illegal means."

"Some big gaps then."

"Right. We felt we had enough to move on Bruno's two henchmen, so we did. They both had priors for armed robbery and burglary."

"Ah."

"So that is where we stand." She placed an empty cup on the table.

"Want a refill?"

Gomez held out a hand. "No thanks."

I was tempted to get another one myself, but judging by her last statement, she might be ready to leave. My cup was empty as well and there were questions I wanted answered. "Can you indulge me in a few more details?"

A strand of hair fell across her face. She brushed it back. "Depends on the details."

"Okay. Dot told me Stanley allowed someone to search her room under the guise of a repairman, and she believed it was her former employer who did it."

"Is there a question in there?"

She didn't brush off the topic, meaning she might have wiggle room. "Yes, did you ask about that?"

"We did." She ran a finger along the edge of the table. "With Stanley being dead and not knowing who the person was who rummaged through her things, there's not much we can follow up on. I spoke with the original investigating officer, and he had little to go on either. They pulled footage from the CCTV and saw the guy, but he was wearing a gray hat, glasses, and a maintenance outfit."

"Did he arrive in a maintenance vehicle?"

She squinted. "I didn't ask. Good idea." She typed a note into her phone and looked back up at me. "The officer said Dot was livid and demanded Stanley be put behind bars. The problem was the neighbor on the floor below reported a water leak coming from his place and with Dot and her roommates not in the building, Stanley had the responsibility and right to enter their place to limit any damage."

"Was there a leak?"

"There was."

"What caused the leak?"

"A broken pipe under a bathroom sink."

"Could the pipe have been broken on purpose?"

"It's possible."

"Did you go back and ask the guy who owns the apartment and try to gauge his involvement?"

She tapped a finger on the table. "We didn't. Good idea."

"Sorry for giving you more work to do."

"Don't apologize. It's my job."

One of Gomez's strengths was her thoroughness. If something needed doing, she would do it. Where I came in was from finding seemingly unrelated strings and making them related.

"I get it, but would what Stanley did be enough to murder him?"

"Possibly," she allowed, "but we couldn't connect her to the scene, nor did we find evidence of her owning a gun."

"Roger." I tapped an index finger on the table. "I spent some time with these Silver Girls and the subject came up. What I couldn't figure out was why would Dot's former employer do that unless their parting wasn't as amicable as she let on."

She leveled a finger at me. "Here's the thing. Their parting wasn't cordial. They fired her after some files went missing."

"What kind of files?"

"I can't tell you. Let's just say they involve a high-ranking government official who was doing something he wasn't supposed to be doing with another government."

I blinked several times. "Like spy stuff?"

"More like treason."

CHAPTER
TWENTY-THREE

First, there were possible mafia ties. Then there was embezzlement from the Paradise Hideaway HOA. After that came stringent building violations, and now we have government spies and treason. What next? Nuclear weapons? This was becoming a regular Tom Clancy novel. It wouldn't have surprised me if Jack Ryan himself burst through the front door next.

"What do you mean, treason?"

Gomez leaned forward and rested her chin on top of an enclosed hand. At first, I thought it was an invitation to lean in so she could give me the dirt, so I did. Our heads came mere inches apart. She sighed and understood what I was doing.

"Clark, I especially can't talk about that. The CIA is getting involved."

"What'll happen to Dot?"

"I can't say. Just don't be startled if you don't see her for a while until this blows over."

A chill went up my spine. I poked a finger at the table. "The CIA here in Myrtle Beach?"

"Happens more than you will ever know." She checked the watch on her free hand. "Anything else?"

I relayed the story Marie told me about Karen slapping Stanley in the parking lot the night before his death.

"Goodness, Clark. That's new information."

"This Marie woman suffers from anxiety issues and was too nervous to talk to the police."

"But she'll talk to you?"

I leaned back and held out my hands. "Maybe I'm more approachable. She seemed to feel like she had some duty to come forward."

"Which she did."

"I agree. She was hoping I'd pass along the information to you and that would be the end."

"We must hear it from her mouth. Otherwise, it's hearsay."

"She agreed to speak with you, if I were present."

Gomez's one hand fidgeted with the empty cup. Creases I'd not seen before ran under her eyes. She moved a shade slower than normal and spent the majority of our conversation at the bookstore with her hand on the side of her face to prop her head up. She was exhausted. Moody was away, and she was working solo right now. The same strand of hair fell over her face. As she reached up to tuck it back in place, it reminded me of a dark-haired Andr—

Clark, stop it, I told myself.

When Gomez hadn't responded, I asked, "What are you going to do next?"

She groaned. "Ugh. Follow up on these leads you gave me."

I felt bad for lumping more work on her. After glancing at the wall between my store and Andrea's, I said to Gomez, "Marie said she stays at home all hours of the day and rarely leaves. It's too overwhelming for her to leave the house. Want me to drive you over for a chat?"

She tucked the hair back in place. "I thought you'd never ask."

Where have I heard that before?

***

FIFTEEN MINUTES LATER, we pulled into the Paradise Hideaway parking lot. The sun was shining. Waves of heat radiated off the pavement. Golf carts and seniors wearing broad-brimmed hats scurried about. The aroma of hamburgers on a grill wafted through the air.

I decided not to call Marie beforehand with the fear she would change her mind and not cooperate. I figured she would be at home. Gomez would need a more formal conversation with the shy woman if she refused to talk to us. In this situation, it was better to keep it casual.

We entered the lobby. A few heads turned in our direction, but no one moved to stop us from going to the elevator. Not that Gomez couldn't have flashed her badge to get where she needed to go. We climbed in the elevator, and I pushed the button for the second floor. The door whooshed shut. It was one thing to be alone together in a vehicle. It was another matter to be alone in an elevator. I glanced at the "Emergency Stop" button before looking up at her. Her head was forward, but she was peeking at me out of the corner of her eye.

She averted her gaze.

The awkward ride for both of us was thankfully short. The doors parted. I gestured for her to take the lead, in part because ladies first. The other part was because I wasn't sure what apartment Marie lived in. She said she watched the parking lot from a window above the lobby entrance.

Gomez walked beside me as I navigated to where I figured the front of the building to be. We stopped. The short hallway seemed like it was in the middle of the building, cutting it in half. The hall ended at a row of doors stretching out in both directions. All had numbers on them. Some had decorations. The unit smack dab in the middle, had a CCU flag taped to the door. Marie showed her pride at being a CCU mom with the shirt she wore at the HOA meeting.

"Is this the place?" Gomez asked.

"I think so." I knocked on the door.

The peephole had light coming into it. For a split second, the light eclipsed.

A chain rattled behind the door before the door creaked part way open. Marie peeked out with one hand on the door and half of her face visible.

In a nervous voice, she asked, "Can I help you?"

I put on my best smile. "Hi, Marie. Remember me from last night?"

"I do."

"You said if I brought a friend from the police department whom I trusted, that you might answer a few questions. Are you up for it? Is this a good time?"

She hesitated. "As good a time as any, I reckon."

Gomez held out a hand. "Hi, I'm Gina. The lead detective with the MBPD. Mind if I ask you a few questions? It won't take long or be difficult. I promise. Clark tells me you saw some things out in the parking lot, and I was hoping you might shed more light on them."

Gomez introduced herself by her first name only. Every other time I've heard her introduce herself, she'd been more formal.

Even when we first met.

"Well, I...," Marie's mouth closed. "Did he tell you what I saw about Stanley?"

"He did," Gomez said.

"Then you know all I know." She closed the door an inch.

"That may be true," Gomez said, "but I need to hear it from you. I'm an experienced interviewer. I may be able to get more from you than Clark." She placed a hand on my upper arm. "No offense."

"None taken," I said, not minding her touch. Then to Marie, "I told her everything I could remember you telling me, but she's right. She's good at this. Give her ten-fifteen minutes, and we'll be gone."

We didn't need to look at each other for confirmation. I knew full well if Marie started talking, the conversation might last longer. Didn't need to tell Marie that up front.

The door swung back open by an inch.

"Colton is in his room," Marie said. "Does he need to leave?"

"Not at all," Gomez said. "In fact, maybe I can speak to him while I'm here."

Marie's hand hesitated on the door. She raised her hand on it while keeping the palm in place. Gomez and I watched the hand with great interest. If it came back to the door, all it would need is a gentle nudge to open it all the way.

Marie let out a breath. "Okay. Come on in. I reckon I can tell what I saw."

Her fingers pressed against the side of the door, opening it for Gomez and me to enter.

CHAPTER
TWENTY-FOUR

WE STEPPED INTO a *Hoarders* episode. I've never watched the show but knew enough about it to understand the gist of it. The show finds people who collect things, sometimes odd things, to a degree where it takes up their lives and homes.

Marie hoarded items from Coastal Carolina. What should feel like a large apartment seemed tight among a teal and bronze collection of kitschy items, posters, banners, and other decorations. They covered all the furniture in the same busy pattern of Chanticleer mascots. Teal kitchen towels hung from the stove with Coastal Carolina embellishments. The toaster was topped with a Chanticleer's head. The ceiling fan had bronze blades with Chanticleer painted along their length. They painted the walls teal. All the door hardware was bronze. My eyes hurt.

Not even my dorm room over twenty years ago had this much teal and bronze decor. Gomez hesitated as she took in the visible living space, as did I. Marie lived with an anxiety disorder. Part of me wondered if an overabundance of teal and bronze and Chanticleer mascots brought it on.

"Come on in," Marie said.

"Thank you," Gomez responded, taking a hesitant step forward. "I appreciate you speaking to me. I understand this is difficult for you."

"That's not the half of it." Marie's face pinched as she turned to Gomez. "Were you the one who interviewed Colton?"

I glanced at Gomez. She had kept the information about interviewing him compartmentalized. She didn't look at me but held her focus on Marie.

Gomez smoothed her ponytail. "Yes, that was me and my partner, Detective Moody."

Marie wrung her hands together. "Do you need to chat to him again?"

"Maybe," Gomez responded, "but not right now. I want to follow up with you first. Then I'll decide if I need to converse with Colton."

"Okay," Marie said. "He was just so torn up about her death."

"Emilie's?" Gomez asked.

"Uh-huh." Marie attempted to smile. "She and my Colton dated freshman year at Coastal."

"Such a tragedy," Gomez said. "They broke up and then ended up working together at Tidal Creek for a while a few years later."

"What was Colton's job there?"

Marie waved a hand. "Nothing glamorous. He bussed tables, washed dishes, cleaned the bathrooms, and such."

"Why did he leave there?" I asked.

"He got a job as a mechanic's assistant over here at the airport. Putting his degree to some use."

"Good for him," I said. It was always nice to hear good news about someone from my alma-mater, even if it was the first stop on a longer journey. "Does he still go back to Tidal Creek?"

"Every once in a while," Marie answered.

"Did he go there the night of the murders?" I asked.

She shook her head. "Nope. Was here with me. Watched a Metallica concert on YouTube together."

"Nice," I said, if only to keep her talking. "Did you ever have any run-ins with Stanley?"

She huffed. "Yes. I did. He fined me for having pumpkins on display outside our door two days after Halloween."

I couldn't help but look at Gomez to get her reaction. To her credit, she didn't smile or flinch and pulled out a small voice recorder.

"Clark tells me you watch the comings and goings of people in the parking lot."

It wasn't a question, more of an open-ended invitation for Marie to speak.

"Y-yes." She stared at a spot on the floor. "It calms me."

"Like watching the waves come in," I said.

Marie's head angled up. "I figure so. Although, I'm not a fan of seagulls."

"Why is that?" Gomez asked.

"I got pooped on by one over at the state park pier," Marie answered. "Haven't been to the beach since."

Gomez held a hand up to her mouth, either to show sympathy or to cover a smile. "Oh. When was the last time?"

Marie cocked her head to the side and peered at the ceiling, doing the mental math. "Five years."

"A long time to not go to the beach," Gomez said.

The ocean was a short golf cart ride away from where we stood. I would hate to live this close to the ocean and never see it. Hearing Marie talk made me appreciate not having an anxiety disorder such as hers.

Gomez was playing the role of trying to gain Marie's trust by displaying sympathy and understanding. It appeared to be working.

Marie placed a hand on her head, perhaps remembering where the seagull made its mark. "Y-yes. Thank you."

"Can you show me where you look out the window?" Gomez asked.

"Yes, of course," Marie replied. "Right this way."

She led the way through their apartment, through layers of CCU themed surroundings. It reeked of cigarettes. A yellow patina clung to the ceiling. We passed by a closed door on the right. The thumping rhythm of raging guitars laced with deep bass vibrated through the door and walls. Two posters featuring heavy metal bands and scantily clad women were taped to the door, canted at crooked angles.

"Colton's room," Marie explained. "The music is his way of staying grounded."

Gomez and I exchanged glances but continued to follow the small woman to a large picture window overlooking the parking lot. One chair from their dining room table with a chanticleer face on the seat sat in front of the window, facing toward the right. Marie could sit off to the side and watch people while being out of sight. A tall light with a teal lampshade sat beside it. A stack of paperback books was underneath the chair.

"Here is where I do my people-watching," Marie stated the obvious. She reached her hands into both pockets and withdrew a cigarette and a lighter. "Do you mind?"

Before I could answer, Gomez said, "It's your house."

A large parking area interspersed with short palmetto trees and flowers in beds bordered by concrete spread out before us.

The lot held cars, trucks, motorcycles, and golf carts. At present, it was half-full. White numbers were painted at the front of each space, designating where people parked.

"Okay," Gomez said, and then gestured at the chair. "Have a seat."

Marie said, "Sure" and lit up. She sat, rubbed her hands along her thighs down to her knees. "Now what?"

Gomez started the recording device and had Marie say her name, time, date, and location of the interview. She then guided Marie through an almost verbatim retelling of what she told me. At first, the interviewee had trouble getting the words out. After a few minutes, she got comfortable and had more confidence in herself. The cigarette shrunk as she took long drags. Her fingers trembled as she puffed. Gomez had a light touch with her questions, and that eased Marie. The second half of the cig took longer for her to puff through. She talked about the conflict between Violet and Stanley, ending with her shooting him in the back with a finger gun, and about watching Stanley and Karen come and go on various nights, culminating with a slap in the face the night before his murder. Gomez recorded Marie's entire statement.

Gomez considered Marie's story while watching people come and go out the window.

"Is that all?" Marie asked Gomez.

Before she could answer, I said to Marie, "Tell me, were you sitting here the night of the murders?"

She gulped and lit a second cigarette. "Y-yes. I was."

Now it was my turn to ask a few questions. "Did you see anything out of the ordinary?"

"N-no. Don't think so," she said with a nervous shake of her head.

"Were you watching out the window between nine and eleven that night?"

"Uh-huh."

Gomez said, "From talking to the folks at Tidal Creek, Stanley was a regular customer and there almost every day. He had a car and a golf cart he drove. They believe he came on the cart when visiting the brewery. Did you see him leave here that evening?"

"I didn't," Marie said. "What time did he go there?"

Gomez looked at the police report on her phone. "He was first seen on camera at sixteen after six, entering Tidal Creek. We can't tell if he took his cart or vehicle or walked there."

Marie blew a burst of smoke out between her lips. "That fat Stanley walked nowhere except from the door to his vehicles in the parking lot. Most of the time, he parked his golf cart in front of the door in the fire lane."

"Did no one ever report him doing that?" Gomez asked.

"Report it to who? Him?"

"No," Gomez said, "To us."

"Not that I'm aware of. We couldn't call the HOA about it. He was the HOA."

"I see." Gomez crossed her arms, holding the recorder in one hand.

"If you say he got there a little after six," Marie said, "I was cooking dinner for Colton and me around that time. Stuffed peppers and asparagus. Wouldn't have been at the window."

"I see," Gomez said.

"What did you see that evening?" I asked Marie.

The woman tilted her head forward and rubbed her fingers on her forehead. The cigarette dangled between them. Gray smoke curled off the end. I had to stifle a cough.

"There were the usual comings and goings." She swiveled her head at me. "Saw you walk Andrea home."

Heat spread across my face. I didn't respond.

"You did, did you?" Gomez said, uncrossing her arms.

"Yeah," Marie said. "She gave him a kiss on the cheek and everything."

"You have an excellent memory," I said in a flat tone.

Gomez shifted away from me. "Did you see when the Silver Girls came home?"

Marie's head bobbed. "Violet and Beatrice came home in front of Andrea and Clark. Karen didn't arrive until sometime later."

"Was she with anyone?" Gomez asked.

"Not as far as I could tell. It was getting dark around then," Marie said.

At once, the music emanating through Colton's bedroom walls ceased. His door opened, and he emerged, shouting, "Ma!"

Marie centered a finger on her lips and stood. "Shh! Quiet down, son. You'll wake the dead."

The thought of Colton sitting in his bedroom listening to heavy metal music turned up loud took me back to when I survived an explosion on the Atlantic Avenue Causeway in Garden City at the beginning of this month. My eardrums ruptured, among other injuries, and I couldn't hear well for days while they healed. Everyone around me said all I did was shout for days because I couldn't hear myself talking. Some of the wounds were still healing. I wondered if Colton shouted because the loud music had damaged his hearing.

His hair was a greasy mess. He stared at us through Coke-bottle glasses with his mouth hanging open. A lit cigarette stuck out from his fingers. "Oh. Hey."

"Nice seeing you again, Colton," Gomez said.

"Uh-huh," he said without conviction.

Gomez stuck her hands in her pockets. "Your mom was just filling us in on what she saw the night of Stanley and Emilie's murder."

"Uh-huh."

I didn't know what to say to someone who had an ex-girlfriend from years in the past die. It was part of Gomez's job to know what to say in situations like this. She had a future in writing Hallmark cards.

She said, "I hate it happened. Her loss is being felt by the entire community."

Colton stared at Gomez for a few seconds with his mouth open. He hadn't shut his mouth since he left his room. I bet he caught a lot of flies. He responded with a low, "Thank you."

"You know," Marie said. We turned to her. "Now that I think about it, I did see something odd that night."

"What was it?" Gomez asked.

"Well, it's just." Marie placed a finger on her chin. "It's just someone else brought Stanley's golf cart back here."

Gomez crossed her arms. "Did you see who it was?"

"I did," Marie said, "but don't know who it was. They don't live here. That's for sure, but I've seen them drop Stanley off late at night before in his car. Someone followed the guy on the cart here in a big, black car. The guy parked Stanley's cart in his parking spot, then came into the building. He left a few minutes later and climbed in the front passenger seat of the other car and drove away."

"Hold on." Gomez pulled out her phone and tapped on the

screen for a minute before finding what she was looking for. She held it up to Marie. "Was it one of these men?"

Marie took the phone, lifted her glasses, squinted, and brought the phone close to her face. She handed the phone back to Gomez. "Mighta been the guy on the left."

"Great. Thank you for this," Gomez said.

"Who is it?" I asked.

She held out the phone for me to see. The picture showed Tony Bruno standing between the two men arrested for Stanley's murder.

CHAPTER
TWENTY-FIVE

WE EXITED MARIE'S apartment a few minutes later, feeling like Indiana Jones escaping the Temple of Teal-and-Bronze Doom. I needed to go home and grab a shower or douse myself in cologne to mask the cigarette smell clinging to me.

Gomez sniffed the sleeve of her navy jacket and made a disgusted face. "Have to take this one to the cleaners tomorrow."

After we climbed back into the Jeep and headed back toward Myrtle Beach Reads and her Camry, I asked, "Can you tell me what Colton said when you interviewed him?"

She stared ahead and seemed to consider her next words. "Might as well tell you. You've got yourself involved in a murder case, again."

"Sorry," I said and meant it.

She held up a hand in my direction. "Don't apologize. He told us he was there that night and saw Bruno's men sneaking around Tidal Creek."

"Sneaking around, how?"

"Right before they closed, Colton saw Bruno's men exit through the back door. Bruno himself finished his beer and walked out the front door and across the street to where they were parked. Because of the sightlines of the cameras at Tidal Creek, we lost track of his flunkies for a few minutes."

"And you believe they killed Stanley and Emilie during that time?"

"That's our assumption."

"Didn't you say you don't know how Stanley arrived at Tidal Creek?"

"Yes, but we know now because of Marie."

"Why would they murder him and then take his cart back home?"

"Unknown. Marie stated she'd seen the men bringing Stanley home late at night in a similar manner before."

"Stanley hung out at Bruno's restaurant. Maybe he would have too much to drink, and they would bring him and his car back here so he wouldn't drive drunk."

"How responsible of them." Gomez tapped a finger on her knee. "It doesn't answer why they would kill him and take his cart back to Paradise Hideaway."

"Another way of looking at it is, why would they kill a man who they would go to the lengths they did to see he got home? Doesn't that suggest a certain kinship?"

It took her a moment before she admitted, "It does."

"If they killed him, why bring his cart back and hang his keys from the hook in his apartment?"

"Fair question."

"Maybe we should try to talk to Bruno," I suggested.

Gomez shook her head so violently that her ponytail whipped her in the face. "Nope. Not happening. Let Moody and I deal with this. I don't want you involved. These are dangerous men."

"And you're only trying to protect me? Is that right?"

We came to a red light at Kings Highway and Farrow Parkway

intersection, passing by the warplanes on display at Warbird Park. A bright yellow Spirit Airlines plane came in from the direction of the ocean and landed at the airport on our left. I kept in the lane to go straight onto Ocean Boulevard. It would take longer to get to our destination by going the scenic route, and we had much to discuss.

"Yes," she answered. "Do you own a gun?"

"I've only touched a gun twice. Once when I was a kid and when I took the murder weapon out of Erin Howard's hand." The left arrow turned green, and two rows of vehicles crept out onto Kings Highway. I watched them go and said, "It was my grandpa's service revolver from the Korean War. He let me hold it. Other than that, I had no desire to be around them."

"For me, they're necessary."

"Have you had to use one before on duty?"

She sucked in air through her tongue. "Once."

The way she said the word told me not to ask any follow-up questions, which I was glad not to.

She asked, "Have you had any self-defense courses?"

"Nope."

"I figured. The point is what I do is dangerous. You've been fortunate in the cases where you've helped. The suspects involved weren't criminals before the murders happened. This thing with Stanley involves the mafia." She rested a warm hand on my arm. "I just don't want to see you get hurt, especially after what happened on the causeway."

I looked down at the hand she held flat against my forearm. The hand with the engagement ring on it. Our moment of passion after the causeway case came about after she'd admitted she didn't know what she would do if something bad happened to me. Here, she displayed the same protectiveness. It caused emotions to stir in my chest I could do nothing about.

Our light turned green, and I took one last glance at the diamond ring before returning my attention to the road.

"Okay," I said. "I hear you. I'll stay out of it."

She removed her hand from my arm. "Thank you."

Desperate to change the subject, I brought up something I had wanted to ask her but hadn't because we hadn't been in contact.

"Thank you again for giving me Brenda Banner's phone number."

"You're quite welcome. Did you learn anything from her?"

"I did. Do you remember telling me Banner had made several calls the evening you and he investigated Autumn's death?"

"I do."

"He made them to the same number that sent the threatening text messages to Autumn the night before her death."

She held a hand up to her mouth. "Oh, my goodness. Did Brenda know who it was?"

"She didn't."

"Goodness," she repeated. "Then whoever it was had to have followed up on their threat."

To me, there are always multiple ways of looking at things. That's what made the events surrounding Autumn's death so frustrating. On the one hand, I had uncovered threats around the time of her death. I had discovered nothing through my research or by questioning her friends and coworkers that indicated she'd gotten mixed up in some foul plot, but it didn't mean a reason or motive wasn't out there.

Even with all the energy and time I'd put into investigating what happened to Autumn, I still had to admit she *could* have died of a heart attack.

"It seems very possible," I said.

Traffic along Ocean Boulevard crawled as was typical for this time of year. Tourists paraded the sidewalks, schlepping towels, beach bags, and umbrellas or pulling beach carts loaded with all the above. Families and groups of friends puttered about on rented golf carts, smiling, and having good times. The sky was a light Carolina blue. Seagulls flapped about while fighting a soft onshore breeze.

"Can you give me this phone number when you get a chance?" Gomez asked. "I'll see what I can find."

"Sure. I know it."

"Figures," she said and pulled up a note app on her phone. "Tell it to me."

I recited the number to her from memory.

"Thank you."

It was my turn to graze her arm. She seemed to lean into me when I did.

I said, "No, thank you."

She held a hand over mine and said, "You're quite welcome."

I dropped her off at her car, where we thanked each other for everything that had transpired today. Conflicting feelings tore through my every being. I seemed to have a good thing with Andrea. Gomez was engaged. Off the market. However, even though we had confronted the rift between us and were well aware of the situation, neither of us could help but to get a little handsy and flirty. A deep gravitational pull seemed to connect us. Could I fight it if we were forced to spend more time together? Could she?

I stared at the back of the lengthy building containing the Shops on the Boardwalk. Teresa was throwing out cardboard boxes with a cigarette hanging from her mouth. A worker from the ice cream shop sat on their back stoop, staring at his phone while on break.

On the other end, the delivery alcove of my bookstore remained still. Since discovering Paige Whitaker's body there, I almost never went near it. I no longer entered the bookstore from the rear, only through the front. It inconvenienced UPS and FedEx, but I no longer accepted deliveries through the backdoor either.

In between my store and Teresa's I Heart MB Tees shop was Coastal Décor. I wanted to go speak with Andrea and tell her about the conversation with Marie, but with the stirring of feelings I had now, I couldn't bring myself to do it. Nor did I fancy a return to the bookstore. I sent Winona a text informing her I would see her tomorrow and started for home at Surfside Beach.

Little did I know the conversation Gomez and I had about whether I owned a gun would be relevant half an hour later.

CHAPTER
TWENTY-SIX

A DARK RANGE Rover with tinted windows pulled out from a spot three cars down as I pulled away from the sandy lot on Flagg Street where employees of the Shops parked. It was an unfamiliar vehicle for this lot. I may not know all the people who drove the cars who parked in our private lot, but I was familiar with all the vehicles.

The Range Rover did not belong.

I took a glimpse in the rearview mirror as I drove down 4th Avenue North toward Kings Highway. Two men occupied the Range Rover, their gaze pinned to the rear of my Jeep. Both wore dark sunglasses on their expressionless faces. The tinted windows made it difficult to make out what they were wearing, but it wasn't bright Hawaiian shirts with flowers on them.

My finger stopped halfway as I started to press the voice command button on my steering wheel to call Gomez. No need to panic. Could be some random tourists who found a place to park where they thought they could get away without paying.

I came to Kings Highway. To my joy and to quell my stomping heart, fortune was in my favor. I had a clear path to the southbound lane without waiting at the stop sign. The tires on the Jeep squealed. The men in the Rover had to wait for a line of passing motorists.

A breath of air escaped my lips, and I turned on the radio. A Nirvana song played on 104.1, again making me feel old. It was the music of my youth now played on what I used to consider a station for old people. In the last few years, I listened to more classic rock and less new music. What was happening to me?

When I pulled into my driveway, I hopped out of the Jeep and went to check my mailbox. Eight black mailboxes stood on a wooden platform on my side of the street. I lived in a sort of cul-de-sac containing five houses. Across the street was another cul-de-sac with an identical number of houses, but not identical houses. Deerfield wasn't home to cookie-cutter homes like the new subdivisions that had popped up around the Grand Strand in the past decade.

The mailbox contained the usual assortment of bills and junk. I flipped through what the mail carrier brought today, while strolling to my front door. As I climbed the two steps to the front porch, a familiar black Lincoln and the same Range Rover that followed me from the parking lot pulled to a stop behind my Jeep, blocking me in.

My heart leapt into my throat. I could panic and run inside to call the police while evading the men in dark suits exiting the two vehicles, or I could play it cool and stand my ground. If I ran, they could start shooting at my back. What worried me more was a stray bullet going through a neighbor's wall or window and hitting them.

One important factor in my fight-or-flight decision was, well, I *really* had to pee. The sooner I talked to them, the sooner I could hit the bathroom…I hoped.

I twisted to face the four men who climbed from the vehicles. One hung back by the rear passenger door of the Lincoln with his hands crossed at the wrist. All the men wore sunglasses. None of my neighbors were visible, which was typical of this section of my street. I was all alone in whatever was about to happen.

Three of them walked up to within ten feet of the porch and stopped. The tallest man, with an athletic figure and impeccable hair, stood in the middle. I took him to be the lead henchman. The other two could have been pudgy twins with dyed black combovers and rosy-red cheeks.

"Can I help you?" I asked.

The henchman cleared his throat. "The Boss would like to talk to you."

"Who's the Boss?" I had almost asked if their boss was Tony Danza or Bruce Springsteen, but I valued my life.

"Mr. Bruno."

"I've heard of him. Why does he want to talk to me?"

"You'd have to ask him that yourself." He brushed the lapel of his jacket aside to stick a hand in his pocket. When he did, I spotted a gun wedged into his belt.

I gulped. "Do I have a choice?"

"'Fraid not," he said.

"Okay then." I squared my shoulders in as masculine a move as this bookstore owner could. "Let's chat."

Goon Number One turned and tilted his head to the man standing by the Lincoln who nodded back and then opened the door. A man wearing a dark pinstripe suit emerged. He had a full head of dark hair, was perhaps a few pounds overweight and of average height, and he wore a thick mustache, flecked with gray hairs.

He stood to his full height and buttoned the top button of his suit. The other men maintained serious demeanors. I'll confess.

Bruno's smile frightened me. He reminded me of the Cheshire Cat in a gangster suit.

His three flunkies parted to let him through. He stopped in front of them and looked me up and down. The first words out of his mouth were a complete and utter astonishment. "I like your book."

***

THE SIX OF us stood inside the door, clustered around the tiny foyer. They smelled of onions and garlic. My front door opens to a long hallway leading to the living room. I tried to edge away from the men, but the guy who had guarded the door of the Lincoln stayed with me like my shadow.

"Is there somewhere we can make ourselves more comfortable?" Bruno asked.

"Yeah, the living room is right this way." I led them fifteen feet down a hallway between the front door and the living room.

"Nice floors you got here," Bruno said. "What is it? LVT?"

I tried to hide my nervousness. "Y-yeah. I think it's called 'Driftwood.' My wife and I got it from Home Depot."

Bruno gave his approval. "I like it. My wife and I are looking to remodel. Maybe I'll bring her here to check out your floors sometime."

Let me know before you come, and I'll have the SWAT team waiting outside. I didn't say that. Instead, I said, "Sure."

The three men and the doorman made themselves comfortable in my living room. The two twins were on either end of the sofa. I'd already gotten them jumbled as to who was who. I mean, they probably *weren't* twins, but they shared almost identical features.

One guy plopped down on the end of a loveseat. The lead goon remained standing with Bruno.

He gestured for me to sit in between the twins. "Have a seat."

I maintained eye contact as best I could, but my eyes were swimming. "Listen, you gotta let me go pee before we talk. I'm busting."

Bruno nodded to his lead goombah. "Fine. Carlo here will accompany you."

I held out a placating hand, palm-down. "I can assure you I'm potty trained and can manage myself."

Bruno performed a soggy sniff through his nose and cocked his head to the side. "I'm sure your momma trained you well. Be that as it may, I'd be more comfortable if Carlo went with you. Wouldn't want you to get lost on the way now, would we?"

Yeah, he'd be more comfortable. What about me? I wasn't lying. I did have to go with an urgency I've discovered was more pronounced in my forties. Another reminder for the day that I was getting older.

Carlo stepped forward and waved a hand like Vanna White, gesturing down the hallway. Did they already know where my bathroom was? It wasn't visible from the front door. Carlo didn't speak. I supposed Mr. Bruno liked it that way.

When I go to a public restroom, I hate using the urinals. One, I didn't like guys coming up behind me or passing by while I was doing my business. The other reason was because I detested the dude who had to engage in small talk while he was taking the same action. I almost always opted for the stalls.

The bathroom we entered was the small one in the house. As much as I wanted to escape, it was too high and narrow for me to climb through. The en-suite bathroom off the master bedroom was larger, but I didn't want Carlo here rummaging through my sleeping quarters. Besides, I hadn't made my bed in three years.

"Is this necessary?" I asked Carlo.

He sniffed. "If the Boss says it is, it is."

"Does this make you as uncomfortable as it does me? I mean, do you really need to be in here with me? There's nowhere to go."

With a dip of his shoulder, he said, "This is not the first time."

I had no snappy response and accomplished the task I'd set out to do.

"Make sure you wash your hands," Carlo said.

"Always."

After drying my hands, Carlo had me lead him out to the living room. The goombah in the recliner had turned on the TV and found a Yankees matinee game on ESPN.

"Make yourself at home," I said to him, unable to mask the sarcasm in my voice.

He sat back, propped his feet up on the recliner, and crossed his hands behind his head. "Don't mind if I do."

Bruno snapped his fingers at the man. "Hey, Joey. Show some respect."

Like a lightning bolt, Joey's hands unwrapped themselves, and he lowered the recliner lift, placing his feet on the floor. "Yes, sir."

"Good boy, Joey." Bruno turned his attention to me. "I must apologize. We're in the middle of a four-game series against Boston. This is important."

By "we're," I assumed he meant the New York Yankees. "I'm more of a Braves fan myself."

"I can respect that," Bruno said. "Need I remind you what happened the last time your boys played my boys in the Series?"

I tried to smile. The last time the Braves met the Yankees, New

York won, and I had just finished high school. "No, you don't."

Bruno and his men had a laugh at my expense, like I held a stake in the Braves organization. My dad was the bigger fan. I was more of a casual observer, but I tried to talk the talk here to find some common ground.

Carlo held out a hand to the empty spot between the twins on the couch. "Have a seat."

I sat and crossed one leg over the other. Focusing on Bruno, I said, "What's this about?"

He sat back in his chair and steepled his fingers together on his chin. "I need a favor."

CHAPTER
TWENTY-SEVEN

IT WAS THE second surprising thing Bruno had told me. First, he liked my book, and now, he needed me to do something for him.

I crossed my arms. "Like what?"

He pointed at the two men flanking me. "Clear my boys' names."

They didn't so much as glance in my direction. They focused their attention on the baseball game being played on the TV mounted on the wall, as if what Bruno was asking was no big deal.

I played ignorant. "Clear them of what?"

"This charge they have against them for killing Stanley and the girl."

That's where I figured he was going with this. There were holes in the police's case against them, such as, no clear link to the scene of the crime. Bruno had the means, motive, and opportunity to have Stanley whacked that night at Tidal Creek, but there was no clear evidence linking them to the garbage corral. At least that Gomez has revealed.

"Why would I do that for you?"

He grunted. "I know about you. You're a nice guy who wants to see justice done. The cases you've solved. Asked around. You can go into this with no preconceived notions, and I know you're already involved. I got sources."

"Except you used the threat of your gun to trap me in my house. That doesn't make you look suspect at all." I risked a little sarcasm. It's my modus operandi.

Bruno spread his hands. "Maybe my associate was just showing you what color belt he was wearing, and you saw the gun and took it as a threat. We didn't unlawfully detain you. You invited us in. It would be in your best interest to keep your mouth shut. Carlo, show him your gun."

Like it was high noon, and we were gunslingers at the O.K. Corral, Carlo whipped out his gun and shot me in the chest.

"Guh!" I shouted. My heart rate thumped to a thousand beats a minute as my hands rushed to my chest.

What struck me wasn't a bullet. It was water.

Bruno's men hooted and howled. The Boss himself didn't. He only smiled.

"Carlo," Bruno said, "go get this man a towel."

Carlo tucked the gun back into his belt and began slinking out of the living room in the bathroom's direction where we'd just been. "Sure thing, Boss."

When the men stopped laughing, they moved their attention to the TV. Water soaked my shirt and dripped onto the couch. Thank goodness for Scotchgard.

Carlo returned a moment later with the hand towel I had dried my hands on and tossed it in my lap. "Here you go."

"Thanks," I said without conviction, taking the towel and pressing it to my chest to sop up the water. I had already planned a shower to scour off the cigarette smell from my skin, and this sealed the deal.

"I'm sorry," Carlo said, "I had to do that to you."

My forehead creased. "Did you *really* have to?"

Carlo's head wavered from side to side. "No, I guess not, but it was fun, wasn't it boys?"

The three other flunkies shared their agreement. The Boss didn't agree with Carlo's explanation. He held out a hand to Carlo. "Give me the gun."

"But Boss, c'mon. You told me to show him my gun, so I did."

"Yes," Bruno said. "I said to show him the gun, not use it. Now hand it over."

Carlo twisted his lip but did as he was told. He handed Bruno the gun and went back to standing at his side.

Bruno examined the water gun for a moment and then shot Carlo in the face.

"Ah!" Carlo yelped. His hands rushed to cover his face as the water splashed and dripped onto my LVT flooring.

The men guffawed harder. This time, Bruno did too. I smiled at seeing Carlo get a taste of his own medicine.

Carlo ran back toward the bathroom, presumably to see if he could find another hand towel to dry himself off with.

"Grab a paper towel out of the kitchen!" I called after him. I'd rather he do that than waste a clean towel. The less dirty laundry, the better. Speaking of dirty laundry, I asked Bruno, "What happened that night?"

Bruno spread his hands. "It's all circumstantial, I assure you."

Rather than take him at his word, I said, "Then assure me how they're innocent? I will not chase ghosts trying to clear their names. How did they place your men at the scene of the crime? I heard at the end of the night at Tidal Creek, you went out the front door while your boys here went out the back. Where were you all going?"

Bruno looked at the men to my left and right and then focused on me. They were statues. "We love Tidal Creek. Well, I love Tidal Creek, not sure about them, but for reasons from my past, I don't like for people to know where I park. You know the tree line that runs behind the brewery, separating it from the business next door facing Shine Avenue?" I nodded. He continued, "It's some sort of time-share office. Anyway, they're closed in the evenings when I decide to take a break from my restaurant, so their parking lot is always empty. My boys drop me off at the front door of Tidal Creek, go around the block, and park in the time-share lot. They cut through the trees to get back to the brewhouse."

"And that's what they did?"

Bruno leveled his gaze at me. With a hardness to his voice, he said, "You have my word."

I maintained eye contact, locked in a staring contest to see who would blink first. He won. "Okay then. Tell me your version of what transpired that evening."

He sat back in the chair. "We'd had a crazy dinner rush, and I needed to unwind before going home to the missus and the bambinos." He motioned to the twins flanking me. "So, Angelo and Carmine here and I headed over."

Everyone in the room's focus was on me. I scanned the other men. The Yankees game droned on in the background. At least now I had names for the twins, but I wasn't sure who was Angelo and who was Carmine. Did they know?

"Where were they?" I said, inclining my head in the other cronies' directions.

"I was off work," Carlo said.

One guy in a dark pinstriped suit said, "Me too."

Joey crossed one leg over the other. "I stayed behind and finished cleaning the kitchen."

The police likely verified the other guys' alibis. Whether through asking family or video from Bruno's restaurant.

"What do you all do there?" I asked.

"I manage the place," Carlo said.

Joey tipped his chin. "I'm the head chef."

Bruno pointed at the dark suit guy who had only spoken once since entering my house. "Frankie here is the sous chef. Assists Joey. Doesn't say much."

Frankie squared his jaw and shook his head in a brief motion. A silent agreement with his boss.

"Okay." I nodded to show them I accepted their responses. "I'm aware Stanley was in your restaurant the night before his death, and you ended up throwing him out. What happened?"

Bruno tilted his head. His neck cracked with the motion. "Ah. Stanley was two sheets to the wind. He came in, already liquored up, and started grousing about his woman."

"Karen?"

"Yeah, that's the dame. He'd been bringing her by for months, wining and dining her, trying to get something going, know what I mean?"

"Sure."

"That night, I was sitting at my customary reserved table in the corner of the bar when Stanley came in, demanding a drink. He was loud and brash as it was, but I could tell he'd already hit the sauce."

"What was your relationship like with Stanley before this?" I asked.

"Stanley and I went way back."

"How far?"

"To Queens. I owned a construction company there."

"Were you part of the mob?"

CHAPTER
TWENTY-EIGHT

MY QUESTION CAUSED the other men to gasp and turn to their boss. Bruno kept his eye on me and paid them no attention.

Before he could answer, I said, "I hear from the police that they've been in touch with an Organized Crime Task Force in New York. They said you and Stanley used to be part of the same Frontino Family. True?"

He squinted like I'd inflicted pain, looked at his men, then at me. "This doesn't leave this room, capisce?"

I shifted my head forward. "Of course."

"Yes, I was involved in the family. I ran a business there and was a capo to the don."

"I thought no one left the mob?"

He gave a frightening smile and grasped the lapel of his tailored suit jacket. "The don himself investigated me after I was wrongly accused of something by another member of the family. Once I cleared my name, I told him I wanted out. When you see what I've seen, and know what the boss has done, it's in their best interests to let me walk away. He knows I'm an honest man." He chuckled. "Take it for what it's worth. I may have been involved in some not so legal situations, but I always did what was right by the code. When I told the don I was quitting and would keep my mouth shut, I meant it, and he trusted me." He leaned forward. "That doesn't mean he doesn't send some associates around now and then to intimidate me and make sure I'm keeping my word."

To hear him talk about his experience with the mob sent a chill down my spine. I didn't want to know what the accusation was.

He gauged my reaction and then said to ease my mind. "I'm straight now. Ask my boys. I do everything on the up and up."

I would not let his past intimidate me on my home turf. "Including blockading my driveway and intimidating your way into my home?"

"Except for that maybe," he admitted and repeated with emphasis, "I *need* your help."

We had gotten off track. Righting the ship, I said, "Back to Stanley and the night at your bar. What happened?"

"Like I said, he was already two sheets to the wind, on his way to being sloppy drunk. We let him have one drink. It was busy. He was causing a scene, complaining about Karen breaking up with him."

"In his drunken state, did he say why she did it?"

"She figured out he was taking money from their homeowners' association."

Something she hadn't said to this point. As I wondered why she didn't report it to the police, I said, "Why didn't you report it?"

He jabbed his fingers to his chest. "With my background? Who am I to rat some guy out for petty theft?"

"He stole over fifty grand."

The whites in Bruno's eyes appeared before he masked his astonishment. "I wondered where he was getting all his moolah."

"How did she figure it out?"

"Stanley didn't know. Just said she confronted him about it.

He lied to her and said there was nothing to it. She slapped him, and then stormed off."

That would fill in the conversation Marie couldn't hear when she watched the scene unfold from her window. "Then he came to your restaurant?"

"Yep."

"And you didn't go to Tidal Creek to track him down and execute him?"

"The thought never crossed my mind. I had him thrown out the night before because he was disturbing the clientele and embarrassing himself."

I bit the inside of my cheek and drew my eyebrows together. "If your boys here went one way and then you went the other, why were you all seen driving Stanley's golf cart back to Paradise Hideaway?"

Bruno didn't hesitate or stumble over his next words. "It was common for Stanley to come to the restaurant and get too drunk to drive himself home. On more than one occasion," he raised two split fingers, indicating the twins to either side of me, "I've had them drive Stanley home and make sure he gets into his apartment safely."

"Very noble of you," I said. "But why drive his golf cart back? He wasn't at your restaurant, nor was he your responsibility."

"Good question. Great question, actually." Bruno looked at each one of his associates before settling back on me. "Everyone in this room, besides you, knows Stanley was an alcoholic. We've met up at Tidal Creek before."

"Witnesses say you and he didn't come into contact that evening."

Bruno raised a finger. "No, he didn't speak to us. We were

there to have a drink and unwind after a busy day. He saw us at one point but ignored us. He was stumbling around and talking to everyone except us."

"Still upset at us throwing him out the night before," Carlo said.

"Did you do the designated driver thing with him then and take him back?" I asked.

"We did," Carlo said.

I wondered if Marie saw him get dropped off. If so, she didn't mention it. Might have to talk to her again. "How often did you do that?"

"It didn't happen as often as you might think," Bruno said. "We'd cut him off and hand him a strong cup of coffee to sober up before letting him get behind the wheel."

It was a nice thing for them to do. "Still doesn't explain why you drove his golf cart back."

"How do you know we did?"

"Someone saw you do it."

Bruno took a deep breath. "I walked out the front door and saw his golf cart parked there. The key was in the ignition. We looked around but didn't see him. We figured he'd passed out somewhere. I talked to the boys, and we agreed we didn't want him getting back on his cart and trying to drive back to his place."

"Isn't that theft? Taking someone's golf cart?"

"That's one way of putting it." Bruno and I stared at each other before he answered my next question before I could ask it: "It's not the first time it's happened. If you say someone saw us bring his cart back that night, then I know there's people who live there who can say they've seen us do it before."

I studied his face for any sign of mistruth. I saw none. "Okay then. I believe you, but I will ask around to verify."

"I would expect nothing less of you, Mr. Amateur Sleuth."

His boys had a laugh.

I weighed him and his request while surveying his boys. If Bruno's story was true, then the twins sitting next to me were innocent. Gomez's case depended on finding evidence that they pulled the trigger. There wasn't enough evidence to hold them without bond, and Gomez hinted that there were holes in their case.

I asked Bruno, "Why not wait until trial? All of what you told me will come out and these guys will remain free."

He pursed his lips and held up two fingers. "Coupla reasons. I don't need my old boss coming around here to check up on me. He's gotta know by now we've spoken to the police. There's nothing about this murder of Stanley linking back to the don, but I still don't want him poking around my business, supposing I've broken the code of silence." He shoved a finger into the collar of his shirt and pulled, as though letting go of stress. "If he presumes his name came up, it could spell trouble for me. I'm telling ya, I'm clean. Besides, these shyster lawyers are expensive."

I chuckled.

His forehead creased. "What's so funny?"

"You."

After I spoke, Carlo's and Joey's hands whipped like lightning to something behind their backs. Angelo and Carmine shot to their feet faster than I thought possible for the two roly-poly men and shifted to face me.

Both of my hands shot in the air. My heart leapt into my throat. Or was that bile? "Whoa now!"

Before Carlo and Joey could reveal what they were reaching for, Bruno waved them off. "Down boys. I wanna hear what's so funny." He rubbed a hand across the pleat in his pants over his knee. "Well, what is it?"

The air in the room grew thick. Everyone was on edge now, except Bruno. The twins leaned forward to face me. Joey and Frankie got up and stood beside Carlo. I paid them no heed and weighed my next words. If Bruno needed me to help, then shooting me would not do him any good.

I leaned forward, toward Bruno, and laced my fingers together in front of me. "It all flows downhill, doesn't it?"

"What flows downhill?"

"Intimidation. Fear."

"Psh." He batted a hand. "What do you mean, *fear*?"

He didn't deny the intimidation, but I let it be. "This. What you're doing. You come into my home and ask for a favor while telling me, in no uncertain terms, I don't have a choice in the matter."

"Oh, yes. You have a choice."

"Yeah? And what if I tell you no?"

"Unpleasantness may occur."

"See, that's a threat."

"No, that's a statement. I never said who the unpleasantness may occur for." It was clear Bruno's experience with evading arrest trained him on how to avoid saying or doing things that could implicate himself in a crime.

"Sure, we can keep dancing around, but all of us know what's going on here. Could I have you arrested for this? Probably not. You're smart enough that you could talk your way out of it. It'd be your word against mine."

Bruno held my gaze but didn't reply. Joey, Frankie, Carlo, Carmine, and Angelo looked down at me. Not since I found Paige

Whitaker's body and started solving murders had I been in a position such as this with my death a pull of the trigger away. I breathed a few deep breaths through my nose to center myself. I could get out of this. They don't want to kill me.

The Boss realized how having his guys standing over me appeared. He motioned them back to their stations. As Carmine sat down next to me, I noted the rectangular outline of a fat wallet sticking out of his right rear pocket. The wallet was so fat it caused him to sit at a slant. I'd chuckle about it later.

"What was the other reason?" I asked.

"Oh. Two others," Bruno said, remembering he hadn't finished his thought. My question and his response eased the tension in the room a smidge. "Stanley may have been a lotta things, but he was my friend. I've known a lotta people through the years, but few I could call friends. Stanley was one of them. I want justice done the same as everybody else."

"Why not let the police handle it?"

"Don't trust them. Never have."

I regarded Bruno. His face gave away nothing. This could have been a conversation about the weather. He possessed a good poker face, but I couldn't detect any trace of lying. He evaded one topic, and I would not agree to anything until he spit it out.

I leaned forward and placed my elbows on my thighs and hands under my chin. "I'll say it again. The police wouldn't arrest anyone without hard evidence placing them at the scene of a crime, which took place in Tidal Creek's garbage corral. If what you say is true and you all didn't go near that specific area, why did they make an arrest?"

Bruno looked from me to Carmine and back. "They found Carmine's wallet there."

"His wallet?" I rotated my body to the aforementioned twin. "How could you lose anything that fat? I just saw it as you shifted in the seat."

"Someone stole it that night," Carmine answered.

"How was it stolen?"

His lips puckered. "Beats me."

"Did you rub up against anyone?"

"Tidal Creek was crowded. I bumped up against several people. Coulda been any of them."

I looked at Bruno for confirmation. He tilted his head forward.

"If it was stolen, then someone tried to frame you," I said.

"Now you see," Bruno said. "The cops got this wrong, I'm tellin' ya."

"Mmm hmm." I could sit here and recount all the good things Gina Gomez has done and her record, but I knew one thing in life. If someone has their mind made up about something, there's no changing it. I asked Bruno, "If everything you've told me is true and these guys are, in fact, innocent, then where would you suggest I start?"

His answer was what I expected.

He cackled. "I'd start with that dame, Karen Govern. He ticked that lady off *bad*."

CHAPTER
TWENTY-NINE

A WHILE LATER, Bruno and his boys left the house. He told me the "old him" might have gone to extreme measures to get the cops off their back, but he was an "honest" businessman, Lorenzo Bruno, now. He left with the veiled threat against mentioning all this to the police, unless and until I figured out what happened that evening.

Which wouldn't be a problem, as Gomez told me to stay out of it.

It was a coincidence Stanley and Bruno were at Tidal Creek that night. It's a small town if you forget about the millions of tourists who visit. Around thirty thousand people live in the area full-time. Odds are, if you're out and about, you're going to see the same person on more than one occasion. Things like this happen. True, in the summer, I was less likely to run into people I knew, but Tidal Creek was also a local hangout.

After our *relaxed* conversation, I had the sense that Bruno and his goons were innocent, at least of this murder. I had been to his restaurant before. The people who work there dressed like gangsters. Their wardrobe here today was likely their work uniform as well and why they reeked of garlic. I should have told Bruno I knew they had been watching me. I recognized Carlo as the one who had parked across from the bookstore earlier today.

After I closed the door behind them and locked the deadbolt, I went straight to my refrigerator, pulled out a tall IPA from New South Brewing, popped the top, and took a big chug. Felt better already. I grabbed a second can, shut the fridge, and padded out to the deck on the back porch and sat down. The change of scenery was much needed.

The blazing sun was still high in the sky. Its light glittered off Lake Vivian. The body of water was nothing more than a large retaining pond for the defunct golf course that used to be here. A paddle boarder coasted along in the middle of the lake. I had an orange kayak I'd take out now and then for some exercise and to get out on the water. Not today, though.

I took another swill of the refreshing beer and leaned back on the Adirondack chair, trying to get a sense of what happened in the twenty-four hours before Stanley's death. Karen slapped Stanley at Paradise Hideaway, and he left the parking lot. He must have gone to Bruno's restaurant afterward to get drunk, or drunker, as Bruno told it.

Gomez didn't give me enough information about the crime scene to piece together how the murders were committed. Stanley had volunteered to help Emilie collect the garbage, an old holdover from his past trash collecting life. It wasn't the first time he had done that, according to Erica Sullivan's report. Someone must have either been waiting in the garbage corral for Stanley to come or followed him in. It wasn't clear at what point Emilie had entered the picture. They could have been together the entire time, or they could have collected trash from separate areas and came together.

It occurred to me if anyone else had shown up on the various camera angles leaving the facility around the time of their deaths, then the police would have interviewed them. Three of the people they had seen leaving the brewery around that time were Lorenzo Bruno and his two flunkies.

I took another sip of the beer and held the cold can between my hands. Condensation from the can rubbed off on my hands. Nice and cool.

Their actions in my home puzzled me. They had let on like they were on the up and up, but Bruno having Carlo follow me to the bathroom to prevent me from escaping or calling the police wasn't something normal people did. Then, when I'd made the comment that something Bruno said was "funny," his men had instinctively reached for something hidden behind their backs. Had to be guns. Real guns. Not like the water gun Carlo had tucked into the front of his belt.

He must use that prop at the restaurant to provide some realism before a laugh. All in good fun. Well, it was fun there, not here at my house.

If it wasn't Bruno? Then who? The only names which kept coming up were those of the Silver Girls. Karen Govern seemed like the most obvious suspect. The others all had their clashes with Stanley. Karen had lied, saying she'd never had any problems with him while also withholding admission of their relationship. That's two lies. What else could she be lying about?

I finished the beer and cracked open another one. The unplanned meeting with Bruno called for two beers. If he'd told Gomez and the police the same story, then why arrest Angelo and Carmine? It's possible the cameras saw them go out the back and disappear into the trees. To me, that would seem suspicious. I got that, but enough to charge them with murder?

There had to be more to the story than Gomez had told me. I couldn't believe she'd be able to arrest someone on such circumstantial evidence. That wasn't the detective I knew.

An egret took flight from the right edge of the lake and flew across my field of vision, heading due east toward the ocean. It clutched a limp bass in its beak. The tang of salty air wasn't present today but being less than a mile from the ocean as the crow flies, if the wind blew the right way, I sometimes could smell it. The evening air caused my shirt to stick to my skin, a sign a steamy night was on the way.

I'd met Stanley that night at Tidal Creek. I had sat on one side of the patio table with Andrea between Karen and me. He had come by making his rounds. Prior to his appearance, I recalled the Silver Girls having a conversation about Karen's recent lack of a love life, which turned out to be a lie. She hadn't divulged her secret romance with the soon-to-be dead HOA leader to her roommates.

They'd let on with the thought Stanley would like to get with Karen, and she had played dumb. I remember he came by and offered to buy Karen a drink after making his rounds. They had a falling out the night before, where she'd slapped him before he went to Bruno's restaurant. Looking back, they both played it cool, not letting any shared animosity show. At that point, Karen had been aware of Stanley's embezzlement, but hadn't mentioned it to anyone. Why?

When Andrea and I left Tidal Creek, Karen had stayed behind with Stanley. Perhaps she had wanted to hash things out with him after their altercation the night before. It occurred to me I did not know when she went back to Paradise Hideaway. If it had been before the brewery closed, then she would be in the clear. I had to find out.

There were a couple of different ways of getting to Karen. I pulled out my phone and brought up my most recent calls, which coincidentally had been to Gomez and Andrea. Either could get me access to Karen.

My finger hovered over the two names on the screen. My finger wavered before jabbing at the one who I most needed to speak to at this moment.

CHAPTER
THIRTY

"CLARK, HOLD ON. I'm pulling dinner out of the oven for Libby and I."

"Of course," I said. The paddle boarder had made it to his dock on the other side of the lake and was pulling his board out of the water. A brown dog scampered from out of nowhere and greeted its owner with a wagging tail. John Fogerty's ragged voice singing *Fortunate Son* played loudly in the distance from someone's speaker system at the golf villas near where the paddle boarder had climbed onto his personal dock. A dragonfly flew past the porch.

The sounds of her phone being placed on a countertop were followed by an oven opening and closing, Libby's insistent calls for food, and the clinking of dinnerware came through the phone speaker. Andrea told her to hold her horses and the little girl stopped complaining. Their voices sounded like they were coming from the end of a tunnel.

"Here you go. Blow on it if it's too hot," Andrea said, and a moment later, her voice came through louder and clearer. "Sorry."

"Did I catch you at a bad moment?"

She breathed into the receiver. "No. Just inopportune."

"Want me to let you go so you can tend to Libby and eat?"

"No, it's okay. I'll put you on speaker, and we can pretend

you're a ghost having dinner with us."

The thought of the girl pretending I was a ghost in the room made me smile, which was what I needed and hoped for when I called her. Andrea had a sense of humor I liked. One of the many things I liked about her.

The intention of my call was to ask her about Karen. I didn't need to bring up Andrea's upstairs neighbor, she did it herself. "Hey, I was delving through more records today and found something interesting."

"Yeah?"

"Karen hasn't paid her HOA dues in months."

"Was she one of those who paid monthly or once or twice a year?"

"I went way back. She paid every month every year since she moved in."

"Was her last payment a lump sum? Like she was paying ahead."

"Nope."

"When was her last payment?"

"November."

Stanley's shift to using HOA funds for personal gain had begun around the same time. If he already had been playing loose by the rules for his own gain, why not let the woman who had captured his interest skirt by without paying her dues? Marie had mentioned seeing Karen and Stanley cavorting around at night, going back several months.

I shifted the phone from one ear to the other. "I bet Stanley let her slide on the dues, so she'd snuggle up with him."

"Sounds about right."

"You never know. Karen's financial status could have changed."

"She had a sizable estate left by her dead husband. I can't imagine the well running dry."

The sports world was filled with stories of star athletes who made millions of dollars during their careers only to file for bankruptcy a few years after retirement because they couldn't handle money. Karen could come from the school where she believed money grew on trees.

"Could be." I took a sip from the can. "How well do you know Karen?"

"Reasonably well. We play cards together down in the rec room on weekends and hang out by the pool. All the Silver Girls and I."

"Are they regular meetups or what?"

"One of them will call if they're going down to the pool and see if Libby and I want to tag along."

Today was Monday. Andrea kept Coastal Décor closed on Tuesdays, and Ed Piotrowski's forecast for the next day was for a scorcher.

"Think they'll go to the pool tomorrow?" I asked.

"Is it supposed to rain?"

"Just saw the weather. The forecast is hot and sunny."

"Is it a day ending in Y?"

I smiled. "More than likely."

"Then chances are they'll be by the pool."

"What about you and Libby?"

She echoed the words I had just said. "More than likely. Wanna come?"

"You know it."

I let her go before her dinner got cold. She said she'd check in tomorrow with a meetup time.

Karen seemed like a woman who loved a cocktail. If I joined them by the pool and she had a few, then it might be easier to pry some information out of her. I reminded myself that if she was the killer, then she knew how to use a gun. I had to figure out a way to ask her questions without arousing her suspicions. I'm sure I could come up with something.

All of this was to find the motive for Stanley's murder. Motive is one thing. Opportunity was another. Karen had said she'd left Stanley that night before Tidal Creek closed. If true, then she couldn't have killed him and Emilie. It occurred to me she could have been so enraged at him and went home, and then came back with a gun. Paradise Hideaway was two minutes away from Tidal Creek by car. If she had spent any late evenings with him there, she would have been aware he sometimes offered to help with the trash collection and at what time he did it. Karen could have timed her second arrival so she would be waiting for him at the trash corral. It was a shame that Emilie came in too.

The thing tugging at my brain was that Stanley was a much bigger person than Karen. Did the threat of the gun keep him from trying to escape or overpower her? They killed him execution style with two shots to the back of the head.

The thought of the friendly, outgoing Karen doing that and then killing Emilie in cold blood didn't jibe with my impression of her. Like I've learned from past cases, you never know what a person will do if they're trapped in a corner. It's possible Stanley had something he was hanging over Karen's head. It would have to be something big enough where it kept her from going to the police about Stanley's embezzlement. But what?

I finished the second beer and went back inside. Reflecting on everything that had happened today, I let out a deep breath.

It had been a long and eventful one.

I went to bed thinking about what the next day might bring. If nothing else, at least I'd get to see Andrea in a bathing suit, which would leave little to the imagination as to her figure. A beautiful view and a mystery to solve? What more could I ask for?

CHAPTER
THIRTY-ONE

LIBBY WORE BLOW-up floaties on her upper arms, lavender goggles, and a little purple swimsuit as Violet taught her swimming lessons. The little girl squealed with glee, not quite taking the lesson seriously. Neither was Violet. She wore a navy-blue rubber swim cap with a periwinkle flower pattern over her hair. How she got the thing to cover her entire mop of hair without a single strand falling out was beyond me.

Andrea sat on the edge of the pool, wearing a baby blue tankini with her legs plunged into the water, watching her daughter play. Made my day already. Karen had made a pitcher of strawberry daiquiris to bring poolside. We sat at a table together under an umbrella. I was pretty sure when we walked out to the pool, a sign with the pool rules said no alcoholic beverages on the top line. Looking around at the various people enjoying the pool, being of the older and retired variety, the rule was being ignored. Maybe they were partying now that Stanley was gone. Even the new HOA president, Paul, held a beer can in a koozie in his hand as he chatted with a couple friends.

I wore a Hawaiian shirt with flamingo print, unbuttoned, wayfarer sunglasses, and a pair of Ron Jon board shorts. My customary flip-flops sat on the cement patio beneath my chair.

A cold daiquiri oozed condensation onto my hand. My legs were up on the seat of an empty chair. The area smelled of coconut sunscreen and grilled hot dogs. The party was on at Paradise Hideaway. I could get used to this.

Dot had taken her mom, Beatrice, to a doctor's appointment. The older lady was disappointed she couldn't be here the entire time, as she loved to swim. She said she used to swim in the shores off the coast of Naples as a child, and it's what kept her youthful well into her nineties. Dot liked to mingle by the pool, not in it.

Before he left yesterday, Bruno had given me an ultimatum. Angelo and Carmine had a preliminary court date scheduled for next Monday at 10:15 in the morning. He wanted their names cleared by then or he would make my life miserable. For someone who let on like they were a reformed and now honest businessman who upheld the law, Lorenzo Bruno's words, actions, and threats ran to the contrary. If I was to believe he was a changed man, then I assumed his warning was nothing more than a bluff. However, if he still had a dark side to him, the pressure was on to comply.

The odds were if he had people watching me like I suspected, then they knew I spent time with Andrea and Libby. A more sobering thought was they would know who my parents were. I took a long sip of the daiquiri.

I couldn't go to the police with details about Bruno's visit. If they pulled him and his cronies off the street, who is to say he didn't have more out there capable of following up on this threat? This seemed like a situation where, if you cut one head off the hydra, two would grow back in its place. I slept little last night.

Karen took a seat in the plastic chair on the other side of the table and sipped her beverage. After taking in the view of the people having a good time in and out of the pool, she said, "Oh, I just love this. I didn't imagine this aspect of Southern living before I came here from Indiana, but I've gotten used to it."

I reached my daiquiri up across the table and we clinked, more like clunked, our clear plastic cups together. "Here, here. I'm from Southern Ohio, and yeah, it could get hot there during the summer, but nothing like this."

"How long have you lived in the South?"

"More than half my life." I reflected on my past for a moment. "It's like, yeah, I know where I'm from, and I love my home state, but now that I've spent so many years here in Myrtle Beach, I consider myself more of a South Carolinian than I do an Ohioan."

Karen sniggered and sipped from her straw. "I have quite a few years to go before I can make that claim. Don't know if I'll reach it, but I'm going to try."

"That's the spirit." With Andrea, Violet, and Libby out of hearing range and the other residents not paying us much attention, I needed to use this opportunity to get some answers. Andrea had set us up perfectly without realizing I was in danger. "So, you had mentioned you had nothing to do with Stanley."

Karen wore sunglasses, so I couldn't see all of her expression, but her lips tightened around the straw sticking out of her cup. Her gaze stayed forward, away from me. "As little as possible."

A rather portly man, bald on top with gray hair around the sides, no shirt and wearing a Speedo, did a cannonball into the pool, drenching two women floating on noodles. People around them laughed and smiled. The two victims, not so much. A huge smile lit up the man's face as he emerged from the depths. One of the now soaked women put her hand on top of his head and shoved him back under. Everyone was having fun.

Except Karen after I mentioned Stanley's name. "That's odd."

This time, she turned to me. "What's odd?"

I took a casual sip from the cup. "It's just after the big HOA meeting, one of your neighbors told me they saw you coming in late at night with him."

"Which neighbor?" she demanded in a hushed, harsh whisper.

"I won't say. From your reaction, I'd say it's true."

Her mouth hung open while trying to think of what to say next. "Who knows about this?"

"Your neighbor and me." I left out the Gomez part. She didn't ask for everybody's name. Her mistake.

"Yes, it's true. Stanley and I dated for a while, but we broke up."

"From what I heard. Your breakup might have happened the night before his death when you slapped him."

Karen raised her voice, "How did you—-!" She stopped as she realized people had turned their attention to us. After letting their short attention spans go about their merry ways, she said in a softer tone, "Someone must have seen us come in."

From our spot by the pool, the front of Paradise Hideaway lay behind us. It had three sections forming a large U and rose three stories. The pool was positioned in a private courtyard in the concavity between the wings, open to the east.

She twisted, raised her sunglasses, and glared at the front part of Paradise Hideaway. The parking lot lay on the other side. Looking back at me, she said, "There are only so many people who could have seen me. I'll figure out who."

"And do what?"

"Not kill them, if that's what you're thinking. No, I would deliver them a stern talking to and tell them to mind their own business."

She took a moment to cool off. I gave it to her because I needed her cooperation.

Marie said she had this crippling anxiety. The last thing she needed was a heated Karen in her face. "I'll leave it to you, but I would suggest letting bygones be bygones and let it go."

"Maybe you should mind your own business too," she suggested.

I took a deep breath. "You say you had broken up with him, but I also know you stayed with him after Andrea and me left Tidal Creek. You wouldn't have done that if you didn't have lingering feelings for him."

"You know too much," she said matter-of-factly.

"Meh. It happens."

She turned to me and pulled her sunglasses down so I could see her eyes. "Look, I want whoever killed Stanley locked up as much as the next person. Yes, I cared for him."

"I sense a 'but' in there."

"Yes, there is a 'but,' Stanley's thieving, conniving butt was stealing money."

"Did you find out before his death? Was that why you broke things off with him?"

She bit the corner of her bottom lip. "I'd spent enough time with him to realize he was spending more money than what he could have been raking in from his retirement account."

Now that Karen had settled in and started talking, I hoped to see what else she would reveal. The half-drunk daiquiri in her hand was her third overall. She had been heavy on the rum when mixing it. Time to go fishing.

I set my finished cup on the table. She didn't offer to refill it.

I laced my fingers behind my head. "You are aware I helped Andrea sift through the HOA bank statements?"

Karen kept her gaze locked on the pool and sipped her drink.

I leaned closer to her over the table. "We know now he was using HOA funds for himself, but I suspect that wasn't the only time he bent the rules, like in who paid or didn't pay their HOA dues."

The comment hung in the air for a long second. She said nothing, so I did. "What came first, your relationship with Stanley or you not paying your monthly dues? And yes, we know you paid every month on the same date until late last fall, which was right around the time my source said they started seeing you with Stanley late at night."

Her mouth fell open. She stammered, "A-after. Our relationship started afterward."

"What happened? Money trouble, or did he offer to look the other way in exchange for your company?"

"B-both."

My eyes narrowed, thinking about where to go next while processing this information. "Tell me what happened at Tidal Creek after Andrea and I left."

"N-nothing." The hand that held her cup shook. "He bought me a beer. He apologized, and I left."

"Did you accept his apology?"

"I did."

"Why didn't you tell the police about him stealing the money?"

"Gracious, Clark. I'd just found out about it. There hadn't been time to process everything. Part of me was afraid I'd either get thrown out of my home for not paying my dues or get arrested." She gestured toward Violet. "If they throw me out, the rest of the girls are homeless, too."

A couple ambled past us holding hands on their way to a set of empty lounge chairs on the other side of the pool. They said hello to Karen. She was too shaken to respond. They gave her and me an odd expression and continued on their way.

"I'll accept that. So, after your beer and his apology, what did you do?"

"I went home."

"What time was it when you left?"

"I'm not sure about the exact time, but it was about twenty till nine when I got back."

Pieces clicked together, but I wondered if they went to the same puzzle. "Can your roommates confirm that?"

She thought for a moment. "Violet was getting ready for bed. She saw me come in."

"Where were Dot and Beatrice?"

"I didn't see them. I assumed they were both already in bed. They're both early to bed, early to rise types."

"What did you do after you got home?"

"I told Violet goodnight and went to bed. I was plumb exhausted."

"After the twenty-four hours you had, I can't blame you."

She reached over, grasped my hand, and gave it a squeeze. "One thing all this reminded me of again, especially after losing my husband, is to treasure the ones you're with." She nodded at Andrea and Libby over by the pool. "Take it from me. If they're your future, then you'll have struck gold."

I watched Andrea laugh after Libby splashed Violet again. We'd only known each other a short time, but Karen's words rang true. The newcomer in my life had left an impression I'd only felt one other time, and that was when I first met Autumn. My attraction to Gina Gomez grew over time. Not a long period of time, but over time.

Her fingers scratched the tabletop. "You know, it's interesting."

"What is?"

"All of this mafia talk involving Stanley."

"What about it?"

"It's just I remembered Beatrice telling me one time when it came up for discussion about having the mafia around where she grew up in Italy."

I thought about the small-statured but feisty woman. "I can see her causing trouble in her early years."

"Pshaw. She's a troublemaker now. She didn't care for Stanley or pretty much anyone else who told her what to do."

"Interesting."

I could think of nothing else to ask her at the moment. The brief show of affection toward me on her part told me there were no hard feelings. By this point, she knew about my recent history of nosing around murder investigations and perhaps thought I was just doing my thing, in which she would be correct.

One thing I've learned in the past year is most suspects in a murder investigation have secrets they lie about until the truth gets revealed. I'd uncovered Karen's secret relationship with Stanley and her not paying her dues, but it left me to wonder if she held any more secrets.

The night of the murders, Karen said she didn't see Dot or Beatrice upon returning home or while saying goodnight to Violet. Then Karen closed her bedroom door and presumably didn't emerge until the next morning. Just because Karen didn't see her other roommates that evening, didn't mean they were in bed.

Which begged the question: what did the other Silver Girls do after Karen closed her door?

CHAPTER
THIRTY-TWO

THE SWIMMING LESSON ended, and Violet climbed out of the pool. Libby continued to splash and play. Another little girl had joined her, and they were having a grand time. It put a big smile on my face. Almost as big as the one Andrea wore.

I hopped up from my chair, allowing Violet to sit after drying off. Karen greeted her with a daiquiri.

The sun was high in the sky. A few thin clouds drifted overhead, coming in off the ocean. A pair of seagulls cruised by on an updraft, angling for the beach. Heat radiated off the areas of concrete away from people and the pool.

Andrea motioned for me to join her. An invitation I was happy to accept. I sat down beside her a few inches apart. We watched Libby play with her friend for a few moments before Andrea turned to me with a smile. "Thought you would never join me."

"Oh, trust me, you were next up on my to-do list."

She bit her lower lip. "Cheeky today, are you?"

I held my hands up in mock surrender. "I have no clue what you're talking about."

"Ha ha. Whatever."

"You look good in that swimsuit."

She leaned over and bumped my shoulder. "You're not so bad yourself. Kind of wishing you'd strip off that ridiculous shirt."

I pulled on the hem of my shirt. "What? This?"

She tugged on the hem of my flamingo special. "Yes, that."

I took the shirt off and tossed it back toward the table we'd commandeered. The sun baked my shoulders. "Happy now?"

Andrea gave me a once over. "You bet."

Since I'd met Gomez, I'd tried to take better care of myself. Eating fewer fatty foods, paddling around in the kayak, the occasional sit-ups, and jogging around the neighborhood. Those efforts increased after meeting Andrea. I had to admit, I should have done it sooner. My health and my looks both improved. After Autumn's death, I'd let myself go, hoping I could whip myself into shape in a matter of weeks, until the harsh reality of getting older set in, reminding me I'm not as young as I used to be, and my body no longer responded the way it did to exercise when I played baseball in high school and college.

I leaned over and bumped her shoulder. "Thanks."

"How did it go with you and Karen? Learn anything?"

"I did. Thanks for setting this up." I recapped the conversation. "I'd like to corner Violet, if possible."

Andrea twisted and waved at the batty West Virginian and Karen, sipping from their cups in the umbrella's shade. She returned her attention to me. "Might be difficult here, unless Karen mingles."

"She's still grieving a little, in her own way. She didn't seem like she was in a mingling mood. More of a drown her sorrows in boozy, fruity drinks."

"Sounds about right." She looked up at a bird passing by and then back at me. "I'll see what I can do with Violet. What about Dot and her mom?"

"Them too. I need to figure out if they stayed in their apartment after Karen came in and went to bed."

"Let's say one of them didn't and snuck out to Tidal Creek."

"Okay."

She placed a cool hand on my arm. "Do you think they'd tell you the truth?"

"No, but if one of them did and lied about it, we could figure it out."

"How so?"

I pointed at a spot above the rear exit of the building. "They'd be on camera."

She drew out a breath. "Oh. Wouldn't the police have already done that?"

"Probably."

"If one of the other Silver Girls left the apartment, wouldn't they have been seen on camera and questioned about it?"

I thought about how James pulled off the murder of Paige Whitaker at OceanScapes Resort. He had spray painted the cameras in the stairwell to cover his tracks. I didn't think one of the Girls had manipulated the camera feeds, but it occurred to me that it might be possible. How? I wasn't sure.

When I didn't answer, Andrea asked, "Why not tell the police what you know?"

I stared her in the eye for a moment, daring not to look away. No need to tell her about Gomez and I spending time together and coming here and questioning Marie. Not all the details, at least. She might act jealous again. The memory of Gomez's hand on mine from just before dropping her off at her car raced to the front of my mind. I shook my head to clear away the thought.

I had also not discussed the meeting with Bruno and the subsequent veiled warning with Andrea, and I meant to keep it that way. No need to make her worry about me more than necessary.

I pulled up my sunglasses and squinted in the direct sunlight. "I'm sure they can figure it out. Detective Gomez told me she didn't need my help and to stay out of it."

She placed a hand over mine. "Good. I like that. Don't need you going up against the mafia or whoever killed Stanley."

"Don't forget Emilie."

"Of course. Poor girl."

Something I said a moment ago *pinged* in the back of my head. Right now, while sitting next to this distractingly beautiful woman in a swimsuit, I couldn't place my finger on it.

Libby doggy paddled over to our side of the pool. Droplets of water covered her goggles. A wet, blonde ponytail dangled from where a hair tie separated it from the front of her head.

"Having fun, Junebug?" Andrea asked.

"Yeah!" Libby shrieked, looked at me, and went back to her mom. She motioned for Andrea to lean forward so she could whisper something in her mom's ear.

Andrea listened for a few moments before standing. "Well, come on. Let's get you out of there."

Libby paddled to the edge of the pool between Andrea and me. I reached down, grabbed her under her armpits, and pulled her out of the water in one motion. Water cascaded off the girl and splashed on the concrete. Some got on me, but that was okay.

"Thank you," Libby said.

Andrea stood and reached for Libby's hand and cocked her

head toward the outdoor bathrooms. "Let's go."

"Okay, Mommy." Libby reached up and took Mommy's hand.

As they left me by the pool, Andrea mouthed, "Potty break."

I gave a thumbs-up and off they went. As I watched them go, Violet joined me. She sat down on the other side from where Andrea sat a moment before and stuck her feet in the water.

She held one of Karen's daiquiris in one hand and sipped from the straw. Her lips puckered. "Wow! That's boozy!"

"I'll say."

"I forgot Karen goes a little heavy on the alcohol when she makes daiquiris," Violet said. That didn't stop her from taking another sip.

I glanced back at Karen, who had refilled her cup. "I've counted at least three she's had herself."

Violet *tsked*. "Sounds about right. Karen loves to have a good time."

"Seems like it."

"Now, don't get me wrong. She's not an alcoholic. She doesn't drink every day or gets hammered every time she does. Although, she's been imbibing more recently."

"I understand." It made me wonder if the uptick in alcohol consumption was a byproduct of Stanley's death. It was in mine after Autumn's death. This was not the time to mention Karen and Stanley's secret relationship.

She held her fingertips on the straw as she drank some more and smacked her lips. "Karen and I were watching you and Andrea just now. You sure make a cute couple."

I either needed to reapply sunscreen to my face or what Violet said made my cheeks burn. "I don't know if I'd call us that. We haven't discussed it."

"I don't mean to pry, but maybe you should."

In the South, when someone prefaces a statement with, "I don't mean to pry," the next words out of their mouth went against that, as Violet's did just now. It could have been worse. She could have added "Bless your heart" to the end.

I answered, "Maybe."

"Growing up in Gilboa, if a man came around me as much as you have with Andrea, everyone would say we were courtin' with an engagement in the works."

"I get your point."

"And if he had at least three cows, a handful of chickens, and a parcel of land, a girl would have been crazy not to marry him."

I stifled a laugh. She was serious.

She continued, "What I'm saying is, when a man has something good to offer a woman beyond your obvious looks and charm, they would be fortunate to have your attention focused on them. You own a business, seem to be well off, and you're good lookin'. I know it's a shame you're single, considering the circumstances, but any unattached woman your age would be crazy not to hitch their wagon with you."

"Thanks." I think. What I didn't point out to the romantic in Violet was not every woman around my age without a significant other desired a relationship. They dedicated themselves to their careers or kids. Or they were damaged by a past romantic connection. Everyone my age who was single had baggage somewhere. That baggage was sometimes too recent to move on, or even see someone else worthy might be out there. I had it. Andrea dealt with the sudden death of her husband, although she insinuated his death was his fault and didn't seem sad about it. I still had the door open on learning what happened with Autumn, and I still hadn't decided whether I could move on before closing that door for good.

"The kids nowadays call it a 'situationship.' Where two people are entangled in something, but neither knows how to define it."

I caught her drift. "Let me guess. You've had this conversation with Andrea?"

Violet gave a coy smile but didn't answer the question. We watched swimmers moving around the pool for a few silent seconds. "When I was in the pool earlier with Libby, I couldn't help but notice you and Karen seemed to have a serious conversation."

"We were. Somehow, we got into the night of Stanley and Emilie's deaths." I didn't say the "somehow" was purposeful on my part. "Now it's rattling around inside my head."

Violet sucked the last of the daiquiri through the straw and set the empty cup on the deck between us. "Yup. That night rattles around inside my head constantly. I wish they'd hurry and prosecute those guys they arrested for it."

"Them or somebody. Karen said you were getting ready for bed when she came home."

"That's right. I had just applied my face cream when she came in."

"How did she seem?"

Violet wiggled her shoulders. "Normal, I guess. I can't remember her being or doing anything odd. She seemed like she did when she normally got home from a late night out."

"Did that happen often?"

"A couple of times a week." She leaned toward me and said in a low voice, "Me and the other girls think she had a man she didn't want us to know about."

I stuck out my lower lip. "You never know." I did. "Everyone is entitled to their privacy."

"You're right. Even if we all live together."

"Must make it difficult to keep secrets."

"You don't know the half of it."

Her statement gave me pause. What secrets was Violet keeping? It wasn't about Stanley and Karen's relationship. They seemed oblivious to it. "What happened after Karen came home? Did everyone stay in?"

The lines between Violet's eyebrows crimped. "As far as I know, Dot went to bed. Now Beatrice sometimes goes out for late night walks."

"Isn't that dangerous?"

Her hair wiggled left and right. "Oh, no. Not around here. She goes and takes a few laps around the building and comes back in."

"Did she leave?"

"I couldn't tell you. I went to bed right after Karen came back." She kicked her feet in the water. "I'm glad this didn't happen when I worked there."

"Someone mentioned that you used to work there." I wasn't going to tell her that the person who told me was investigating this case for the MBPD.

"A couple years back. Tended bar for a few months one summer when they needed help, just as something to do."

"Nice." A thought struck, causing me to stare forward with wide eyes, focusing on nothing. Like most employees trying to sneak food, drink, or a smoke while on the clock, Violet *could* have known where the blank spots were in Tidal Creek's security coverage.

CHAPTER
THIRTY-THREE

Before I could ask her about it, Dot and Beatrice arrived. Karen had a drink ready to go for Dot, who accepted the beverage with heartfelt thanks.

"Every time I go to that doctor's office with Ma, I expect to die of old age while waiting," Dot said.

Beatrice shucked off her fanny pack and swimsuit coverup, draping the fabric over the pack to hide it in an empty chair. "You'll die of old age? Where would that leave me? Waiting for you on the other side of the River Styx?"

Dot rolled her eyes. "Come on, Ma. You know what I mean."

"I do. But waiting for Dr. Shank's smooth touch is worth the wait."

"For you maybe, but not for me."

"Schedule an appointment with him. It'll change your life."

"Sure, I'll fake gallbladder problems just so I can see him. My Medicaid would love footing *that* bill."

Beatrice walked by Dot on her way to the edge of the pool. "If you only knew." She jumped into the deep end with the ease of someone half her age.

The demographic of year-round residents in Myrtle Beach skewed older. I've been around many living in their eighth or ninth decade on Earth in my twenty-plus years of living in the Grand Strand. I couldn't believe my eyes. The small woman swam with a grace and ability I hadn't seen for a person of her age. She used to swim every day in the waters off Naples before her parents brought her to the United States. Not a bad way to grow up.

We settled in and enjoyed another hour of life by the pool. Dot immersed herself in a book on an e-reader while Violet and Karen gossiped. Beatrice continued her laps. Libby got sleepy. Andrea took her daughter up to their apartment to put her down for a nap. I offered to help, but she told me to stay by the pool, knowing the full reason I was present.

I wanted to resume my conversation with Violet about her having once worked at Tidal Creek, but she had snagged a seat with Dot and Karen at the table under the umbrella. They were having a good time eating cold-cut sandwiches Violet made before coming down to the pool. I didn't ask Violet pointed questions, with the other two clustered around.

However, I accepted a BLT and a bag of small potato chips from Violet. While they chatted, I monitored everyone having fun at the pool. Beatrice had swum to the deep end and had one hand placed on the deck to hold herself in place. Marie's long-haired son, Colton, made an appearance, having escaped his darkened lair. He wore a rock t-shirt and a pair of jeans — not quite swimming attire — and was making a lap around the outside of the pool. He didn't talk to anyone, except he said "Hello" to Beatrice as he passed by before leaving the area. His abrupt appearance and exit seemed peculiar. Almost as much as his random stopping and speaking to Beatrice.

I said almost to myself, "Why would he do that?"

"Why would who do what?" Karen asked.

I gestured toward Colton's back as he closed the gate door on his way back inside. "Him."

"Who Colton?" Dot said. "Yes, he's an odd one. What did he do?"

"He came out here for less than five minutes." I waved a hand, outlining the path Colton took on his lap. "He drifted around the pool, said something to Beatrice, then exited the way he came."

Violet crooked a finger. "Yeah, he's an odd one."

Karen and Dot whipped their heads around at their roommate. I could guess why they reacted the way they did.

Dot explained, "Ma befriended him. She saw he didn't like to talk to anyone, and his mom had her own set of problems, so Ma wanted to help him come out of his shell."

"Still has that motherly instinct," Karen said. "It never goes away."

I swung my head to look at Karen. "Wouldn't his mom take exception to another woman treating Colton like her offspring?"

"If Marie knew about it, perhaps," Dot said. "Ma took him under her wing after she learned his mom did little for him."

"I've spoken to her," I said. "She has her own set of problems she deals with."

"All the more reason to help the boy," Karen said. "Especially after he got arrested."

"Arrested? What for?"

"For stealing some Northerners' money while working at Tidal Creek," she explained. "He was here on vacation, and somehow or another, Colton made off with six, seven hundred dollars."

"Wow. Did he go to jail?"

"It seems like he did thirty days in the J. Reuben Long Detention Center in Conway."

"Goodness." I had watched the young man with a close eye. With every step, he moved with a slight hesitation. His shoulders slouched. Here was a person who, from all outward appearances, needed as much help as he could get to save him from wasting his life. He'd already spent one stint in jail. I hoped being around Beatrice would prevent him from going back.

Dot slurped from her straw. "It's one of those random things about living in a condominium. We all live in a closed-off space, and sometimes weird relationships develop."

Karen flashed a warning glance at me. We kept our mouths shut.

We munched on our sandwiches and people watched. One of my favorite things to do. They say you can't judge a book by its cover, and while that may be true most times, you can learn a lot about a person by watching their actions.

There was something I needed to learn from Dot, and I spent the second half of the sandwich trying to figure out a way to steer a conversation in that direction. There was no need. She did it for me.

She stuffed a potato chip into her mouth. "Clark, I've been wondering something."

"Yes?"

"Of course, we know how you've gotten yourself into murder investigations. At any point, have you thought to yourself it was dangerous?"

I reflected on the four cases, from Paige Whitaker to Brian McConnell. Each presented their own hardships, trials, and peril. The last time I got involved in a murder case, I almost died. I grasped my ribcage with one hand, recalling the blast that almost did the deed.

I chuckled. "To be honest, the first time I did it, I dove into it without thinking. My dad pointed out to me then that I had no training, either in investigation or self-defense, and I could get myself killed doing it. I've been in a sword fight and survived an explosion." Left out the two times when I broke into places I shouldn't have while searching for evidence.

Dot arched an eyebrow. "What would you do if someone pulled a gun on you?"

Bruno and his men standing over me with guns strapped to their waistbands popped into my head. "How do you know that hasn't happened?"

That caused the three women to sit back in their chairs and regard me differently.

"What did you do?" Violet asked.

"Kept my composure and talked my way out of the situation."

"What are you going to do when you can't talk your way out?" Karen asked.

"I'll cross that bridge when I come to it."

Dot fluttered a hand. "All I'm saying is, I've been around some unsavory sorts. People who lived in their own worlds where violence was a threat."

"Like who?" I leaned in, hoping she would confide in me some of the famous people her security firm helped to protect.

"Sorry, can't tell you for whom we provided protection for." Dot drew from her straw and then continued. "Let's just say we had some who fought in a ring or octagon or rapped about violent upbringings. Behind closed doors, they could be some of the nicest people you'll ever meet, but it didn't mean their public personas didn't bring out the riff raff or others who meant them harm."

I tapped a finger on the table. "Yes, I've been around the people at the Gladiator Games Dinner Show. Very different people behind closed doors. I understand where you're coming from."

"Every person who worked for the security firm had to take self-defense training. Both hand-to-hand and with a gun. Even me, who spent my career there behind a desk in a private office." She leveled her gaze at me. "You play a dangerous game. I encourage you to look into self-defense before you get mixed up with the wrong people."

Too late for that. I didn't want the Silver Girls to know I had been in contact with Lorenzo Bruno. In her warning, Dot answered the question I sought the answer to. She knew how to use a gun.

The questions now were, did she have one and was she furious enough at Stanley to use it?

CHAPTER
THIRTY-FOUR

A*NDREA SENT ME* a text message saying she was going to lie down beside Libby and nap with her. I thanked her for setting up the pool date with the Silver Girls and bade my farewells to them. As it was, I'd spent too much time in the sun this afternoon and hoped I still had a bottle of aloe in the medicine cabinet at home to relieve what I was sure was going to be a bad sunburn.

I drove away from Paradise Hideaway, pondering my next move and what had transpired at the pool. My thumb tapped on the steering wheel as I paused on Phillis Boulevard to let a minivan leave the Barnes & Noble parking lot. When the van pulled out, I pulled in, making the snap decision to go for a coffee in the Starbucks Cafe inside the large chain bookstore. I needed to concentrate and drink something to clear away the rum from the daiquiri. I wasn't drunk, but I was kind of feeling it thanks to the sun and drink combo. It was best not to leave the driving to chance, considering the exorbitant amount of traffic promising to be between here and home.

I realized I had my bookstore where I could go for coffee, but it was farther away than I wanted to drive at present, as was my home in the opposite direction. In fact, I spent many occasions at this Barnes & Noble before opening Myrtle Beach Reads. I didn't perceive them as competitors. We were far enough away from each other where we weren't fighting each other for every tourist dollar. Much of my traffic came on foot from visitors staying at hotels along the Boardwalk. Market Common was one of the shopping hubs in Myrtle Beach and served as a different tourist destination, of which there was plenty to go around.

The parking lot was full, as usual. I had to course through the rows several times before finding a spot. I hopped out of the Jeep and trotted to the front door, where a woman in a blue skirt held open the door for me. After expressing my appreciation, I entered the small lobby and was hit with a wall of pleasant coolness of which I was also thankful for after being outside most of the afternoon.

I wound my way through several tables of book displays, taking mental notes on how we could arrange our offerings. I glanced at the Southern Fiction table to see if they carried my book. They had other local authors, such Lisa Borne Graves and Maegwen Salley-Massey, but not mine. Maybe someday.

The people who worked here knew who I was from having my bookstore. I hadn't worked up the courage to see if they could carry my book.

As I walked past the information kiosk in the middle of the store, an employee whose name tag identified him as "Rob" stood behind the desk. He was wearing a dark denim button-up shirt with an amulet hanging around his neck and possessed bushy, scraggly, black and gray hair on top of his head with an equally scraggly salt and pepper beard. I took one glance at him and decided this would not be the day to approach them about my book.

Besides, in my board shorts, Hawaiian shirt, and flip-flops,

I looked like a beach bum. Not authorial at all. Nor did I have any books with me. I headed for some java.

After grabbing a coffee from the barista, I found an empty table at which to sit. I made myself comfortable and took my first sip of coffee. The cobwebs in my head from the daiquiri cleared away. Readers and coffee sippers surrounded me. They focused their attention on each other and not on me. A Mendelssohn orchestral piece played from the overhead speakers. It wasn't quite the quiet moments of nirvana I experienced during the early hours at my bookstore.

It would do for what I needed at present, which was trying to sort out if any of the Silver Girls had killed Stanley. On the surface, each had a motive. Karen hadn't paid her dues and any potential falling out and sense of betrayal with Stanley could have resulted in her getting thrown out. Stanley had fined Violet for walking her dog too early in the day. Beatrice had several run-ins with Stanley and hadn't tried to hide her dislike for the man. Then, he had allegedly allowed someone from Dot's former employer to gain access to their apartment to snoop around.

They were a tight-knit group of friends, and I had to consider the possibility they had planned out the hit together. Karen said when she arrived home, she saw neither Dot nor Beatrice. Violet was getting ready for bed. Karen had gone into her room and didn't see any of her roommates until the next morning.

There had been time between Karen's arrival and the closing time for Tidal Creek, where a Silver Girl could have slipped out and done the deed. It's possible Violet could have waited for Karen to close her door and splashed water in her face to rinse off the nighttime mask and left. On the flip side, she could have climbed into bed, leaving the opportunity for Dot and/or Beatrice to leave unnoticed.

Supposing Karen was telling the truth and had gone to bed, any combination of Dot, Violet, and Beatrice could have left and gone to Tidal Creek. It was a five-minute stroll from Paradise Hideaway to the brewery. Gomez would know if any of them showed up on the camera feeds.

Speaking of which, Violet had worked for Tidal Creek. She could have known about the blank spots in surveillance coverage. I didn't know if she knew how to use a gun, but I had this vision that everyone who grew up in rural West Virginia was born with a shotgun in their hands. I'd been through the part of that state where she said she was from. Although beautiful, the residents knew how to take care of themselves and loved hunting. Dot mentioned Violet loved to tell stories about squirrel hunting growing up. Dot also had gun training. I wasn't sure about her mom, nor Karen.

None of this mattered if they had all stayed at Paradise Hideaway. If so, then they were innocent. Where did that leave Lorenzo Bruno's goons? If they were the true culprits and I were in Bruno's Italian loafers, then I would try to establish SODDIT as much as possible. That is, Some Other Dude Did It.

I scratched the surface of the table as I realized I'd finished my coffee. Readers and shoppers moved around me, oblivious to the murderous thoughts going through my head. At this point, I only had a partial picture of what happened to Stanley and poor Emilie. Detective Gomez would know if any of the Silver Girls showed up on the camera feeds. The police's focus had been on Bruno's men, Carmine and Angelo.

It was four in the afternoon. Not quite time for dinner. Not for me, at least. My parents, on the other hand, were probably figuring out what they were going to eat. I didn't want to go to their house. They lived on the opposite side of the same neighborhood as me in Surfside Beach. There was a pull coming from Market Common tonight. Something deep in my bones told me to stay here. All the answers were within my reach.

That didn't mean I couldn't use a little help. I might be in my early forties, but it didn't mean I was too old to call the person who could help the most right now. My mom.

CHAPTER
THIRTY-FIVE

UNINTELLIGIBLE MUSIC THUMPED from overhead speakers inside Gordon Biersch. The drone of conversation drowned out any ability to make out what music was being played. From what I could tell, it had too much of a modern beat for my 90s musical tastes.

Low lighting in the restaurant made it difficult to make out my neighbors, which meant they would have a hard time seeing me. I was cool with that. I had an IPA in front of me as I waited for my parents' arrival. Our table had a small lantern hanging off the wall, casting the tabletop in a soft glow.

I enjoyed my beer and watched the employees scurry about from table to table. Mom and Dad climbed in on the opposite side of the booth.

"This is a pleasant surprise," Mom said, picking up a menu. She'd had two bouts with throat cancer but hadn't needed to receive treatment for over two years. It took her a long time to regain her health and ability to eat many foods. Now she was picking up steam and putting back on some of the weight she lost during treatments.

Dad perused the beer menu. He'd remained by her side almost every waking minute since her initial diagnosis. Their fiftieth wedding anniversary was in the rear-view mirror, and they had been high school sweethearts. An old family rumor circulated that they had eloped across state lines, and my dad had falsified his birthdate so they could get married before he went off to Vietnam. They were the symbol of requited love personified. I had always respected their relationship and hoped I could have what they have with each other. With Autumn, we were well on our way until her unfortunate passing. She and I had shared a similar bond.

I hadn't mentioned Andrea to them yet, but my mom was a long-time reader of mystery novels and had a knack for putting two and two together. My suspicion was that she had her suspicions I was seeing someone, but she hadn't verbalized it.

Until now.

"Is your new lady friend going to join us?"

Dad looked up from his beer menu with a jerk of his head. Panic reverberated in the middle of my chest.

There was no point in lying about it. "Uh, no. She's not."

Mom twisted her lip. "Aww. I was hoping this call was to introduce us to her."

"H-how did you know?" I asked.

Mom studied her menu, but said in a calculated voice, "You've been to our house for coffee less recently and haven't called as much. Twice we've asked you over for dinner, but you say you had other plans. Your dad and I know it's been rare when you've had evening plans since Autumn's death. For you to use that excuse twice in three weeks without telling us what those plans were is telling."

I kept my eyes on the menu and pretended what she said meant nothing. "Quite an observation. Doesn't prove there's a woman involved. I could have been up to my ears in paperwork at the store for all you know."

"Not true," she responded. "You've told me about the system you have for getting those odds and ends done on a weekly basis. I know you go in early on Tuesdays for paperwork and payroll duties, and you delegated the ordering of books to Winona last October, so that's no longer on your plate. There's another reason I deduce you're seeing someone."

I crossed my arms. "Why's that?"

This time, Dad answered the question, speaking for Mom. "You seem happy."

My shoulders sank with the realization he was correct. Happy people showed it, and it had been far too long since I appeared that way. "Thank you."

Mom and Dad shared a look and smile. Mom said to him, "Told you!"

They shared a chuckle and then mom asked me, "When do we get to meet her?"

"I don't know you will. We only started seeing each other. I'm not sure she's ready to meet the parents.'"

"I understand. We won't bite." Mom flipped her menu over and scanned the other side.

"Ha. I know."

Dad laid down his menu. "What's her name?"

"Andrea."

"She sounds lovely." Mom smiled.

I tossed my menu on top of Dad's. "You only know her name. How could you know her level of loveliness?"

"Because she's captured your attention, and we know she must be special to have done that, everything considered."

"Perhaps." I was desperate to talk about something, anything else.

A tall waiter with a hipster haircut, beard, and matching sleeves of tattoos came and took our drink orders. Peach sweet tea for mom, a Belgian Ale for me, and a German lager for dad. I faced the main dining room while my parents had a view of the bar and flat screen TVs. A Braves game caught dad's attention.

Before I could ask what had been happening in my parent's life or if they had heard from my brother, Bo, Mom said, "If you won't tell us about your new girlfriend, at least tell us what else has been going on in your life."

I raised a finger. This brought me back to my relationship status chat with Karen. "She's not my girlfriend. It's a situationship. We haven't defined it yet. I will say that she has a five-year-old daughter, Libby. Cute as a button."

Dad perked up when the possibility of a built-in grandchild might be part of this deal. He and Mom had always hoped for grandchildren. My older brother, Bo, was a confirmed bachelor, although it didn't mean there couldn't be an unknown grandchild out there with his DNA. I wouldn't be surprised. I would never tell this to my parents, though. They held him in high regard.

After our drinks were delivered and our food order was placed, Mom asked, "What else have you been up to?"

I bit the corner of my lip. "Another case."

Dad rolled his eyes. Mom sipped on her straw.

"Not on purpose." I held up a placating hand. "It came in a roundabout way."

"Who is it this time?"

"Do you remember the man and woman who got shot over here at Tidal Creek last week?"

Dad didn't watch any news outside of ESPN, so staying up to date on current events wasn't in his universe. Mom did. "Yeah,

I remember. Such a shame. Do they know who did it?"

"They thought they did, and even arrested two men for it, but had to let them go."

"Why?"

"No solid evidence linking them to the crime scene I'm aware of. I don't have all the information the police do."

Dad sipped his lager. "Thank goodness."

"What do you know?" Mom asked.

Her mind worked differently from most people's. She questioned everything and saw things from different angles. She had read mystery novels since she was a little girl and passed on the love of mysteries to me. I've helped the police solve four cases. In every one of them, Mom took the facts of the case, digested them, and offered me a different avenue of investigation. She wasn't right every time, but her ideas eventually had led me to the answers.

As we waited for our dinner to arrive, I went over everything I knew. From Stanley's embezzlement with the Paradise Hideaway HOA to Lorenzo Bruno and my encounter with him and his entourage to the Silver Girls.

We paused the conversation as our food arrived, and dug in. Dad enjoyed his fish and chips. My burger was a flavor bomb and hit the spot. Mom's schnitzel seemed to please her as well.

"So, a lot of these people had motives to kill Stanley, and they confirmed some to have been at Tidal Creek at the time of the murder." I raised a greasy finger from off the edge of my burger. "Here's the thing. I'm still unclear on how the murder went down."

Mom swallowed what was in her mouth. "I don't remember them giving any details about the murders on the news. Only that they had been shot."

This wasn't a proper dinner conversation, and I hoped the surrounding people weren't eavesdropping. To those unaware of the subject at hand, I imagine I sounded like a conspiracy theory nutcase, and my parents were the poor souls who had to listen to Junior go on a rant.

I glanced to my left and right and leaned forward. Mom did too. Dad watched the game and was seemingly oblivious to our conversation. He had a refined sense of selective hearing.

"Someone shot Emilie in the chest. Stanley took two shots to the back of the head, execution style."

Mom didn't blink. "Was he on his knees when it happened?"

"Yes." I explained further, "Stanley volunteered to help take out the trash. He was a lifelong garbageman on Long Island and was a force of habit. I imagine he did it for the occasional free beer."

Dad raised his glass. "If that's all it took for free beer, I'd empty their trash every day."

Mom and I shared a laugh, but Dad appeared to be serious.

"Anyway," I continued, "when he entered the garbage corral, someone was there waiting and made a drop on him. Emilie must have walked in during or after the slaying and took one to the chest for being in the wrong place at the wrong time."

"Poor girl," Mom said and pushed some bits of schnitzel around her plate.

"What's on your mind?" I jammed a fry in my mouth.

"You seem to have a jumbled mess of means, motive, and opportunity. You need to step back and try to look at things differently. How? I don't know. Another question you need to ask is, what if the mafia and Stanley's HOA dealings had nothing to do with this?"

CHAPTER
THIRTY-SIX

WE FINISHED OUR meals. Dad insisted on paying the check. I gave Mom a hug, and we went our separate ways. Fortunately, they had found a spot to parallel park their Tiguan across the street from the Gordon Biersch entrance. My Jeep was still in the parking lot on the other side of Barnes & Noble.

A cool breeze pushed the palmetto fronds around the trees lining Howard Avenue. The falling sun brought out bright pinks and fuchsia streaks in the clouds. Locals motored past on golf carts. A van with Vermont license plates inched its way through the intersection where Nevers Street crossed over Howard Avenue. There was no stop sign on Howard at the interchange, but that didn't keep tourists from stopping anyway. A mom had led her three daughters to the walking path area between the eastbound and westbound lanes of Howard. She was having them pose for a picture in front of a fountain. Two older women got up from a bench and gave each other big hugs before going their separate ways.

A pair of older couples traipsed arm-in-arm across Nevers from Dolce Lusso. One husband carried a Tupelo Honey takeout bag. Five teenagers dressed in black jeans and rock band t-shirts with dyed black hair trundled through the crosswalk. All but one of them had their faces buried in cell phones. A group of kids played tag across the street on the village green at Valor Park. Their parents watched and chatted while the young ones wore themselves out.

I wasn't ready to go home yet. There was a certain positive energy in Market Common this evening, lifting my spirits. With two beers already in my belly and a thick hamburger to soak them up, I decided to grab another at Tidal Creek. I glanced at my watch. It was about half an hour until closing. Plenty of time.

After traversing the length of Gordon Biersch, I crossed over Deville Street and passed a parking lot on my way to Tidal Creek. Only Myrtle Beach would treat breweries like Starbucks franchises with drinking establishments within a stone's throw of each other. I wasn't complaining.

Mom made the astute observation that the killer had to know about the blind spots in Tidal Creek's CCTV. Which narrowed down the suspect list.

As I approached the end of Nevers Street where it dead-ended at Tidal Creek, I saw a familiar face standing on the near corner. Well, I couldn't see her face at present, but I would recognize that dark hair pulled back in a ponytail and navy pantsuit anywhere. Gomez.

She stood with arms crossed, focused on the movements at the brewery across the street.

I snuck up behind her and whispered, "Expecting someone?"

She jerked and gasped at the same time. It was the first time I'd seen anything rattle Detective Gina Gomez. She held a hand to her chest. "Goodness, Clark. You scared the snot out of me."

"Sorry. You, of all people, should have your head on a swivel. Consider that a little self-defense training from me."

She gave me a knowing smile. "Whatever. Good point, though.

What are you doing here?"

I jerked a finger over my shoulder. "Just had dinner at Gordon Biersch. I should ask you the same question. Why are you standing here like a sentinel?"

"Doing something I should have done to begin with. Watching what they do before they close." She glanced at the smart watch on her wrist. "Should be another twenty minutes before they go around collecting the trash."

"Oh." I stood beside her, trying to see what she was seeing. She wore the same intoxicating perfume she had on during our rendezvous in her car. That brought back a pleasant but uncomfortable memory, considering what has transpired since then. "Would you call this a stakeout?"

"Not really. It's not like I'm trying to hide."

"True. No plans with your fiancé tonight?"

Her head snapped in my direction. "No. He has a poker night with the boys. I could ask you the same thing? Where's your girlfriend?"

I almost said Andrea wasn't technically my girlfriend but bit my tongue. "No plans tonight. Hung out by her pool today."

"Sounds nice."

"We weren't frolicking together in the water, if that's what you're thinking." In retrospect, that would have been an acceptable activity.

It took a few seconds before she responded. "Didn't cross my mind."

"Good." I shoved my hands into my board shorts' pockets. "No, I spent most of the time chatting with the Silver Girls."

She pivoted and gave me a stern look. "Not about the murders, I hope. Told you to stay out of it."

"I can't help it if they brought it up."

She gave a knowing groan. "Did they?"

"They did."

"Learn anything?"

"They all had a motive."

"We're aware of how Stanley allowed Dot's former employer into their apartment and some of the ticky-tacky fines he levied against the other roommates, yes."

"Did you know it's possible all of them, except for Karen, might have been present at the time of the murders?"

Gomez bit her fingernail. "They don't show up on any of the camera feeds around Tidal Creek."

"Did you check the feeds at Paradise Hideaway?"

Her head whipped in my direction. "No."

The hair on the back of my neck stood on end. I pointed a finger at the brewery. "We both know there are sizable gaps in coverage of this entire area. It's possible they could have left the Hideaway and snuck over here with no one seeing them."

Before she could respond, a worker at Tidal Creek emerged from the front door. She held a cluster of clear, empty trash bags in her hands. The trash can below the carryout window was her first stop. She took the lid off the trashcan and removed the full bag of garbage it contained, replacing it with one of the empty bags.

Gomez jabbed a hand in the worker's direction. "When we spoke with the owners and manager, they told us the trash didn't get taken out until after closing."

I watched the worker go about her business. "Looks like when the boss isn't around, they try to get out as early as possible. This could have happened the night of the murders."

"It did. They started collecting before closing, but because of the lack of cameras pointing at the garbage corral, we still don't know the exact time Stanley and Emilie entered the trash corral, but we know they disappeared from camera coverage at 8:59 during the collecting."

"So, you just assumed the murders occurred after nine, because you were told that's when the garbage ended up here?"

Gomez did her best Moody impression and grunted. "I'm such an idiot. If they disappeared off the feeds at 8:59, it's possible they entered before then. The coroner believes they were shot between nine-thirty and ten-thirty, but with the warm weather, it's possible rigor mortis could have set in earlier."

I placed a hand on her wrist. "You're no idiot. We both know that's not true. It happens. How would you have known if no one was watching what they were doing and when they were doing it?"

Her shoulders relaxed. "Yeah, yeah, yeah. You're right."

"Don't beat yourself up about it. When did Bruno and his men leave?"

"Three minutes before closing."

"By that point, Stanley and Emilie were grabbing the trash."

"Yes. They were out in the Beer Garden at the moment Bruno walked out the front door."

"Did you see which way Bruno went?"

"Across the street to that parking lot presumably to wait for his friends."

"Where did his friends go?" I asked, knowing the story they told me.

"They disappeared through the trees straight across from the back door of the taproom."

"And you think they circled around, came out where the trash corral is, and jumped Stanley?"

"That's one factor leading to their initial arrest."

"Tell me. Why are they still not in jail?"

Gomez shook her head in disgust. "There wasn't enough forensic evidence to definitively link them to being where the murders occurred."

"You say 'definitively' like there might be something." It wasn't a question, but I hoped Gomez would pick up on where I was going with it.

She did. "Yes. We found Carmine's wallet on the ground near Stanley's body. We believe he carried the wallet in his coat, and it fell out during the hit."

What she just said wasn't right, and what I was about to say would collapse their entire house of cards, propping up whatever case they were trying to compile against Angelo and Carmine. "He doesn't carry his wallet in his jacket."

"How do you know?"

I told her about Bruno coming to my house and how I noticed a thick George Constanza-ish wallet in Carmine's back pocket when he sat down next to me. "There was a faded outline around it. They were wearing their work uniforms, so it was probably a pair of pants he wore often. That impression wouldn't be on that pocket if he kept the wallet in his coat."

Gomez cursed under her breath. We stood there together in the near darkness, watching people get into their cars and leave Tidal Creek. Within minutes, we'd be the only people here.

"Let's see if we can still get in."

Gomez patted the police badge hanging from a chain around her neck. "Trust me. We can get in."

We crossed the street and entered the main entrance to Tidal Creek. The garbage collecting worker had moved around the near side of the building on her route.

Two tables were still occupied in the dining room. One had two older couples chatting. Empty plates and half-empty beer glasses lay on the table. The other had two men. One was a familiar face, and the other was a fashionably dressed, handsome younger man with dark hair. Greg Rowles and a friend. They were bent over a tablet the younger man held between them, discussing something on the screen in-depth. Two full glasses of beer in frosty mugs sat before them. Neither looked up at our entrance.

Gomez strode up to the bar, where a woman of average height with dark hair pulled back into a ponytail was cleaning glasses. Her name tag identified her as "Amanda."

"We're getting ready to close," she said to Gomez, "but I could pour you a draft right quick. What'll it be?"

"Nothing for me." Gomez flashed her badge.

Amanda recognized her. "Oh, yeah. The detective. Can I help you?"

Gomez leaned on the bar and began asking Amanda questions about the early trash collection. As riveting as I imagined that conversation would be, I had something else I wanted to do.

I navigated through the empty tables to the table where Rowles and his friend sat. They looked up from the tablet upon my arrival.

Greg smiled. The other man regarded me with calculating eyes.

"Clark, good to see you, friend."

"Hey, Greg. Fancy running into you here."

"Yeah." He pointed at his friend. "Tony and I get together every few weeks to pre-plan our strategy for my haircuts over at

Dolce Lusso."

Tony smiled and halfway rolled his eyes at me. At least he seemed to get free beer from the meetings.

I couldn't imagine the maintenance which went into keeping that appearance. Greg was paid good money for his various appearances and looking sharp had to be a priority.

I did some quick math in my head. "Was the last time you two got together the same evening you played here, and those murders took place?"

Greg and Tony shared a glance. "It was," Greg said.

He tapped Tony on the arm, letting him know to put the tablet away. Greg's hair plans must be top-secret. He waved a hand at an empty chair. "Have a seat. I assume you're still asking questions about the night of the murders. I'd told you what I knew when I saw you at Shine the next day."

"Thanks." I sat. "I realize that and thank you for taking the time to talk to me."

Tony took a swig of beer.

Greg held his glass to his lips. "No problem."

I made a show of observing the interior of the taproom. "It's just that I thought being here might jog some memories."

"Possibly." Greg drank from the glass. "What do ya got?"

I drummed my fingers on the edge of the wood tabletop. "Right now, I think the police are still trying to determine who was where and when."

Greg tapped the side of his forehead. "Got a mind like a steel trap. I remember the evening as clear as a bell."

I asked if he had followed the case, and he said he had. It had been the subject of several segments on his Carolina AM show.

"Then you might remember where certain people were."

"Between the two of us, we should." Greg glanced at Tony. His quiet friend nodded to me in confirmation.

"There were three mafia looking guys. Remember them?"

"Oh, yes. Lorenzo Bruno. I've dined at his restaurant many times. Not as good as Crave Italian, but that's just my personal preference. I remembered the friends he was with from the restaurant."

"Did you talk to him?"

"No, Tony and I stayed in our little corner over here. We try to sit at this same table every time." The table was in the middle of a row farthest away from the front door. It offered open views of both entrances, the dining room, and people exiting through the door to the brewery. "I had a big campaign to record with Shade and Shutter Expo the next day, and we had to make sure my hair was on point, as the kids say."

"Right," I said, drawing out the word. "Did you see him talk to anyone else?"

"Not that I recall."

"He didn't communicate with the victim?"

"Which one?"

I squinted. Something Mom had said tugged at the back of my head. "Stanley."

"Not that I recall. He came in to use the restroom before he volunteered to take out the trash, and they glared at each other for a moment."

"But they didn't speak to each other?"

"Like I said, not that I recall."

I chewed on that. "You asked a moment ago which victim. Did you see them talking to Emilie?"

"Yeah, Bruno flirted with her every time she came by. She

spent most of her time behind the bar but came out to collect empty plates and glasses."

"Hmm." I crossed my legs. "Do you recall seeing any older women?"

Greg chuckled. Tony followed suit.

"C'mon, this is Market Common. This place is mostly older women." He turned serious. "Yes, there were older women present."

"Did any of them come in around closing time?"

Greg traced a finger on the table, trying to recall who and when. "Not that I recall."

When I thought I'd hit another dead end, Greg continued, "I was parked on the street outside and spent a few minutes getting the music going in my truck before pulling away. At about that time, I saw someone appear from behind the warehouse across the street and cross over in this direction."

When he said those words, everything fell into place.

CHAPTER
THIRTY-SEVEN

GOMEZ ROUNDED UP the suspects the following morning at Tidal Creek. The brewery was normally open for light breakfast and coffee, but one owner, Adrian, placed a sign on the door saying they would open at eleven.

They still made money during our meeting. Almost everyone had a coffee or tea in their hands. Lorenzo Bruno enjoyed a frosty beer, as did Beatrice. It was five o'clock somewhere, or closer to it in Naples, where she grew up. The rest of the Silver Girls were there as well. Karen, Violet, and Dot congregated at a table with the beer-swilling, quirky old woman. Violet cradled her dog, Daisy, on her lap.

Bruno and his henchmen were present. The twins, Angelo and Carmine—the ones accused of the murders—sat side by side at a table. I'd already forgotten who was who. Carlo, the consigliere or underboss, sat by Bruno's side at the same table with the twins. The kitchen staffers, Joey and Frankie, sat in chairs facing the center of the taproom at a table behind the twins.

Grizzled old Detective Moody stood beside Gomez, sipping a cup of tea. His partner nursed a coffee. The brawny officers, Dame and Battles, who tackled me on the Boardwalk during the death on the causeway case, blocked both exits. The owners of

Tidal Creek, Dara and Adrian, stood behind the bar. Adrian sipped beer from a half-pint glass, and Dara clutched a cup of steaming coffee. Both appeared worn and ready to put this story out of their lives. I couldn't blame them. Nothing like a double homicide at your business to make your lives miserable. Their manager, Amanda, was drinking a double espresso. Her bloodshot eyes warranted the extra boost of caffeine. She closed last night, and Gomez and I stayed with her well after she locked the doors. Amanda had gone above and beyond the line of duty as manager of the brewery. If I were Dara and Adrian, I'd give her a raise.

A husband and wife who appeared to be in their mid-forties sat at a table together. Neither appeared to be drinking anything. She had red-rimmed eyes. Must be Emilie's parents.

The last two people of interest present were Marie and her son, Colton. Her hands shook while trying to hold a to-go cup of coffee with a lid. If she had used a mug, coffee might've splattered everywhere. Her nerves had to be vibrating in overtime right now. She didn't know why she was here, but the police compelled her attendance. The view out of her apartment window was key to this in more ways than one.

I didn't invite Andrea because she would need a babysitter for Libby, and this was no place or conversation for little girls. Besides, I could relay Andrea's role in this as I helped her uncover Stanley's misdeeds.

Gomez and I stayed up late last night after leaving here, going over everything at the McDonald's by the airport. She'd brought Moody in too, after he'd missed a few days dealing with his heart doctor. Gomez expressed the tremendous pressure they were under to solve the case since a new police chief had taken over. They revealed to me all the details of the case since I had stuck my nose so far into it that there was no sense in keeping information confidential. I needed them, and they needed me to figure out the killer.

When everyone was present and accounted for, Gomez had Adrian lock the doors so that the people working in the brewhouse would not be allowed into the dining room for the duration of this assemblage. It might take a while as this case was more complex than previous ones Gomez, Moody, and myself had come across. Never had any of us had so many suspects to juggle.

Gomez stepped forward and got everyone's attention. The din of conversation ceased as everyone gazed at her.

"Thank you," she said when all was still. She turned her focus to Emilie's parents. "Mr. and Mrs. Smith, thank you for coming this morning. I wanted you to be here for this. I would have invited Stanley's family, but his only son is in New York and didn't have enough time to get here overnight."

"You're welcome," Emilie's dad said in a solemn tone. His wife clinched a soggy tissue in one hand and nodded her approval.

"We know who killed your daughter," Gomez said, "and Stanley Griffin."

Although her statement shouldn't have come as a shock to those gathered, murmurs of shock still arose. During the investigation, everyone here was at some point aware of the other suspects in the room. Whether or not they were friends, they will forever be linked by the murders of Stanley and Emilie.

"On the evening of Sunday, June 21st, at around nine o'clock in the evening, someone shot and killed Emilie and Stanley in the trash corral in the parking lot between the brewery and the beer garden." Gomez paced left and right as she spoke so everyone could hear her. "There aren't any cameras focused on the corral or that area of the parking lot. It's one of the blank spots in their CCTV coverage. We don't know exactly what time they entered the corral or when the murders took place. The coroner placed their time of death between nine-thirty and ten-thirty. For a time, we ran under the assumption the killings took place after nine, because Tidal Creek's closing protocols called for the trash to be removed after they close at nine. It made it difficult to figure out who might have done it, because from using cameras located elsewhere in the vicinity and speaking to witnesses, it appeared no one was here, that everyone had gone home after Amanda locked the doors."

She held up a finger. "However, we know protocol sometimes gets broken."

Bruno's men looked at each other with their heads tilted forward. The Silver Girls regarded each other with raised eyebrows. Marie drummed her fingers on a table. She separated her pointer and middle fingers in a way suggesting she wished a cigarette was between them.

Gomez held out an arm in my direction. "Most of you have met or know who Clark is, especially after helping us solve several murders. Most of them weren't by his choice, and his involvement with this case came because of assisting a woman with unraveling the HOA records Stanley left behind."

Gomez did not mention Andrea by name. Was it because she wanted her name withheld, or some latent jealousy because Andrea was attached to me?

Gomez continued, "Without Clark's help, we wouldn't be here this morning."

I gave a tight smile. This wasn't a joyous occasion. It was as serious as it gets, and I appreciated Gomez's kind words. Seeing

Emilie's parents sitting there with reddened eyes and occasional sobs strengthened my resolve to say what I had to say. They needed closure on their daughter's death, and I was here to provide it, as I hoped someday to get with Autumn's.

"Mr. and Mrs. Smith," I said to Emilie's parents, "It's a genuine tragedy what happened. I've been in your shoes when a loved one has been ripped away at too young of an age. I feel your pain, and I hope today will be a big step in being able to reconcile what happened."

"What happened, precisely?" Bruno asked. Having the former mafia member present, someone who spent a lifetime figuring out how to avoid the police and jail time, was like having a criminal attorney in the room. He was someone who knew the ins and outs of the legal system and how to skirt it.

I let Gomez take this part. It would be painful for Emilie's parents to hear, but this part had to be told to understand who committed the crime and why.

"The corral has walls ten feet high on four sides." She raised her left hand high above her head to show the walls' height. "There is a door on the front that uses a metal peg which goes into the concrete to keep it shut. Anyone can enter the corral at any time because the gate doesn't have a lock."

She cast an accusing glance at Adrian and Dara for this lapse in security. In their defense, I couldn't imagine why people would want to break into an area meant for trash and kitchen grease disposal, unless it was a homeless person scavenging for scraps. To my knowledge, Market Common didn't have much of a homeless population, and many of the restaurants held food back to help those in such need. If the trash corral had always remained locked, then anyone who needed access would have to track down a key to open a lock. I viewed the lack of a lock as a tradeoff between ease of access and security to an unappealing area.

"The killers did just that. They snuck into the corral and waited for Stanley and Emilie to arrive." Gomez paced from one side of the taproom to the other as she talked. "We believe Stanley arrived first, and they were executing him when Emilie arrived. The murderer shot her in the chest from between five and seven feet, which was the same distance between Stanley's body and hers. The question is, why?"

She turned to me. I was up.

I took a drink of coffee. The warm liquid flowed its way to my stomach, providing a sense of calm and relief. It allowed me to center myself.

Before speaking, I cleared my throat. "Stanley was the president of the Paradise Hideaway homeowners' association. After Covid hit, the other members of the board either moved or passed away and communication between the HOA and residents of Paradise Hideaway ground to a halt. He was the only one remaining, and for the residents, if the trash was removed and the grounds were well kept, they didn't care what was going on with the association. Stanley knew this and used it to his advantage.

"After his death, my girlfriend, Andrea, called upon me to help with going through the bank records for the HOA." Gomez shifted her stance away from me, and I realized why. I'd just referred to Andrea as my "girlfriend" without thinking about it. It seemed like the natural and proper thing to say at this point. The "situationship" picture became clearer. Gomez had a "fiancé," so any negative reaction on her part to what I said was her problem. This thought went through my head on the fly, and somehow, I kept my line of thought. "Andrea found some discrepancies in the statements she hoped I could help her reconcile. We figured it out and learned Stanley had been embezzling substantial sums of money from their accounts. Sums so large that if anyone found out, they might be angry enough to kill him for it."

"How much?" Dot asked.

"Andrea and I figured it had to be near fifty K," I said.

"More like seventy-five," Moody added from nowhere in a gruff voice. Everyone stared at him. "We did some digging ourselves and uncovered more."

His words caused a stir.

"It's true," Gomez said to me. "We have more tools at our disposal."

I whistled. "I don't know about you all, but if I learned the president of my HOA had stolen thousands of our collective dollars, I'd be miffed, but enough to kill someone? Beats me. Learning of what Stanley was doing might have been enough *if* someone already held a grudge against him. As it turned out, Stanley was not the most likable of HOA presidents. He rubbed many residents the wrong way by handing out what many felt was petty fines, even if he was going by the letter of the covenants and bylaws of the building." I scanned the room and zeroed in on one person. "Like Violet, for example."

CHAPTER
THIRTY-EIGHT

SHE JUMPED IN her chair and held a hand to her chest upon hearing her name called. "Me? I had nothing to do with Stanley's murder."

I raised a finger. "You had a reason to be upset with him."

"I don't know what you mean." Violet said, stroking Daisy's fur in more of a soothing motion for herself than for the dog.

"Did Stanley have reason to fine you?" I asked.

Everyone's attention swung to Violet, who shrunk like her namesake flower in her chair.

"Y-yes."

"Why?"

She ran a hand over the pooch's head. "For walking Daisy too early in the mornings. He said it was in the building codes because people didn't want to be woken up by dogs barking that early."

I hooked a thumb in one of my pants pockets. "Did that bother you?"

Violet cast a glance at Gomez before coming back to me. "Darn tootin' it did. Daisy is the sweetest little dog that ever lived."

Dot rolled her eyes. Bruno's boys snickered. Dara hummed in sympathetic agreement. Beatrice drank from her beer glass.

Karen remained still.

"Not enough to kill him, if that's what you're getting at," Violet said in her defense. "Besides, they were killed when I was getting ready for bed. Karen came into the apartment while I had my night cream and bathrobe on."

"Night cream, which could have been washed off, and a robe that could have hidden other clothes underneath." I let the comment hang in the air for a moment.

Violet opened her mouth to talk, but no words emerged. The act of me focusing on her left her flabbergasted and confused. As she should be. I was laying the groundwork to arrive at the killer. I targeted Violet as my first suspect because it would give a glimpse into the building Stanley controlled.

"Tell me," I said to her, "growing up in the farmland of rural West Virginia, did you ever learn to shoot a gun? I've traveled through the area where you grew up, and it seemed like every other truck and four-wheeler had a rifle rack on their backs. I bet deer hunting is big around those parts, aren't they?"

She stared at me with an open mouth at length before saying, "Y-yes. It is. I admit, I used to shoot squirrels with my daddy every fall. He gave me a little pea shooter, but lordy, I haven't fired a gun in, has to be sixty-plus years."

I pursed my lips, walked to the Silver Girls' table, and rested a hand on it in front of Violet. Looking down at her, I said, "I believe you're telling the truth. You didn't commit the crimes."

Violet rested back in her chair, expelling a relieved breath. Karen rested a hand on her shoulder in a comforting gesture. Violet reached up and squeezed it. Karen would need comfort in a moment. As I planned out what I was going to say, Karen's part had to come later.

"Dot," I said, shifting to a different Silver Girl. "You made it clear you didn't care for Stanley, and in your shoes, I wouldn't either. He picked on your friends and let some guy from your old security firm into your apartment when you weren't there to go through your things. Violating privacy would be enough, especially if they were after something you needed to be kept secret."

Dot possessed a level of poise and quiet confidence, unlike her friends. She focused on me and didn't seem to care if my revealing of a motive alarmed others for murdering Stanley. I wouldn't want to be in a high-stakes game of poker against her, but she had reason to be self-assured.

"That's all true." Dot straightened her back and held her head high. "But I didn't do it."

I ticked off the points on my fingers. "You had firearms training from your previous job. When Karen came home, she didn't see you. She assumed you were in your room, but we know assumptions can often be incorrect. You could have already snuck out, and she didn't see you in passing, or you were waiting for everyone to be in bed before you emerged from your room to leave for a return visit to Tidal Creek to kill Stanley."

"You're right," Dot admitted, "I could have."

"We both know you were probably lying in bed reading a book. Is that so?"

"Yes, I was, as a matter of fact. Catching up on Amor Towles' newest book."

"On your tablet?"

"Yes."

I glanced at Gomez. "That can be confirmed, couldn't it? That she was reading at the time of the murders."

Gomez glanced at Moody for an answer, who had a baffled expression. He still used a flip-phone. She said, "Seems plausible. I'll ask my fiancé."

My brain went to a screeching halt. What would her fiancé know about getting data off of a device? There was only one answer I could surmise, and I didn't like it. I made eye contact with everyone and knew I couldn't stop and follow up on what she just said. It would have to wait.

I zeroed in on Dot. "Did you know about Stanley's emptying of the HOA bank account?"

She leveled her gaze at me. "No, I didn't."

I held up a finger. "I discovered that she didn't have knowledge of the embezzlement until it was revealed at the meeting after his death."

"True." Dot crossed her arms. "I was as dumbstruck as anyone else in that room. I wouldn't put it beneath him. Stanley always seemed like a smarmy guy."

I took a step toward her. "I don't think you did it, either."

Dot's demeanor relaxed. "Good."

"Which brings us to Karen." I stepped back to stand beside Gomez, but not as close as I had before. Taking a sip of coffee, I continued, "Of everyone at Paradise Hideaway, she was the closest to Stanley."

"Yes, close enough that we found her fingerprints all over his apartment," Gomez added. She revealed this to me last night. The police had already deduced that they were having a fling, as most of the prints were concentrated in Stanley's bedroom. I wasn't going to include that detail. These people were smart enough to connect the dots.

Dot was the first and loudest to hum "Mmm hmm" while

casting a judgmental eye at her roommate.

Karen glanced back at Dot and didn't blink. "Yeah? What about it? We were both single and liked to have a bit of . . . *fun.*"

Karen said that last word in a way that made me, and most everyone else in the room, uncomfortable. Except for Frankie, the quiet sous chef. He swiveled in his chair and regarded Karen in a new light which seemed inappropriate for the occasion, but the ring finger on his left hand was bare.

I paced toward her. "What of it? You and Stanley got into a fight the night before his murder when you learned of his embezzlement. You confronted him, knowing he was living beyond his means when he confessed how he'd been doing it. You felt violated." I glanced at Marie, then back to Karen. "You were seen slapping him in his car in the Paradise Hideaway parking lot before storming inside. We know he'd been letting you slide on your HOA dues. You had to realize if he wanted to, he could have your place foreclosed upon for not paying your dues, leaving you and the Silver Girls homeless. You couldn't let that happen."

Karen lifted her chin. "No, I couldn't."

"And you did something about it, didn't you?" I leaned down toward her, in as opposing a manner as I could.

Karen's chin quivered at the implication. She peeked at Emilie's parents.

To Gomez and me, she said, "I did."

CHAPTER
THIRTY-NINE

AFTER EVERYONE HAD a moment to collect their breaths, I said, "After I and the other Silver Girls left here, Karen remained behind to talk with Stanley. Isn't that correct?"

Karen nodded.

I continued, "And you two made up right before his death, didn't you?"

Her chin continued to quiver. A tear ran down her cheek. She sobbed. "We did. I told him what he was doing was wrong. He told me he had gotten in so deep, he didn't know how to get out. I told him there was only one thing he could do, and that was to turn himself into the police the following day."

"What did he say to that?" I took a sip of coffee.

"He'd do it."

A gasp came from one of the Silver Girls, but I couldn't make out from who.

"What about you not paying your dues?" Gomez asked. "You knew that this would be found out, eventually? Also, you didn't tell us any of this in our interviews. We're going to have a conversation after this."

Karen gulped. "Yes, he said he'd doctor the records before turning himself in to show I had paid. He wanted to protect me."

"How noble of him," Moody said.

Tears brimmed in Karen's eyes. "I-I loved him, and he loved me." She cried, and Violet took her in her arms.

While she did that, I said, "Another explanation could be, since Karen was a former bookkeeper, she could have killed him and doctored the records herself."

Violet glanced up and for a moment realized she could be consoling a murderer. "Did she? Kill him?"

I shook my head. "No, she didn't."

Violet, Karen, and Dot let out sighs of relief. Beatrice, the mother of the group, finished her beer, reached over, and patted Karen's arm.

Karen held her head up and asked through the sobs, "Why are you pickin' on us?" Then she pointed at Bruno's table. "What about those mafia lookin' guys? Weren't they arrested for it to begin with? Why aren't they in jail?"

"Because the evidence we had wasn't enough to not grant them bail," Gomez said. "They're out on bond awaiting a hearing."

"That's next week," Bruno said. The twins shifted in their chairs. They were the ones who would face the judge.

"What linked them to the scene of the crime was two things," I said, directing my attention to Karen. "First, they were seen going out the back door of Tidal Creek minutes before it was believed the murders took place. Second, the police found Carmine's wallet dropped in the corral."

"What was he doing in the corral?" Karen asked.

"We don't know that he was there," Gomez said.

Neither Bruno, Carmine, Angelo, Joey, nor Frankie showed any sign of emotion. The employees of Luciano's might have committed their fair share of crimes, but killing Stanley and Emilie was not one of them. Carmine's wallet was what this entire case hinged upon.

"Carmine didn't drop his wallet there. Someone stole it." I explained how Carmine and Angelo tag-teamed to bring Stanley's golf cart back to Paradise Hideaway after seeing him drunk and how doing it was a regular occurrence when Stanley used to go to Luciano's.

The reaction to that revelation was about as I expected. Bruno and his gang remained stoic. Others, including Dot, Violet, and Karen, gasped or looked at each other in shock.

Only three people in the room were unmoved.

"Carmine got his wallet back from the police," Bruno said, "but we were never clear on how it ended up there."

"It was odd." Gomez stood in place. "We found his wallet there, but there were no prints on the outside. We found Carmine's all over the inside, including on the three-hundred and sixteen dollars in cash."

"Someone stole his wallet, but left that much cash in it?" Dot said. "That's unusual."

"No, it was a timely and perfect setup."

"You're going to have to clue us in how that is, Mr. Thomas," Bruno said.

None of the three people who failed to act surprised when I said someone had stolen the wallet had added anything to the discussion. They were Marie, Colton, and Beatrice. I locked my attention on those three. Marie and her son sat at a table behind the Silver Girls and Beatrice. Colton's mouth hung open like he was trying to catch flies. It wasn't out of worry or shock. That was his normal appearance. The thick lenses of his glasses hid whatever expression his eyes might give, if any.

"And then there were three," I said. "Well, two. Marie didn't do it. She was watching out the window of their apartment because she was waiting for Colton to come home."

If Marie was relieved, she didn't show it. She reached over and grasped her son's hand. His long, oily hair fluttered when he whipped his head in her direction. His Adam's apple bobbed up and down. Beatrice drummed her table with the fingers of both hands, waiting for what I was about to say.

After narrowing it down to those two, I regarded them both before shifting my gaze over at Emilie's parents who hung onto my every word. They held hands together on the table. I could see the young woman's resemblance to her mom. If the genes would have held to form, Emilie would have aged well and went onto become a beautiful, vibrant woman.

If it weren't for Beatrice and Colton killing Stanley and then Emilie for walking in at the wrong time.

As I swung my head back to peer at Colton, I had an epiphany.

I was wrong.

Everyone was wrong about this entire case.

Stanley wasn't the intended target.

It was *Emilie* all along.

CHAPTER
FORTY

My heart palpitated. It's quite a thing to stand in front of a room of people gathered to hear you speak about what they believe will be the truth when you realize halfway through that what you were planning to say is wrong. I hoped no one would notice if I talked my way through it and adjusted on the fly. I'm not as experienced with these summations as, say, Hercule Poirot. Then again, he's a fictional character. I'm not. At least I didn't think so.

"What is it?" Gomez asked.

The room was quiet. All eyes were on me, and I knew it. My entire theory just went right out the window, and I had no time to deliberate about what direction to take next, so I just started talking after taking the last drink of coffee in the cup. It helped strengthen my resolve.

I started pacing back and forth in front of everyone's tables. The act helped me to clear my head. "This entire time, we've gone under the assumption Stanley was the target of the execution and Emilie had been an unfortunate witness. She was in the wrong place at the wrong time. We figured it took at least two people to carry out this crime. Someone to subdue Stanley, and another person to either keep watch or be the shooter, which is why it was easy for the police to finger Angelo and Carmine for it.

"Over the past few months, Beatrice took Colton under her wing." I looked at Colton's mom. "No offense, Marie, but he needed support in a motherly way that maybe you weren't well enough to provide. And that's nothing against your disabilities. It's just the way it is."

Marie's eyebrows narrowed in anger, but she remained silent. Sometimes the truth hurts.

I turned on my heel and paced back toward Emilie's parents. "Did you know Colton and your daughter dated at one time?"

They craned their necks to regard the gawky young man. "No, we didn't," her dad answered. "When?"

"It was during their freshman year at Coastal," I answered. "It didn't last long. Colton, you haven't had a girlfriend since then, have you?"

Emilie's mom opened her mouth and worked her jaw as she gazed at Colton. She might not know Colton, but I could tell that what I said hit a note and she was trying to work something out in her mind.

Black hair wavered across his face as his head fluttered back and forth. "N-no. I haven't."

"How long ago was that?"

I watched as the creaky cogs in his brain tried to do the math. "Five years."

"You worked here with Emilie for a time, didn't you?"

"I did." He reached up and wiped tears away from his eyes with the back of his index fingers.

"Why did you stop working here?"

"We fired his behind for stealing a customer's wallet," Dara spoke up. A vein throbbed on her forehead.

Everyone gaped at her and Adrian standing together behind

the bar. I turned to them. "How did you learn he had stolen the wallet?"

Adrian answered. "He stole it from a tourist. The guy came in the next day and asked if we had his wallet. He explained he'd had a few too many and didn't recall the events from the previous night. I went through the tapes and saw where Colton brushed up against him and grabbed his wallet while he was bussing tables. We turned him into the police and fired him on the spot."

"Thank you. Colton spent thirty days in jail for the offense." I paused and said, "Let's reset. Colton worked here. Which meant he knew the blank spots in the camera feed and what everyone's responsibilities were. Even who took out the trash."

Amanda volunteered, "Em loved taking the trash out. I always thought she was an oddball for liking that task, but if she wanted to volunteer to do it, no one was going to stop her."

"How long has she been taking that role at closing?"

Amanda's eyes bulged as she thought about it. "It seems like she's been doing it since she started here. She and Stanley had that in common since that's what he did up north before retiring here."

"He did," I confirmed and directed my next question to her, Dara, and Adrian. "Did Colton and Emilie work here at the same time?"

"There was some overlap, yes," Amanda answered. "They rarely worked the same shifts. She was here before him. Em came to me when he started and told me about their brief history together. Said it was a sorority dare or something to ask him out. She did and liked him at first, but decided soon thereafter she wasn't interested."

"Did something happen between them?"

Amanda looked at Emilie's parents before answering. "Yes, she alluded to an unpleasant encounter, but didn't elaborate. Said she decided it would be best if they didn't see each other anymore and broke up with him."

"Sound right?" I asked Colton.

His long neck flushed. "I don't know what she's talking about."

"Did she break up with you?" Gomez asked.

Colton must have known from his time in jail not to lie to the police, especially when in a room full of witnesses. Gomez told me they questioned him after seeing him on video, but he said he went home before Tidal Creek closed. That was a lie.

In a quiet voice, Colton answered, "She did."

"Have you had feelings for her since then?" I asked.

His mouth must have gone dry. He took a drink of water and then answered, "It's possible."

I allowed a few beats for his answer to permeate before directing my next question at Beatrice. "I hear you like to go on late night walks?"

"Who told you that?" she replied.

The fact she responded in that manner was enough. "I have my sources. You also enjoy being up early for swims, right? You told me you used to do that growing up in Naples, and Stanley had fined you for getting into the pool before it opened."

She gritted her teeth. "That's right."

"Didn't he also fine you for having the wrong color flowers outside your apartment?"

"That mook was happy as the Lord of the Manor," Beatrice said.

"You told me you didn't like him," I said.

"No lie there," she said.

The thing about Beatrice was, she spoke her mind and didn't care what anyone thought. When a person reached a certain age, they said what they wanted, never mind the consequences.

I stepped in her direction. She watched me with glasses that magnified her eyes, like the ones Colton wore, just in a women's frame. She showed no fear.

"What made you gravitate toward Colton?" I asked.

She reached back to where Colton sat at the table behind her and grasped his hand. Turning back to me, she said, "Look at him. He needs all the help he can get. Deep down, I'm still a mom, and I saw a boy who needed guidance with his life."

More like she was bored and searching for something to do, I thought. "How did you do that?"

"We had tea together, and I would tell him life lessons." She fingered the pearls around her neck.

"Were they life lessons, or were you reminiscing about your past?" I asked.

"Both," she answered. "You can learn a lot from history. Colton had little real-world experience or knowledge. His poor mom is a wreck." She swung to Marie. "No offense."

Creases formed on Marie's forehead. "None taken."

"Tell me," I turned to Beatrice, "growing up in Naples, were you around the mafia?"

Her eyes darted to her daughter, Dot. For the first time, Beatrice's visage cracked.

"They were around," she answered in vague fashion.

I rubbed my hands together. "Do you know the power of a simple Google search?"

"Look wise guy. I might be in my nineties, but I'm not oblivious."

I shifted my focus from her and spoke to all in the dining room. "When I met Beatrice, she mentioned growing up in Naples. The other side of the conversation at the time was about Stanley and his ties to the mafia. So, I searched for Beatrice using her maiden name and included Naples in it. As I did my search and clicked through the results, I had a craving for a cappuccino."

"Why would you need that?" Dot asked. She had to be aware if I was talking about my internet browsing here and now, that I had to have unmasked something. Which I had.

"Because, Dot," I answered, "I found an old newspaper clipping from a newspaper in Naples in 1938 of Beatrice getting arrested for suspected theft. She had a large amount of money she was ferrying across town for the Cappuccio crime family. They thought an eight-year-old girl ought to be able to move about unsuspected by the *polizia*. They were on to her and arrested her as part of a larger investigation into the crime syndicate."

Dot glared at her mother. "Ma! Is this true?"

The corner of Beatrice's lip curled. "Yeah. I almost got away with it. They promised me a position working in the house. That would have been big for a girl like me."

Dot said to Gomez and me, "Ma grew up in a poor family. Grandpa was a no-good alcoholic who never had a stable job. Grandma was the obedient housewife who didn't say much."

Beatrice must have taken after her father more.

"All I wanted to do was help the family. I got pinched for it."

I scratched the side of my face. "Did you go to jail? The article only said you got arrested."

"No, they let me off."

"How did that happen?"

Beatrice refused to blink. "The Don had a lot of influence."

I understood the implication. "Did you keep working for them?"

Beatrice laughed. "Nope! Getting arrested once was enough for this girl. I was only eight. I didn't know what I was doing."

"Bet it made you grow up fast. Didn't it?"

"Darn tootin' it did. I helped Mom and Dad make ends meet in other ways. Being around the Cappuccios taught me how to be resourceful and quick on my feet."

I had laid the groundwork. Now it was time to put it all together. I strode to the front and set my empty coffee cup on a table and said, "Here's how it went down."

CHAPTER
FORTY-ONE

"On the night of the murders, I was on a date with Andrea, where we were joined by the women sitting at this table, minus Beatrice. She was taking care of Andrea's daughter." I waved a hand at Violet, Dot, Karen, and Beatrice. "Colloquially known as the Silver Girls, because they all seem to share similar attributes to the famous Golden Girls. Violet is kind of like Rose. Karen gets around like Blanche. Dot is the serious and level-headed one, like Bea. And Beatrice, well, look at her. She's the spitting image of Sophia. Is even native to Italy. And they all live together."

I paced a few steps toward Emilie's parents. "That evening, Andrea, Dot, Violet, and I left here around fifteen after seven. Andrea needed to get back and put her daughter to bed. Karen remained behind and went off to speak with Stanley where they made up."

I had Bruno say that he and his boys were sitting at the same table they currently occupied. One with a view of the bathrooms. I'd already heard this from him but needed to get it out for others to hear.

"For the benefit of everyone here, let's explain your dealings with Stanley around the time of the murders to the others. Tell us, did you have an altercation with Stanley the night before his death?"

If Bruno could have shot lasers from his eyes, I would have a hole in my head. But he couldn't. "We did. At my restaurant."

"Can you tell us what happened?"

"Yeah, Stanley came in, already as drunk as a skunk. Raised a ruckus. He was complaining his girlfriend had just broken up with him and wanted to drink to the point of passing out." Bruno crossed his arms and peered over at Dara and Adrian. "We don't operate that way at Luciano's."

The implication he threw down was that Tidal Creek was a place to get rip-roaring drunk and go nuts, which I knew was the complete opposite. I watched Dara glare at Bruno when he said that. Methinks the former Mafioso might not be welcome here after this.

Bruno continued. "I had Carmine take Stanley home. He was enough of a regular at the restaurant and an old acquaintance from Long Island where we helped him like that. Angelo followed behind in Stanley's car."

"Was he mad at you for kicking him out of your bar?" I asked.

Bruno chuckled. "Sure was. I bet he didn't even remember it the next day."

I meandered over and stood next to Bruno at his table. "Did you see him the night you were here?"

"I did."

"Was anything said between you two?"

Bruno hooked his thumbs on the lapels of his pinstriped suit jacket. "Nada. We made eye contact and nodded at each other as he went into the bathroom over there."

"When he and Emilie left to take out the trash, did you have Angelo and Carmine follow him?"

"No. We finished our beers, paid the tab, and left." He added,

"All while Stanley was in the bathroom."

"How did you leave?"

He stuck out a thumb at the front entrance. "I went out that door and waited on the sidewalk across the street for them to come get me."

I raised my chin and asked the Twins. "What about you guys?"

Angelo answered. He had a deep Italian accent. "We left through the back door over there."

"Why did you separate?"

"I had them drop me off first and go around the block and park in the lot of some timeshare place. It was an old holdover from my, let's just say, more questionable days as a business owner in New York where I never got into a car before the driver turned the ignition. Because, you know." His hands mimicked an explosion. We got the point.

"Were you part of the Frontino Crime Family?"

Bruno's eyes darted to those gathered in the room. "I got out scot-free. Let's leave the details out of it, capisce?"

I tilted my chin in his direction. "No need to. While you were across the street waiting for the Twins to pick you up, did you see something?"

"Yeah," Bruno said. "Saw Stanley's golf cart parked right in front of the door on the street. He'd parked it at a funny angle, like he'd already been drinking when he got here. He must have been drunk because the cart key was still in the ignition. Anyone coulda removed it."

"What did you do?"

"I had Angelo drive it back to Stanley's apartment complex." Bruno's head pivoted to get his next words across to everyone

DEATH AT TIDAL CREEK

in the taproom. "I figured, as drunk as he appeared, he was in no shape to drive the cart back to Paradise Hideaway. It was close enough he could stumble back there on foot."

"It is less than a five-minute walk between here and there," I said, for those unfamiliar with the distance between Paradise Hideaway and Tidal Creek. To Bruno, I asked, "What if he wasn't drunk? What if he had gone outside and believed his cart had been stolen—wouldn't he have been upset?"

Bruno gave a wry smile. "Let's just say maybe it was payback for him for causing a stir at my place the night before."

"A prank. I get it. After you took his cart back, did you go back to Tidal Creek searching for him?"

"Nope. Me and the boys went back to my restaurant before we all went our separate ways."

"So, you didn't see Stanley after he entered the bathroom?"

"No, sir. We left while he was draining the lizard or whatever."

"Thank you. I believe you." I pivoted and paced in the opposite direction.

Bruno sat back and steepled his fingers together. The Twins relaxed.

I pointed at Karen and asked Bruno, "Did you see her with Stanley?"

He bent his neck to get a better look at Karen. She stared back at him with a blank expression.

He smacked his lips. "You know, I didn't see her wit' him, but saw her leave a'fore I saw him go into the bathroom."

"How much before?"

He wiggled his hand. "Ten, fifteen minutes."

"Which was around eight-thirty." Moving back to everyone else, I said, "The feeds showed three minutes after Bruno, Angelo, and Carmine left, Stanley got together with Emilie to go gather the trash. At the same time, back at Paradise Hideaway, Beatrice stalked out the front entrance wearing a dark jacket with a hood, like she would when she goes out for nighttime walks. Colton left out a side entrance around the same time wearing a dark t-shirt and pants."

I looked at Bruno and the Twins. "It was at the same time you took Stanley's golf cart back to the Paradise Hideaway parking lot. You just missed each other."

Beatrice's face had turned red. Colton's mouth hung open, which wasn't much of a departure from his normal expression.

"Why didn't the police see that in the footage earlier?" Dot asked.

Gomez spread her hands. "We were focused on the camera feeds coming from Tidal Creek, the Market Common parking garage across the street, and a camera on top of Yoga in Common. They went behind the warehouse next to here, which was out of view of cameras. We didn't see them leave on the Paradise Hideaway camera until last night, when Clark came to us and asked to inspect the footage."

"Yes," I said, "and this is where I believe Marie started covering for her son and how she had to know about this scheme."

Marie's jaw dropped. She looked ready to catapult herself out of her seat and lunge for the front door. Officer Dame stood in front of the door, daring anyone to try it. He wagged a finger at Marie, and she stayed put.

I took a few steps over to their table and stood beside her. She smelled like stale cigarettes. "Marie overcame her crippling anxiety and came to the HOA meeting where Stanley's embezzlement was divulged. The question in the back of my head was, why would she do that? I believe the answer was to see if they said anything about Colton so she could help cover for him and perhaps her anxiety isn't as bad as she lets on.

"She stays up, watching the parking lot from her window. Her condition keeps her from sleeping, and that's how she passes the time. She told me several interesting things she saw, including Angelo and Carmine dropping off Stanley's golf cart. Them doing that and Beatrice coming out the front occurred three minutes apart. If she was still at the window, she would have had to have seen Beatrice walking out the front door. Her apartment is right above it. She would have also known Colton left their apartment, but she didn't tell us that in any interviews."

Everyone saw where this was headed, but I still had a few surprises to reveal.

CHAPTER
FORTY-TWO

"*I had a* conversation with Greg Rowles, who was sitting over here." I pointed to the empty table where Rowles and Tony formulated the plan for his next haircut. "Bruno, he saw you, Angelo, and Carmine leave. He watched Stanley and Emilie gather what they needed to go collect the trash. He saw one other thing as well."

"What's that?" Violet asked.

I tilted my head at Beatrice and Colton. "He saw *them* crossing Knoles Street beside here, coming from behind the warehouse across the street just after they locked the doors. An area where there is no camera coverage." I focused on the young man. "Didn't you?"

Colton shook.

Beatrice held my gaze but kept silent.

"A blank spot that someone who works here, or used to work here, might know about," I said. "When I thought about who might know about the areas without camera coverage during the investigation, I leaned toward Violet since she used to work here. At the time, I forgot about Colton being an employee."

Gomez stepped in. "I spoke to Rowles last night and showed him pictures of you two. He was positive it was you. He said nothing about seeing you in our interview with him because we asked him what he saw when it came to Stanley, Emilie, Bruno, Angelo, and Carmine."

"Wait a second," Carmine said, shifting from Colton and then to Angelo for confirmation. "Is that the guy we literally bumped into after we left here and were going back to the car?"

Angelo squinted at Colton, who twirled his head away. "Yeah. You know what? That's the guy!"

"Carmine, that would be the moment your wallet was stolen," I said. "A wallet which was dropped in the garbage corral when the murders happened."

The dining room was still. No one stirred. The hum of the HVAC was the only sound.

"The trash corral is another area without security coverage." I turned on my heel, treading in the opposite direction. If this went on much longer, I would wear an indention into the tile floor, but it wouldn't. I was almost done. "Colton used to work here. He had access to that information. He also knew Emilie liked to gather the trash on nights when she closed. She closed every Wednesday night, which he would also know."

"Wait." Emilie's dad asked, "Why is this relevant? I thought the target was Stanley."

"So did everyone else," I explained, with my attention now focused on him and his wife. "At the beginning, we couldn't find anyone with a motive who'd want to murder Emilie. We focused on Stanley and his background and possible mafia ties, his embezzlement from the homeowners' association, and his actions as the HOA president. Many people might have liked to have seen him dead — not to mention the way in which he was murdered — but he wasn't the intended victim. Emilie was."

The revelation caused a stir. I waited for the room to calm

down before continuing. "The person who did this had to have been someone who knew that when Emilie closed, she took out the trash. We've talked about Emilie's past relationship with Colton." I moved closer to him. "Tell us, did you try to resume that relationship?"

If possible, his jaw slackened a little more. Perspiration beaded on his forehead. He gulped. "Uh, I asked her out again, if that's what you're meaning."

"That is what I'm meaning. What was her response?"

Colton looked at Emilie's parents first and then answered. "She laughed at me. It was humiliating."

"Did that anger you?"

His head tipped forward. Stringy hair fluttered. "It did."

It was me and him now. Everyone else was a witness. "You and Beatrice had grown close. Is that correct?"

"Uh, yeah. She gave me advice."

"What type of advice?"

"Uh, like how to get a job and stuff."

"By stuff, do you mean relationship advice as well?"

Beatrice turned to Colton. "Hold your tongue."

Marie swung around at Beatrice. "Watch your mouth, you old bat!"

The tips of Beatrice's ears grew red. She was aware she was my focus at the moment and controlled her temper.

Colton glared at Beatrice, who searched the bottom of her beer glass for another drop, before answering. "Uh-huh."

"Did you tell her about getting turned down by Emilie?"

"I did."

"What advice did she give?"

"Maybe the world would be better off without her."

Emilie's dad got up and lunged at Colton and Beatrice who were seated near each other. Battles expected what was coming and wrapped a thick arm around him in restraint. Her mom wailed.

Once he got settled back in his chair, I addressed everyone gathered. "Colton and Beatrice came here to murder Emilie. She entered the trash area first and found them waiting. I imagine they exchanged some words before she got shot in the chest."

"Wouldn't someone have heard a gun being fired?" Dot asked.

"Not necessarily, in this case," I answered. "When Greg saw Beatrice and Colton, he said he looked like they just came from the pool. Greg didn't think it was weird at the time because pools stay open until around then, and we're so close to the beach. People dressed in swim attire is a common sight. Beatrice was wearing a pool cover up with her fanny pack and Colton wore swimming trunks and a black t-shirt. He also had a beach towel flung over his shoulder. The towel and fanny pack are the keys to this entire thing."

"How so?" Karen asked.

"Beatrice and Colton knew if they were going to corner Emilie in the trash corral, they were going to need some way to suppress the gunshot. If you wrap a towel around the barrel of a gun, it does the trick," I explained. "It wouldn't silence the shot. There would still be a *pop*, but it wouldn't sound any different from the engine sounds from one of the many motorcycles cruising in and out of Market Common.

"I'm not sure who pulled the trigger on Emilie. If it was Beatrice or Colton. However, I'm reasonably sure she used the threat of the gun on Stanley after he appeared in the corral to get him on his knees before shooting him twice in the back of the head. The gun belonged to Beatrice." I scrutinized her. "Is that right?"

She stared back. "I don't know what you're talking about."

"Can you stand up?" I asked her.

She didn't budge.

Gomez took a step toward her. "On your feet."

Beatrice's magnified eyes flickered between Gomez and me. We stood side-by-side over her. Beatrice knew better than to resist the command from a police detective, especially with Dame and Battles closing in on her and Colton.

With hesitation, Beatrice found one drop at the bottom of her glass and slurped the last sip and set it on the table. It might be the last drop of beer she ever tasted. She pushed the seat back and stood. The rhinestone covered black fanny pack hung around her thin waist.

Gomez reached into her pocket and retrieved a set of clear plastic gloves. As she pulled them over her fingers, she said to Beatrice, "Remove the fanny pack and hand it to me."

Beatrice's bottom lip quivered, but she complied, unhooking the strap and handing Gomez the storage bag.

"Thank you," Gomez said without conviction. "Let's see what you have in here. Clark told me he already has a good idea of what we'll find inside."

"What's that?" Dot said with genuine concern for what the answer meant for her mom.

Gomez unzipped it and reached her hand inside. After a moment of digging, she withdrew her hand and held it up for all to see.

In it, she held a small Smith & Wesson pistol.

CHAPTER
FORTY-THREE

BEATRICE SHOWED NO emotion. Colton put his head down on the table. Marie's face didn't betray any shock, either. Karen and Violet held their hands over their mouths.

Dot straightened her back in her chair. "Ma! How could you do such a thing?"

"The boy had become family to me," Beatrice said. "When he told me about what happened between him and her in college and how she laughed in his face when he asked her out, I took offense."

"So much offense that you would have her killed?" Gomez asked.

"Hey, I learned in Naples that you don't mess with family," Beatrice replied. "She humiliated him. Twice. It had to be done."

Emilie's mom got to her feet and jabbed a finger in Beatrice's direction. "No! It didn't! Emilie was the sweetest girl. Colton tried to take advantage of her."

Colton's head remained glued to the table, like an ostrich burying its head in the sand to avoid what was happening around it.

"Explain," Gomez said.

After all the crying and sobbing, Emilie's mom had strengthened her resolve now that the killer had been unmasked. "Emilie told me about some boy — but not his name. During her freshman year at Coastal, they went on two dates. On the second date, the boy tried to force his way on her. She kicked him in his nether regions and got away. It must've been him."

"Why didn't she call us, or at least the campus police?" Gomez said.

"She was terrified. We tried to get her to file a police report, but she wouldn't."

We all watched Colton. The back of his head jerked around as he sobbed into his crossed arms on the table, proving in fact, it likely had been him who had committed the assault. Beatrice remained unexpressive. A cold-blooded murderer.

"What about Stanley?" I asked her. "Why did you kill him too?"

Her eyebrows pulled together like the answer should have been obvious. "Stanley? That loser had it coming. The world's better off without him."

"No, it's not," Karen said. "Stanley may have been a lot of things, but that's not true. He was a kind and funny man . . . just had a habit of stepping on the wrong toes."

"He stepped on my toes one too many times," Beatrice said. "Besides, it's not like they were the first ones."

"The first ones, what?" Gomez asked.

By now, Dot, Violet, and Karen had gotten up from their chairs and stood back from the table, leaving Beatrice to sit by herself. Marie rubbed Colton's back.

"That I've killed," Beatrice answered, and then explained, "I did more than run money back and forth for the Cappuccio's when I was a little girl. They called me the *piccolo assassino*."

"The Tiny Assassin," Dot translated with a note of awe in her voice.

"Wait a second," I said. "I read about you when I did the Google Search for you and the mafia in Naples. After I found your one arrest and nothing else, I went down the rabbit's hole and saw the Cappuccio's involved in a lot of articles involving an assassin tied to them. What I read wasn't about you specifically, because the police never learned who the Tiny Assassin was. They knew the killer had to be small because the person hid in small spaces while waiting for their intended victims. Why confess to that now?"

Beatrice peered down at her empty beer mug and back at me. "Look, I'm ninety-three. Who knows how much time I have left on the planet? I figured if I was going down for this, I might as well fess up." She turned to her daughter, Dot. "Maybe I'll get a Wikipedia article out of this. Go down in history."

Sometimes, at this point, I would say something snappy as a last word to the killer before they're hauled away, but I regarded Emilie's parents, huddled together, and back at Dot, who was about to lose her mother to prison. The normally composed woman shook with fear at what was about to happen. This was a somber moment, and no place for my sometimes-smart mouth. I stayed quiet and let the police do their jobs.

Gomez said to Dame and Battles, "Get the cuffs out and take them away."

Dame gathered Beatrice and Battles grabbed Colton while reading them their rights.

* * *

AFTER DAME AND Battles took them away, Gomez told me to meet her at the police station. I had to give a statement about my role in solving the case. It was crazy to think I'd gotten used to the process and knew what to expect. I told her I would see her there. She and Moody left.

Emilie's mom gave me an enormous hug and told me they would have me over for dinner as a thank you. Her dad shook my hand and told me he'd have me out for a round of golf at the Dunes Golf Club. I looked forward to dusting off my clubs to play on the legendary course.

Amanda, Dara, and Adrian thanked me and then went about the tasks of opening the brewery. A few other workers appeared from the kitchen and prepped for the day. Amanda warned us they were going to open the doors in five minutes, giving us a few more minutes of privacy.

Bruno sent Angelo and Carmine out to fetch the car while Joey and Frankie remained with him.

The former mafioso and current restaurateur approached me. The first time I met him, he oozed confidence. Right now, after learning what happened that night, seeing the effect it had on Emilie's parents and the Silver Girls, he showed compassion.

"Clark." He shook my hand with a forceful grip and released it. "That was so hard, seeing that poor girl's parents go through that. I just gotta thank you for doing what you did. You held up your end of the bargain."

I almost said it was a one-sided bargain slanted in his favor, but let it slide. "Welcome. It's good to help bring closure to this."

"Bet it feels good, doesn't it?" He placed a thick hand on my upper arm. Like a father having a tender moment with his son. Here, the father might have been packing heat. *Nothing strange here.*

I glanced at Emilie's parents as they walked out the front

door. Her dad had his hand on the small of her back to guide her through. She glimpsed back and smiled at Bruno. A smile which would be more common now that their daughter's murderer had been uncovered.

"It does." I relaxed my shoulders, studying Bruno. Here was a man who might know certain people who know certain people. Now that I had helped him, I took a chance on him helping me. "I helped you. Now, I want something in return."

His eyes narrowed. "Like what?"

"A person such as yourself seems like you operate in the gray." I recalled my conversation with Detective Ed Banner's wife, Brenda. He had been the lead investigator on the night of Autumn's death. Gomez confided in me he had acted strange, making several hushed phone calls to a number that had sent Autumn threatening text messages the night before her death. The next week, fifty-thousand dollars showed up in their checking account, which he had Brenda promptly move elsewhere. We discussed how her husband sometimes operated in the gray.

"What are you implying?" Bruno said.

"You blockade me in my home. I believe that's called illegal seizure. You flash your guns and force your way in."

"As far as we're concerned, you let us in. As far as flashing guns, my man just scratched and itched on his hip. You just happened to see what he had there."

"Your word against mine, huh?"

A shrug. "If you say so."

"Do you know about anything going down at the courthouse about three years ago? Something people would kill over."

Bruno shifted a foot. "That's one place I try to keep my paws out of, period. You think I'm shady? Meet some of them down there. Look, I'm legit. I try not to do anything to get me on the other side of the law. Doesn't mean I don't know people who will. Let's just say there's someone controlling this town. In fact, there's two of them." He cracked his knuckles. "Let's equate your situation in mafia parlance. You have the don and the underboss. I know who the underboss is. The don, I'm not so sure. Not so sure I wanna know. Know what I mean?"

"You're saying that's not mafia controlled?"

"Correct. This is something else. Maybe like an old boys' network."

"Locals?"

"You didn't hear that from me." He peered at his goombahs. They remained stoic like good guard dogs. To me, Bruno said, "You're something like a Sherlock Holmes. And you know, for every Sherlock Holmes story, there's a Professor Moriarty."

Goombahs one and two gaped at their boss.

He lifted his shoulders to his earlobes. "Hey, I read."

I kept my attention on Bruno. "What are you saying?"

"All I'm saying is when you set off a trip wire and then tread into the wrong territory. Someone is keeping their eye on you." He took a step closer so no one else could hear, "When I inquired about you, I heard some things. Watch your back. Be careful. Trust no one."

A chill crept up my spine. Before I could ask him what things he heard or who the "underboss" was, he thanked me once more and told me to come by his restaurant some time. I told him I would. He gathered his cronies and left as Amanda opened Tidal Creek for business.

Bruno's comments shook me. I knew I had to get to the police station, but I was frozen in my tracks. What I had thought might be a case of murder with Autumn to cover up a case from getting to court now went much deeper. The gravity of what I'd stumbled into pressed down on me.

As I gathered the resolve to leave, I looked over at the Silver Girls. They still hovered near the table where they sat during my summation. Violet and Karen huddled around Dot, who cried and cried. Even the toughest of people had their limits, and Dot had reached hers. A tear formed at the corner of my eye, watching them. Three of the closest-knit people I had ever encountered.

Dot composed herself and said to her two roommates, "I'm so glad to have both of you right now. Thank you for being a friend."

CHAPTER
FORTY-FOUR

THAT EVENING, AFTER leaving the police station, I had dinner with Andrea and Libby at their apartment. She made spaghetti with garlic toast and salad. Libby wouldn't touch the bread or greens but put a killing on a bowl of *pisgetty*.

When dinner ended, I helped Andrea clean the dishes while Libby played. It seemed natural and comfortable. Family-like.

Later, we sat out on a wicker sofa on her balcony and watched the sun go down over Market Common. I sat between the two, with one arm around Libby. She cuddled up to me and fell asleep within minutes.

The night was set to be an unseasonably cool one as a cold front moved in. A hint of ozone was in the air. Rain was coming. Clouds gathered in the distance without obscuring the sunset. We could use the break after the sweltering heat wave we'd undergone in the past two and a half weeks.

Andrea held my right hand in her left and rested her head on my shoulder. I met her and Libby a few weeks ago, and both had already changed my life. For the first time since Autumn's death, I could say I was happy. It felt good.

As I looked over Market Common spread out before us and the daylight waning, fortified by the warmth of Libby to my left and Andrea to my right, I thought, "I could get used to this."

* * *

A SEARCH OF Colton's room uncovered a beach towel with holes blasted in it from shrouding the barrel of the gun. He had tossed it in a corner of his cluttered room without a care.

Beatrice confessed to both shootings, and Colton was charged with murder, even though he wasn't the one who pulled the trigger. Allegedly. In South Carolina, if two people conspire to kill someone, and only one does the actual slaying, if the other person who helped plan it was present, then they were also considered a principal in the crime. He'd go down for second degree murder. If convicted, he faced life in prison, unless he pled to a lesser charge. At Beatrice's age, having been accused of first-degree murder, she would die behind bars.

The FBI was called in to help in the investigation into Stanley's embezzlement. Using the alternate email address I gave them from the community board in Paradise Hideaway, they found an offshore account in the Cayman Islands attached to him holding over seventy-five thousand dollars. Much of the money was returned to the residents of Paradise Hideaway. The biggest pool party in the complex's history ensued.

Two weeks passed since the gathering of suspects at Tidal Creek. That Friday, I received excellent news from the contractor I had hired to outfit the interior space of Garden City Reads. He'd finished his work and was ready to hand the space by the pier over to me. Now all I had to do was fill it with books and decorate it. It made me miss Autumn being here. She would have shouldered most of that burden and had fun with it—especially the books part.

Expanding to a second location as a way of honoring her. She would have loved knowing we grew the business and spread the love of reading. When we were married, I always wondered which she loved more: me or reading. I would never know the answer to that question, although I had my suspicions, which made me smile.

***

You could cut the humidity this afternoon in Downtown Myrtle Beach with a knife. It didn't matter what you wore, you were going to sweat. I cranked the AC in the Jeep to full blast as I stared at the side of City Hall. They had invited me to a ceremony in Mayor Rosen's office to receive a commendation for my role in apprehending Colton and Beatrice.

The occasion would mark the fifth one of these I'd done. Each was as surreal as the first. This one promised to be different. They appointed Sue Miller to replace the retired Chief Kluttz. The mayor and city council appointed her. Miller had a different way of doing things than Kluttz and wanted more positive press for the police department when possible. That a citizen helped to solve the Tidal Creek murders was one such occasion to celebrate.

At the other commendation ceremonies I had attended, it was mostly just Detectives Gomez, Moody, a reporter from the newspaper, the mayor, and myself who attended. The mayor would shake my hand, give me a plaque and a check. There would be a few pictures taken, and we'd go about our merry ways.

For this, they had planned more of a reception with light hors d'oeuvres and beverages and invited police officials, council members, and other representatives from the press. Receptions were held in a conference room usually reserved for meetings to decide the future of Myrtle Beach. Today, they were celebrating the work Detective Gomez and I had done in closing the case.

I entered through the front doors of City Hall into a cavernous lobby. A young guy with curly hair and glasses sitting behind a reception desk recognized me and led me back to the conference room. I'd been held up at the bookstore prior to coming. Humphrey was late to work. Again. I was fine with it because it meant less time I'd have to spend schmoozing with city officials, some of whom still held a grudge after kicking me off the Myrtle Beach Downtown Development Corporation for breaking into an executive office at OceanScapes Resort during the Paige Whitaker investigation. At least I didn't get arrested for it.

Therefore, I was the last to arrive at today's ceremony. I wore a polo shirt, robin's egg-colored Bermuda shorts, and a pair of flip-flops for the occasion. My normal wardrobe for these events. Andrea was tied up at her store and couldn't come. She joked she would come for the next one of these events. *Hardy har har.*

When I entered the conference room, everyone turned my way and began clapping. My neck and cheeks flushed. I had the urge to run. Seeing Gomez's smiling face among the crowd kept me here. I held up a hand and said, "Thank you." The people resumed their conversations.

Arrangements of various foods and beverages filled the conference room table. No one sat.

Mayor Rosen was the first to greet me with a sturdy handshake. "Clark! Good to see you again. This is becoming a regular occurrence. We might as well designate you your own parking spot outside."

"I don't know about that." I released his hand.

Rosen had been a district attorney when Autumn died but had thrown his hat into the ring for mayor. He won a hotly contested battle with the incumbent mayor, but I had to admit, he did a good job running the city during his tenure.

"We'll get started here in a few minutes," he said. "In the meantime, help yourself to some food and drink if you'd like."

"Thank you," I said as we parted ways. One glance at the proffered food on the table did nothing to entice me, so I made my way to the person in the room I knew best and was most comfortable with, even if it came with a caveat after our — ahem — meeting, in her car last month.

I said a few words to people I barely knew as I made my way over to Gomez and Moody who were standing in a corner. Knots of people stood on either side of them. If the guest list for this shindig had been any bigger, they would have needed a banquet hall to accommodate everyone.

When I reached her and Moody, she finished speaking to a council member I recognized. When he drifted away, Gomez turned to me. "Clark."

"Gina."

Moody grunted.

"Hi, Detective," I said to him.

"Hi, Clark," he mumbled. "Nice job. Again."

"Thanks," I replied.

Gomez sized me up and down. "We make a pretty good team."

"Great minds think alike."

Before I could ask her how she was doing, a man sidled over to her side, breaking off from a cluster of people next to us. He was tall and had dark, slicked back hair, a square jaw, and had the appearance of a man used to getting his way. I disliked him instantly.

Gomez grabbed his hand, causing my stomach to harden. She said, "Clark, this is Lucien. My fiancé."

We shook hands. He had bulging veins in his forearm and had a vise-like grip. "Nice to meet you."

"Yes, Gina has told me about you." His voice oozed confidence. "You've done some great things for the department."

"It was nothing." I almost said she had given next to zero details about him to me.

"It was definitely something," Gomez said with a warm voice.

I said noncommittally to Gina, "Sure." Then to Lucien, "What do you do?"

A dimple appeared on his jaw. "I run the forensics lab."

The hair on the back of my neck prickled. "Oh. Cool."

Gomez said, "He's the person I gave Autumn's phone to."

I regarded Lucien. He met my gaze, unwavering, as the recollection of Bruno's final words of caution sent a chill down my spine. *"Trust no one."*

ACKNOWLEDGEMENTS
and a Note About West Virginia

First, I want to thank Karen Govern for her donation to the Horry County Literacy Council and winning the drawing to be a character in this book and to everyone else who participated.

Writing a book is a lonely job. I sit at a computer for countless hours creating these stories, but it doesn't mean that I don't have help. In this book, I would like to thank Dara Liberatore for allowing me to kill people at her business. I often get asked by readers if the places in these books are real. The Tidal Creek Brewery used in this novel is real, and it's spectacular. I urge you to make it a regular stop when you come to Myrtle Beach. Maybe I'll see you there.

Thanks to Amanda Post for the grand tour of the Tidal Creek Brewery. All weaknesses in their security are fictional. The place is a regular Fort Knox.

Also, Jessica Dalske for the ins and outs of an HOA gone wrong. That part is based on a true story that happened in my neighborhood and poor Jessica was one of the people who had to put on their real-life sleuthing caps and figure out where our money went. The case is ongoing.

I appreciate Mike Dame for keeping me in-line with police procedure and operations. Thank you to Christine at the Veranda at Market Common for her assistance in how a community such as Paradise Hideaway pays its power bills.

As for the West Virginia jokes and references. I grew up in a tiny community in the center of that state. My dad's first job was to milk cows at a dairy farm. We lived around several wheat fields at my house, and I enjoyed helping throw hay bales in the back of trucks during the harvest season and going on the occasional horse ride. I haven't lived in the state for most of my life, but it is still in my blood. There are many great and wonderful people who live there. All references made in this book to Violet's heritage are taken from stories and experiences I grew up with. Sometimes the best stories are true stories.

Sometimes.

All books in the series are available on Amazon, Barnes and Noble, Books-a-Million, and wherever books are sold. Don't see them in your local store or library? Ask the bookseller or librarian to order them for you.

Learn more on his website at calebwygal.com.

ABOUT THE AUTHOR

Caleb is a member of the International Thriller Writers and Southeastern Writers Association, the author of nine novels, social media marketer, woodworker, occasional golfer, reacher of things on high shelves, beach walker, shark tooth finder, and munchkin wrangler.

His two Lucas Caine Adventure novels, *Blackbeard's Lost Treasure* and *The Search for the Fountain of Youth*, were both Semi-Finalists for the Clive Cussler Adventure Awards Competition.

He is currently at work on the next book in the Myrtle Beach Mystery Series.

He lives in Myrtle Beach with his wife and son (the munchkin).

Visit Caleb online at
www.CalebWygal.com

*If you enjoyed this story please
consider reviewing it online and at Goodreads,
and recommending it to family and friends.*